CONTACT!

She laughed, a queer, wild little laugh. "You're not going to believe it. I think what we thought was a flare is some kind of a—I think it's a ship."

There must have been a glitch in transmission. "What did you say?"

"I said I think it's a ship. A spaceship." She paused. "Not one of ours."

SECOND STAR

SECOND STAR

DANA STABENOW

ACE BOOKS, NEW YORK

The quote that appears on page 19 is taken from *Time Enough for Love* by Robert A. Heinlein, copyright © 1973 by Robert A. Heinlein, and is used by permission of the Putnam Publishing Group.

The quote that appears on page 78 is taken from *Disturbing the Universe* by Freeman Dyson, and is used by permission of the author.

The quote that appears on page 169 is taken from *Broca's Brain* by Carl Sagan, copyright © 1979 by Carl Sagan, and is used by permission of the author.

This book is an Ace original edition,
and has never been previously published.

SECOND STAR

An Ace Book / published by arrangement with
the author

PRINTING HISTORY
Ace edition / June 1991

ISBN: 0-441-75722-7

ACE®
Ace Books are published by The Berkley Publishing Group,
200 Madison Avenue, New York, New York 10016.
ACE and the "A" design
are trademarks belonging to Charter Communications, Inc.

PRINTED IN THE UNITED STATES OF AMERICA

10 9 8 7 6 5 4 3 2

For Tim and Esther Grosdidier
and their world to come

— 1 —

Homecoming
and Housekeeping

There is no land uninhabitable or sea unnavigable.
—**Robert Thorne**

My full name is Esther Natasha Svensdotter but if you want to live you'll call me Star. Star is what Esther means, it was the first word I ever said, and when I'm feeling romantic I like to say that among the stars is where I live.

It was the first day of the new year and ten minutes out of LEO Base the gee forces on the *Ted Taylor* Express were discouraging to both my stomach and my disposition. I moaned a little. No one in the cockpit paid me any attention. I moaned a little more. Crip, the lean, graying captain of this happy ship, turned from his console to give me an unfeeling grin. "Happy New Year, Star."

I opened my eyes with an effort and gave him what I hoped

1

was a damning glare. "Yeah, right, you asshole. Welcome to the twenty-first century."

"Hang in there. It's time to give us another boot." I swore at him feebly. He gave a fiendish laugh in reply. His right hand gripped the lever rising up between his seat and the copilot's. "Ready to boost?"

"Ready, Captain," she replied crisply.

"Okay, kick it!"

I held on to my liver and followed the propulsion process in my mind. When Crip hit the glory button one of the bombs—pardon me, Colony Control prefers that we refer to them as ECFCPCs, or Express Class Freight Carrier Propellant Charges—anyway, at boost one of the bombs in the fuel bay was expelled by compressed nitrogen and ignited about a hundred feet below our ship's pressure plate. The controlled-velocity distribution of hydrogen pushed against the plate and we bounced farther away from Terra. I moaned again. The piston shock absorbers between the payload and the fuel bay took most of the blow, but it was still a bouncy ride.

I was riding the bare duralumin jumpseat against the cockpit aft bulkhead. Crip and his copilot and navigator were between me and the only port on the *Taylor*. There wasn't much of a view, black and more black. I didn't care. After two interminable weeks of kissing babies on Terra I didn't care what kind of infernal machine got me there, all I wanted was home. I closed my eyes and tried to forget how cold, how hard, and how small the jumpseat was.

My hair woke me up. I had forgotten to bind it that morning like I always do first time up and out after a spell downstairs. In the zerogee it was floating around my face in a tangled mass, and the ends were getting in my ears and up my nose and in my eyes. I sneezed, like I always did, and, silently cursing my own vanity in refusing to get it cut, fumbled in my pockets for a hair ribbon or a piece of string. When I finally had the blond mess braided back and the end secured with a length of the gray tape found on any self-respecting spaceship's flight deck, the view through the port had improved immeasurably. I gave a sigh of pure joy and I could the hear the smile in Crip's voice when he spoke without looking around. "Not bad, huh, Star?"

Not bad? Home had never looked so good. At first it was only a smooth, slender twinkle in the far distance, to the right of Luna and dimmed by her radiance. As we approached it filled the port, no longer a smooth column but a hexagonal cylinder. Against the blackness of space the rotating sides reflected the sun's light in sharp, glittering bursts. The solar mirrors flared out from one end like the skirts of a girl at her first dance. Stabilizers, antennae dishes, handgrips, tool racks, and airlocks protruded from a surface already lumpy with an uneven layer of porous moon rock—LIMSH, courtesy of Colony Control, or Lunar Insulating Material for Space Habitats. Acronyms are Colony Control's life.

Home again, home again, jiggety jig. Home was Ellfive, and Ellfive was the first of two planned space colonies circling Lagrange Point Five, maintaining a stable orbit between the conflicting gravitational pulls of Terra, Luna, and Sol, traveling sixty degrees ahead of Luna as the third point of an equilateral triangle of which the other two points are Terra and Luna. I had to swallow hard. The sheer immensity of the mere idea of Ellfive, when I had time to think about it, made me feel the size of a gnat and about as significant. But home is where, when you have to go there, they have to take you in, gnats and all. I shifted in my seat, straining at the harness with my feet braced as if I could help push the ship in quicker.

Crip warped in closer to the North Cap, its six-and-a-half-kilometer diameter dwarfing the *Taylor*, and the transmitter erupted with the traffic-alert whistle that sounded like the combined efforts of a stall signal on a Super Cub, air squeaking out of a balloon, fingernails scraping a blackboard, and teeth biting down on aluminum foil. Cockpit crews hate the whistle and curse me en masse for requiring its installation on every ship doing business with Ellfive, but it is a clamor impossible to ignore and so admirably serves its purpose. "Ahoy the *Taylor*, ahoy the *Taylor*, this is Ellfive Traffic Control."

"Go ahead, Control," Ariadne responded from the navigator's console.

"Be advised, there is a hold on your docking, *Taylor*, I repeat, a hold on your docking. Proceed immediately to

Transient Parking Area Number Three. You are cleared for approach and orbit."

Ariadne swore roundly and fluently, the harsh words sounding worse in her musical contralto, and looked around at Crip. "Ellfive Control, this is Captain Young, commanding the *Taylor*. What's the problem, Bolly?" he said. Over his shoulder I watched him bring up the approach vectors for the Warehouse Ring on his screen and punch in the coordinates. The maneuvering thrusters kicked in, sounding like incoming mortar fire outside the hull. The old girl shuddered once in protest and began changing direction slowly. "I say again, Bolly," Crip repeated, "what's the problem? Are we early?"

"No, you're not early, Crip, the *Thunderbird* is late and the hangarlock won't be free for at least another hour."

I could see Crip's shoulders stiffen, but his voice remained calm. "Ellfive Control, are you aware that we have the boss on board?"

The traffic controller's voice was no less grim than his own. "We know, Crip. The *Thunderbird*'s captain insists she is unable to pull back from the lock for another hour."

In moments we were stationary, floating free in Park Three, still sixteen klicks from home. Crip hushed his mike and swiveled his seat to speak to me. His voice was polite and furious. "This is the third time in a month the Patrol has put me behind schedule, Star. Just what the hell is going on?"

"It's not your fault, Crip," I said, fighting back my own annoyance. Annoyance does not sit comfortably on top of a hangover in zero gravity. "It doesn't have anything to do with you."

He looked at me, frowning, but his crew was there so he said merely, "We could rustle up a solarscooter for you."

I shook my head and immediately regretted it. "I'll ride in with you." I sat back in that Iron Maiden of a jumpseat and tried to get comfortable.

Unfortunately, the *Taylor* had not been built with my comfort in mind. The entire vehicle was 125 meters long and looked like the bishop piece from a chess game, with an aft pusher plate that was 57 meters across. We rode up front, with the freight modules between us and the fuel storage, and the freight modules and fuel storage and the pressure plate between us and ignition. It never felt like nearly enough of a safety margin. After Hiroshima and Pyongyang there wasn't enough room in the universe to put between me and fission. Once they work the kinks out of the Martin-Bond deuterium-helium fusion nuclear pulse rocket, or figure out a way to make solar propulsion push a spaceship along at speeds comparable to that of an Express, I'm jumping the fission ship.

Still, we were lucky to have the Express ships, and no one knew it better than I. When The War of the Worlds nonsense broke out in 1992 after Odysseus II intercepted the message from Betelgeuse, the absolute necessity of fielding some kind of force into space to act as a Terran reception committee became obvious to those of the most limited intelligence, and even to a few congressmen. Some bright soul remembered a plan by General Atomic in the late 1950s to build a ship powered by nuclear bombs that would put payloads larger by a factor of two or even three on Luna than would a chemical rocket of the same mass at launch. Congressional leaders in their infinite wisdom fell on Project Orion with loud hosannas and began to hurl funding at it in that odd but seemingly innate American conviction that enough money can cure anything. In the resulting rush to construction plans for padding crew seats were inexplicably lost.

Two interminable hours and seventeen minutes later the *Taylor* docked, its nose nuzzling comfortably into the North Cap hangarlock. The little man inside my head had set aside his piledriver in favor of a meat tenderizer but was still thumping away with unflagging energy. I couldn't unstrap fast enough. "Very nice trip, Crip, as always," I said, turning to pull myself through the hatch.

"Liar," he said, his usual good humor restored with our safe arrival. "You didn't think so."

"My stomach didn't think so," I protested. "Stop by for dinner next trip." I could see a polite refusal forming and added, "I'll get Charlie to whip up something."

He brightened perceptibly. "In that case I accept."

I slapped a bicep with one hand and jerked my forearm in his direction. He saluted smartly in return. I waved good-bye and pulled myself down into the payload bay, an immense cavern stripped to the essential shell, stark and bare and filled with freight strapped into nets, most of it mining equipment bound for the Trojans on the next SeaLandSpace freight tender. I didn't mind the lack of passenger amenities; the *Taylor* was an Express-class cargo ship, not some posh TAVliner where flight attendants served saki nonstop from Tanegashima Spaceport to Tranquility Base, discounts available for frequent flyers. And the truth was that if necessary I would have ridden a mass capsule home today.

The polysteel diaphragm of the North Cap's transitional hatch enclosed the *Taylor*'s bow, the atmosphere pressured up, and the cargo door dropped down slowly to become a ramp. I could see the arm of a Clark hoist floating outside, surrounded by a dozen waiting longshoremen in heavily padded overalls. I pulled myself down via the handholds and the three other passengers followed me out. One of them was a big dark man in a scruffy gray flightsuit too short for his arms and legs and too tight in the butt. He had yet to learn that you don't use your legs in zerogee and he kept getting tangled up with himself and anything else that got in his way. It's always a surprise to me how much one human being can fill up an entire cargo bay, if the cargo bay is on Ellfive and the human being is an Ellfive cheechako. He looked like he was headed for Neptune when one of the longshoremen finally took pity on him and took him in tow with a boathook.

"Where the hell do they get these guys?" Jerry Green grumbled behind me. "I'll bet that jerk's never had on a p-suit in his life." He sighed a deep, sad sigh. "It's not like the old days, Star."

I agreed, hiding a grin. Jerry, an aerospace engineer at Daedalus Flight Service, had been on Ellfive for all of eighteen months and was returning from his first R&R downstairs. He'd been quarantined at LEO Base for ten days for displaying cold symptoms at transfer, and the food at LEO Base had never been anything more than edible. Jerry, whose nature and mass were normally Dionysian in character, was today looking lean, hungry, and definitely unhappy. "Who is he, Jerry, do you know?"

"New rent-a-cop, somebody said," Jerry replied.

"Oh, no," I said.

"What?"

"It couldn't be," I said to myself.

"Probably not," Jerry said. "It couldn't be what?"

The zerogee cheechako being towed briskly into the hangar at the end of a boathook couldn't possibly be the new security supervisor. Helen hadn't found a replacement yet or she would have notified me, I assured myself, and then the lead long-shoreman gave the all-clear. I forgot the cheechako and Jerry and grabbed handholds straight across the floor to the barrel lock. I pulled myself in one side and rolled out the other into the waiting arms of Simon and Charlie. Simon grabbed me by the nape of the neck, brought me right side up, and said deliberately in his basso profundo voice, "Good to see you again, Star." We shook hands in formal greeting. It was about as formal as he got, but Simon always shook hands. "How was the trip?"

"The usual."

Simon examined me closely. "You are not quite your usual bubbling and effervescent Valkyrie self, Star."

"Who is?" I said, annoyed.

"Too much welcome?" Charlie asked, regarding me with a sapient eye.

"Nine Rotary Club luncheons, twelve Chamber of Commerce dinners, fourteen pep rallies, and, so help me, a parade. With fireworks," I added when Charlie snickered. "But that should be the last of them. Helen promised me no more goodwill tours before commissioning. Please God, let's get down to where I can swallow."

"Did you go home?"

"Yes."

"And?" my sister demanded. "How's Mother?"

"Mother's fine. Thinner, and she looks tired, but otherwise okay. I wish—" I stopped.

"What?"

I shook my head. After forty-two years of unarmed sibling combat Charlie knew when to leave well enough alone, and this time actually managed to. What I wished was that there were some way to get Mother more food. Her arm, lifted in farewell, had been almost frail outlined against the clear, pitiless light of an Alaskan winter morning, and I had been thinking of little else since Onizuka Spaceport.

We crossed to a pullbelt, each snatching at a handle as it passed by, and began moving rapidly down the inside of the endcap toward the north end of Valley One. The gravity slowly increased, until my braid lay heavily on the back of my neck. The moment I was able to put my feet down and ride the belt upright, I remembered, "Damn!".

"What?" Simon said behind me.

"I forgot my pack." I half turned to go back.

"No problem," Simon said. "It's Rex's shift. He'll give it to me."

I hesitated. It was my own rule that explicitly ordered that every incoming passenger identify his or her own luggage in person before it be allowed inside Ellfive proper.

"Rank does have its occasional privileges," Simon reminded me.

"Stop being so damn conscientious," Charlie said roughly. "You look like hell. Simon'll get it."

The little man with the sledgehammer switched into a lower gear and settled the matter. "All right. Go ahead."

Simon hopped nimbly across to the up pullbelt; Charlie and I continued down. "What have I missed while I was gone?"

"Not a lot," Charlie said cheerfully. "Impossible as it may seem, we managed to struggle on without you. Construction on Shepard Subdivision has fallen a little behind schedule but Roberta says they should be ready by February first."

"Good." We rode the escalator down to O'Neill Central, getting off on the corridor that ran by my office. The civilizing influence of full gee was mine once more. "Never let it be said that man wasn't meant to live in anything less than full gravity," I said, and stretched luxuriously. "At least never let it be said to me." I headed for my desk and thumped the viewer controls. "Archy?"

"Boss! It's about time you got home! Simon and Elizabeth are all wound up in plans for this mass transfer gadget they dreamed up. Bo-ring. I—"

"Archy, signal Orientale that I want to talk to Commodore Lodge. Now."

"Nice to see you, too, boss," Archy said with what sounded like real indignation, and Lodge's regal head and starred shoulders filled the viewer forthwith. His hair as usual was impeccably coiffed, and I wondered yet again how he kept it from floating around in the one-sixth lunar gravity. Most Loonies shaved their scalps or at the very least cropped their hair short to avoid the fuss. "Greetings, Star," he said primly. "Welcome home."

"Welcome home, my ass, Grays," I said. "Let's cut out the bullshit."

He grinned. It was a wide, white, attractive grin, warm and friendly and infectious. A funny thing about that grin, though, the longer I looked, the longer his canines got. "What can I do for you, Star?"

"You can make your Ellfive liberty shuttles shove off on time from the North Cap hangarlock, for starters," I snapped.

Lodge's grin seemed to freeze in place. He wasn't used to being reprimanded by anyone of less rank than the Secretary-General of the American Alliance. He didn't like it, not one little bit, and wasn't that just too bad. I said, "Crippen Young says the Patrol's shuttles are making a habit of being in the way. In the way of inbound Express ships, in the way of LIMSH tenders, in the way of solarscooters, in the way of mass capsules. In fact, Grays, the only way your people seem able to get out of is their own. It is not an inspiring sight, according to Crip. Makes him lose faith in the legendary competence of Patrol pilots. Says he's thinking about making a formal complaint to the Aerospace Pilots Association."

It may have been wishful thinking on my part but I thought the commodore flushed slightly. "That's Crip's opinion," he said with a contempt that somehow made him seem less handsome. "What can you expect from a civilian pilot?"

"I expect him to meet his scheduled departure times, and he does," I said. "Let me make myself clear, Grays. Your people screw up one more docking schedule in Hangar One, and I'll make it SOP for every in-bound Patrol vehicle from troop carrier to liberty shuttle to the admiral's gig to take on an

Ellfive-certified pilot at the Warehouse Ring. And I'll bill Orientale for the service." I shut down the circuit with my fist and put both hands up to massage my temples. "Oh, God. Is my head still on?"

Charlie regarded me with pursed lips and a disapproving expression. "Something tells me it was more than the Soldotna High School Marching Band that put that lovely chartreuse color into your cheeks." I growled something or other and she said firmly, "Take a light hit. That'll make a start at getting your body clock back on schedule."

"How many candles?"

She shoved me inside the booth that stood in one corner of my office. "I'll do it, I'm the doctor." Short people spend much of their lives with cricks in their necks from trying to look everyone else directly in the eye. This makes them domineering, cantankerous, and natural physicians. I muttered, but let her close the door and set the gauge while I fumbled with the goggles.

"All set?"

I adjusted the goggles. "Green light."

There was a click and a thud and a low whine. I closed my eyes as what felt like a billion candlepower irradiated my poor abused carcass and theoretically rearranged my biorhythms into something approaching normality. Much better than drugs for depression, ship lag, and fatigue, Charlie declared. Well, maybe. My head hurt about the same, before and after. "There should be a law against after-dinner toasts," I said, emerging and pulling off the goggles, "with the penalty for offenders death by drowning in a butt of malmsey." I looked toward the window and felt better at once.

Charlie looked from my face to the view and back again. "Why did you want a window that faced inside anyway, Star? You've always been such a stargazer."

"Outside whizzes by once every two minutes," I said. "Makes me seasick. Besides, when we put on spin there was more free-floating construction debris outside than there was stars. And besides that"—I waved a hand toward the window—"that view's why we're here, after all." I sat down behind my desk and accessed the screen. "Archy?"

"Yo."

"Bring up the Hewies, will you?"

"Can do."

A yellow circle with a dot in the middle of it appeared on my viewer, displayed on a black background. At equidistant points around this circle smaller circles blinked steadily, representing the monitoring satellites of the Helios Early Warning System. The display held for a few seconds, to show all twelve monitors up and running. I punched a button and it was replaced by a rolling readout of the current atmospheric conditions on Sol, monitor by monitor.

"We're only into the fourth year of Cycle 23," Charlie said at my shoulder.

"I never take Sol for granted," I replied. Not anymore, not ever again. Monitor Seven was showing some turbulence. "Archy? Put in a call to Mitchell Observatory." I waited, and Sam's face came on the viewer. "Sam? I'm looking at the Hewie display. What's this I see on Hewie Seven? Area—uh—378?"

A long-suffering sigh gusted down the commlink. "And hello to you, too, Star," Sam Holbrook said. "Welcome home."

"Never mind that, what about this reading?"

"What about it?" he said testily. "It's not a flare, it's not even big enough to qualify as a solar incident. We're keeping an eye on it. Why else did you shanghai me out of my nice comfortable chair at Stanford?"

"To keep both eyes on Sol and anything else that wanders into view," I said. "And I didn't shanghai you, you volunteered. Thanks, Sam. Keep in touch."

"Do I have a choice?" he snapped. My viewer went dark.

I looked at Charlie. "Do I need to access Blackwell?"

"Nah. I medivacked a couple of space-happys, is all. And I've been treating a Frisbee chemist who hasn't been keeping up on his full gee workouts. He's got a mild case of hypercalcemia but we caught it in time. He should be back to work in a couple of weeks."

"What about that rigger, Charlie?"

"Thanks, Arch, I forgot. I've got a rigger on the ward who

ripped his p-suit glove on the framework of Island Two. He's being fitted for a three-finger prosthesis."

"That it?"

Charlie smiled her Cheshire cat smile. "Well, I do have an electrical engineer new hire yelling about violation of his civil rights."

"He doesn't want to pee in a bottle," I guessed.

"I don't care what people say about you, Star, you are too average bright."

"You know the policy, Charlie. If he refuses a preemployment bodily fluids test, and won't agree to random sampling during his employment, kick his application out. And don't make a secret of it, either, downstairs or up."

"And his civil rights?"

Vacuum is unforgiving as hell. Working in it requires, above all else, a clear head and steady hands. "I don't give a damn about his civil rights."

"He will be made aware of that fact."

"Good. That it?"

Charlie regarded me thoughtfully. "Has anyone ever called you overly conscientious?"

"No," I said in genuine surprise. "I don't think so."

"How about a long-nosed, interfering bitch?"

I had to grin. "Only you. But a little learning is a dangerous thing." To prove my point I accessed Demeter, the agronomy program. Demeter informed me that the first batch of *Apis mellifera* had tested the subgee waters of an Express cargo bay with all six sets of toes and had died immediately thereafter of, as near as anyone could figure out, sheer indignation. "A honeybee in zerogee is an unhappy honeybee," I said, sighing.

"Why do we need the damn things, anyway?" Charlie said. She had a tendency to levitate, loudly, in the presence of any creature with six or more legs. When we were kids she swelled up to twice her normal size if a mosquito so much as sneezed in her direction. I sometimes suspect Charlie's main motivation for spacing was the lack of insect life in vacuum.

"The agronomics experts engineered a specific number of pollen plants into the farming toroids," I said, for the two or three hundredth time, "and hand pollination is a bitch—it's boring, time-consuming, and hell on the lower back." I read further. "Interesting. Even if they survive the flight, the bees don't seem to be able to fly."

"They're not supposed to be able to fly at full gee on Terra anyway," Charlie said.

"Aerodynamically speaking, no," I agreed. "You'd think they would take to subgee the way a TAVliner does to orbit. But they don't, it says here. I love my job."

Just then the office door slid open and Simon came in with a face like Zeus making ready to hurl a thunderbolt. He was followed by two massive security guards who dwarfed the little man clutched firmly between them.

"You'd better look at this," Simon said without preamble, and held out my opened pack.

I looked, and felt the bottom drop out of my stomach. Tucked in between my tattered plastiback edition of *The Riverside Shakespeare* and a dozen skeins of bainin was a small cube of gray explosive, a modest detonator, and a timer set for half an hour later. "Looks like a bomb," I said.

"Nothing gets by you, Star," Simon said.

My eyes were burning and I rubbed them with the heels of my hands. It helped, but not much. "Well, at least it's not ticking."

"Not very funny, Star," Charlie said, looking at the little man without expression. From experience I knew she was not really seeing him, that for her he had already ceased to exist.

"No," I agreed. "Not very funny. Where did you find him, Simon?"

"Rex saw him fussing around your bag up in Cargo. You know Rex. He tailed him into the men's room and caught him slipping it into your pack."

I lifted my head to stare across my desk at the little man. Why are fanatics always so short? The eyes are always the same, too, the kind of eyes that see only what they want to see and no more because it might interfere with their vision of what should be. The Luddites didn't have a lot of time to spare for what actually was. The name stenciled over the left pocket of his immaculate jumpsuit, so immaculate that it must have been stolen right off the Supply rack, was J. Moore. I made a mental

note to ginger up the security around Supply. There was as yet
no fear in his face, only pride of purpose and a fervent desire
to immolate himself upon the altar of his cause. "Well, Mr.
Moore, or whatever your name is," I said, keeping my voice
even, "have you anything to say for yourself?" I was miserably
aware that it would have been more appropriate if I had asked
him if he had any last words.

He did, of course. They always do, the Luddites. His
shoulders were back, his chin was up, his syntax perfect and
perfectly demented and impossible to reproduce. Moore believed his was a holy mission—"God has sent me to you." He
made no attempt to deny his culpability—"It was all my idea,
I built the bomb and I brought it up and I waited until
Svensdotter came back and I put it in her luggage." I had no
reason to think he was lying. That unimaginative little lump of
explosive, with no attempt to disguise it, was proof positive.
An engineer would have thought up something much more
difficult to detect, and the Luddites never wasted the few
engineers they managed to entice into the theological fold in
actual execution of a plan. Shortsighted, ignorant, and bigoted,
they weren't stupid. Moore moved from method to
motivation—"This must stop, this abandonment of Mother
Earth, this adoration of the false god of technology." He
begged us to see the light before it was too late, before the
human race had trapped itself in a future that was as unnatural
as it was abhorrent, he didn't say to whom.

I watched him preach on, only half listening. I'd heard it all
before. The Luddites had been trying to destroy Ellfive for
years, in the beginning on the floor of the American Alliance
Congress, and then in more direct fashion, as with the barely
aborted sabotage of the unfolding of the first solar receptor,
and ending most recently with the murder of an astrophysicist
who had, ironically, spoken out against the construction of
Ellfive. Not to mention the last time they tried to knock me off.
You'd think I'd be used to it by now.

"So what are you going to do, Svensdotter?" Moore said at
last with what I was sure he felt was magnificent scorn. "Get
your goons to take me out and shoot me?"

The Luddites had what someone once called the one-syllable

view of life. Yes, no, black, white, good, bad. If only it were
that simple. I fought back a wave of nausea. Charlie, Simon,
and the guards were motionless, staring anywhere but at either
of us. "I couldn't shoot you even if I wanted to, Mr. Moore. If
you had done your homework you'd know there is nothing to
shoot with at Ellfive, and as long as I'm boss here there never
will be."

Something of our tension seemed to penetrate his self-
absorption then, and his eyes darted around the room. "I want
a lawyer. I want to be charged."

I raised my head and looked at him. His features were small
and pinched. "This isn't Terra, Mr. Moore. There are even
fewer lawyers on Ellfive than there are weapons."

He stilled finally and stared at me, uncomprehending. I
elaborated. "There are no lawyers. There is no judge, no jury,
and no appeal. Until commissioning, I am the law on Ellfive.
And the law, Mr. Moore, as provided by the Ellfive charter,
demands immediate execution of a sentence in kind to the
offense. Article II, paragraph three, subsection one."

I set my teeth and my knees and got up to go around the
desk. I nodded at the two guards who stood on either side of the
little man. They stepped back. Simon didn't. I gave him a look
that allowed as how I didn't need a whole lot of help with
someone shorter than Charlie and whom I probably outweighed
by twenty-five kays, and I was right. It wasn't difficult to take
one of Moore's arms and bend it up behind his back. I put my
other arm in a choke hold around his neck, for insurance. I had
to bend over a little to get the right leverage. I forced him step
by step out the door, the guards flanking me on either side,
Simon bringing up the rear. Charlie stayed behind. She always
did. I wished I could.

Rex was leaning up against the wall of the corridor, looking
mean and suspicious. Rex Toranaga, straw boss of the North
Cap security crew and a descendant of samurai warriors by way
of the Maui cane fields, had a naturally mean, suspicious face
and an equally mean and suspicious nature. I liked him, not
least because I knew he wasn't hanging around waiting for his
quota of gratitude. When he saw where we were headed he
gave one nod of grim approval and went back to work. Other

people passed our little procession. A few of them glanced at us and then as quickly away, as if they had committed an act in questionable taste. Out of the corner of my eye I could see that one of the guards was a little green around the gills. I didn't blame her. In thirteen years I had had to space eleven people, four at Copernicus Base on Luna and seven at Ellfive. If I wouldn't let myself remember their names, their faces were imprinted forever on my retinas. I clutched at the little man with sweaty hands and forced him on.

Airlock OC-3 was a scant New York City block from my office, a small room with spacesuits in various states of age and repair hanging from hooks on all three walls. The fourth was given over to the airlock. The room stank of stale sweat. Moore started to make little gobbling noises when Simon cycled the lock. He managed to sink his teeth into my forearm, right through my sleeve, and rip off a good-sized strip of skin. He started to scream when I shoved him inside and slammed the hatch. I didn't look and I tried not to listen but while the atmosphere in the lock was bleeding off he made enough noise for a shower full of people at Auschwitz. When the lock cycled back I had to lean on the flusher for several minutes.

Back in my office I dismissed the guards and went into the john to throw up and change into a clean jumpsuit. When I came out Charlie had her bag open. "Sit," she said sternly, pointing to my chair. When my sister gets in these Hippocratic moods, you can either go along with her or you can coldcock her and carry on. The problem with door number two is that eventually she wakes up. I sat. She zapped my wound with an asceptiwand and smoothed on a layer of shamskin. "That should fall off in a few days."

"Thanks, Dr. Quijance," I said, flexing my arm and wincing. "Let us hope the little bastard wasn't hydrophobic." I rubbed my forehead and said wearily, "Got anything for this headache?"

She rummaged around in her bag and handed me two capsules without comment. I broke them under my nose one at a time and inhaled. The sharp aroma swarmed into my sinuses like a relieving army and the steady throb behind my eyes eased up. "Archy, front and center."

"Yo."

"Archy, send a message to Colony Control. Tell Ricadonna I want that new security supervisor up here as in yesterday. You can make the language as nasty as you want."

A bang on the door interrupted his reply and in marched a stocky little woman in her fifties or thereabouts. She had a full head of flaming red hair, a tiny butterfly tattoo at the corner of one eye, and the inevitable squeebee hooked to her belt. "And so it's the bloody-minded Luddites again, is it now? Then it's a drop of the mountain tay you'll be needing, Star," she said without ceremony. She unhooked the squeebee and handed it over.

I took the bottle, only because I knew it would bring on one of Paddy's redheaded mads if I didn't. I uncapped it, sent up a small prayer, and drank. It went down like liquid oxygen. I wheezed a little, suppressed a gag, and felt hot beads of sweat pop out of every pore. Paddy looked me over appraisingly, gave a satisfied, less-than-maternal nod, recovered her squeebee, and marched out again.

"What does she put in that stuff, anyway?" Simon asked.

"I've always been afraid to ask," Charlie admitted.

"You're responsible for the health of the crew on this project," he said, a little pompously. "That stuff is poison, it has to be. You should shut her down."

"Be my guest." Charlie waved an expansive hand. "Tell Paddy she can't brew her poteen. When she stops laughing, you can track down her still. I figure it's hung on the outside of any one of a thousand Ellfive airlocks. Not including the Frisbee, of course. Or either Doughnut."

Simon subsided, mumbling, and I said to my second in command, "Is there anything urgent I should take care of right away?"

"No, I don't think so," he said. "Not anything that can't wait until tomorrow, anyway."

"Good. Why don't you head on home, then?"

They rose and then hesitated, exchanging one of those comprehensive looks that couples use to communicate with after they've been married for eleven years. Simon cleared his throat and spoke to a nonexistent spot somewhere over my left shoulder, his rumbling voice carefully devoid of any feeling that I might mistake for sympathy. "You sure you wouldn't like to spend the night at our place? Elizabeth's been talking of nothing but Auntie Star coming home for the past two days."

"I'll be all right."

"You're sure?" Charlie said in the same tone of voice, also to the nonexistent spot.

"Goddammit, Charlie, I said I'm all right."

"You don't look even close to all right to me." She was going to say more until Simon placed a firm hand over her mouth and said to me, "Elizabeth took Hotstuff back to your place this morning. She looks ready to pop—Hotstuff, I mean, not Elizabeth—so you might find yourself up to your ankles in baby cats when you get home."

From somewhere I dredged up a wan smile. "I can hardly wait. Now get out of here. Give Elizabeth my love and tell her I'll see her soon."

The firmness of my voice must have convinced them both. They left. "Pull up the drawbridge, Archy," I said.

"Consider it done, boss." I heard the bolts in the door slide home.

My knees unlocked and I slumped down into my chair. I silenced my communit and set my viewer to store any incoming calls. My hand was trembling so much it took me three times before I could set the correct code.

Who would have thought the little man to have had so much blood in him?

— 2 —

Stranger in Town

When a place gets crowded enough to require IDs, social
collapse is not far away. It is time to go elsewhere. The
best thing about space travel is that it made it possible to
go elsewhere.

—**Lazarus Long**

The following week I plunged back into the countdown to
commissioning. It was slow, painstaking, detailed work,
involving checklists that in one continuous printout would
stretch from Ellfive to Terra and back again. The difficulty lay
in getting all the items on one checklist from one department
signed off, punched by the relevant inspector, and cleared by
the oversight committee all at the same time, so as to retire the
list and commission the entire unit once and for all. The
agronomics checklist was only one of many, if one of the most
complicated, especially after I learned that the tomato plants
were refusing to come into bloom and the second batch of bees
died of starvation before we knew what was happening.

19

Conchata Steinbrunner, the agronomics number two, was about ready to commit sideways. "The son-of-a-bitching *bees*, Star," she kept repeating in helpless rage. "The son-of-a-bitching *bees*." H_2O shipments from Luna were still behind schedule, and although we had water enough, or at least ample supplies of hydrogen and oxygen to make enough water to support the recycling systems for the first load of colonists, I didn't like being behind. I foresaw a trip to Copernicus Base in my near future and I wasn't even psychic, and I was spending what I knew perfectly well was far too much time worrying over the solar activity reported on Hewie Seven.

A week after my return I was standing by in the prefab shop watching the carpenters play with one-meter-by-three sheets of sheetrock. It was made of a new silicon-polymer composite a joint team of carpenters and chemists in the Frisbee had literally cooked up. The idea was to employ it as interior walls in residential construction, and today would see if the idea proved out. The carpenters laid out what looked like the entire inventory of the Ellfive tool crib and with great enthusiasm set about hammering, augering, sawing, routing, sanding and lathing, creating large mounds of sawdust and filling the air with cheerful curses.

"That's it, Star," lead carpenter Lee Nakajima said at last. He mopped his forehead, leaving a wet smear of skin showing through the film of white dust. "She tests tougher than cedar, lighter than pine, and she's got a density that makes her almost soundproof. Takes any kind of a nail or screw or bit and won't splinter or split no matter what we do to her."

"Since when is sheetrock a she?" I inquired.

"Since I spent every night for the last month with her at the shop, instead of home in bed with my wife, is when."

"Oh. Zerogee analysis come through?"

"Molecule bleed-off is negligible. Structure maintains integrity to minus-oh-one and it can even keep a seal. For a while, anyway."

"All right, Lee, " I said, clapping him on the shoulder. "Damn good job, and a fast one, too. I'm doubling your crew's bonus," I added, raising my voice, and there was a loud cheer. "How soon can we get the stuff into production?"

Lee grinned and said, "We've already got Dupont pouring it in the Frisbee."

"You were that sure it would test out, were you?" Another grin was all the answer I got and I said, "Okay. Let Roberta McInerny know when to expect delivery of this—uh—we'll call it Leewall"—another cheer went up and Lee actually blushed—"in Shepard Subdivision." I shook Lee's hand warmly, turned to leave, and collided with Caleb Mbele O'Hara.

He steadied me with both hands on my shoulders. "We've got to stop meeting like this," he said.

"O'Hara," I said irritably, "you are beginning to haunt me. I can't step outside my office without stumbling over you. Are you sure you aren't twins?"

"I'm sorry."

He didn't look at all sorry, he just looked big. He had looked big thrashing around on the end of a boathook in the cargo bay the day we arrived, but standing right next to me in the prefab shop the difference in size between the zerogee cheechako and a Kenilworth space tug was hardly worth mentioning. It was rare that I was able to look someone in the eye without leaning down. I could today. The experience was oddly disquieting. I took an unobtrusive step backward and said, "So what's your problem? You're the Ellfive security supervisor now, go secure something. Go find out how that Luddite got his bomb on board last week."

He stepped forward. "Nobody will talk to me about that, so I put Rex Toranaga on it."

I stood my ground. "Oh." Airlock executions were not something we bragged about at Ellfive. I had no wish to become known as the Bloody Mary of the solar system and the news rarely went farther than Frank and Helen on Terra. I could hardly blast my own employees for being loyal and discreet.

"Also," O'Hara added, "I'm just beginning to find my way around. Ellfive's a big place."

I looked at him for a long moment. His green eyes—they were beautiful eyes, large, thickly lashed, and uncomfortably alert—met mine with an expression of bland innocence. I sighed to myself and bowed to the inevitable. "Okay. I'm inspecting Valley One today. You want to ride along?"

"Sounds good." We walked down the corridor and up the stairs to the carport, O'Hara walking in front of me, and it wasn't just my suspicious nature that kept me watching him. He walked like the cat who walked by himself, waving his wild tail and walking by his wild lone. He also walked with the careful nonchalance of someone who is never completely convinced that what is beneath each new step will bear up under the strain. I could relate.

My car choked a little under our combined weights but managed to stagger into the air. As we rose, freed from the centrifugal gravity of the rim, our weight lessened and we proceeded smoothly down Valley One at a cruising altitude of three hundred meters. "What's this thing run on?" O'Hara said.

"Compressed air. Hear the turbines?"

He listened. "That hum?"

"Yes. The air is sucked in through the forward intake, run through a compressor, and pushed out through vents in the hull and the tail. It's the same principle as a balloon, after you blow it up and let it go, only controlled. The higher we get the less we weigh and the faster we go."

"How do you steer?"

"Rudder and elevators, controlled by this yoke and these pedals. This is the throttle, although there are really only two speeds, stop and go. What with the increase in gravity the closer we get to the rim, takeoffs are rough and landings rougher. You haven't taken the security aircar up yet?"

"No."

I shook my head. "Get on the stick, O'Hara. Give Daedalus a call."

"Daedalus?"

"The flight shop. They'll set up an appointment for you with an aircar instructor. Tell them I said you have priority."

"Thank you."

I gave him a sharp look but the expression on his dark face remained uniformly meek. "Aloft, expect everything to happen in slow motion. An aircar's airspeed can be measured in figures of one digit. With that little air pressure against the rudder she handles like an inner tube on the Great Salt Lake."

"Looks kind of like an inner tube, too," he observed.

I couldn't deny it. On Ellfive function won out over form every time. "If you're used to flying planes on Terra, an aircar takes some getting used to. One thing you must remember is to wipe down the intake at the end of each day. Our atmospheric humidity has increased to where the moisture tends to condense on the inside of the vents. It can be a problem if you don't stay on top of it."

"I'll remember," he said obediently, and added, almost as if he couldn't help himself, "I don't want to be forever blowing bubbles over Ellfive."

He went back to looking over the side at the lush vegetation passing beneath us. Lush in comparison to this time last year, at any rate. The sun beat down on our heads from the solar window above us, the golden light only reflected glory in the windows on either side. It was enough to turn the tinted glass of all three a deep, beautiful blue. "Over there," I said, pointing, "that's Clarke Apartments, housing for singles."

O'Hara inspected the collection with interest. "What is that particular architectural style called?"

I winced. "I don't know. Iberian Art Deco is as good as anything, I suppose." Or whatever you call turning loose an architect with visions of Addison Mizner dancing in her head, and then forgetting to check up on her for four weeks. Clarke was colorful, if nothing else.

"What is that big white building there?"

"McAuliffe School, grades one through twelve. Classes begin the second week in February."

"Hmm." O'Hara craned his neck to look from the window overhead to the windows on either side. "This place is shaped like a pencil."

"A pencil thirty-two kilometers long and a little less than six and a half in diameter, with a total land area of thirteen hundred square kilometers," I said dryly.

"How much is habitable?"

"About half. Every second surface of Ellfive's hexagon is a valley three kilometers wide extending the length of the pencil, alternating with windows also three klicks wide. Ellfive's axis points toward the sun and the cape of solar mirrors, one outside each of the three windows, reflects sunlight into the colony through tinted solar windows that makes our sky blue. Computerized adjustment of the angles of these mirrors fakes dawn, dusk, and passage of the sun across our sky, even though we complete a rotation every two minutes, providing the colony with earth-normal gravity. The days and nights are twelve hours long, by design, so that the transition from flatlander to farmer in the sky won't be very traumatic. With a million or so colonists due in at regular intervals over the next year, the less trauma we have, the better." O'Hara was smiling, and I broke off. "I'm sorry. Was I lecturing?"

"You've said all this a few times before, I take it."

"I could recite it in my sleep."

"What's this about flatlander trauma?"

"Terran shrinks have been making dire predictions for years over the prospect of Ellfive raising a population of agoraphobics. Charlie—Dr. Quijance, Ellfive Med—says that's crap. There's six thousand meters of open air between the valleys, and what with more vegetation taking hold every day, the clouds are getting thicker all the time." And then there were the viewports, big enough for two, with the entire universe drifting by the clear graphplex bubble every two minutes. I preferred climbing into my pressure suit and getting right out in the middle of it, although Charlie has informed me with what I can only describe as a salacious grin that the viewports give spectacular new meaning to what the French refer to as "the little death." I couldn't swear to it myself, and it didn't have any bearing on Ellfive security anyway, which was a good thing since I sure as hell had no intention of sharing this titillating little tidbit with O'Hara. I said, "We might eventually have a problem with claustrophobia, especially with the Ellfive-born who go to school on Terra and have to learn to deal with finite horizons. Agoraphobia, no."

O'Hara grunted. "What's that group of buildings? The white ones with the red roofs?"

I answered by setting the aircar down on the perimeter of the housing site with my usual bone-jarring finesse. "Welcome to

Shepard Subdivision. Single-family dwellings built around a community center and playground, close to shopping, restaurants, trolley, bike path, and schools."

O'Hara got out of the car and cast an appraising glance over the development. "I like the architecture. American Southwest, isn't it?"

"Yes. We were concerned with maintaining at least an illusion of privacy, and enclosed patios seemed to be the best way to go."

"What's the material? It looks like adobe brick."

"It's supposed to."

"Star!"

I turned and waved. "Hello, Roberta. Caleb O'Hara, this is Roberta McInerny, Ellfive's architect for family housing. This is Caleb O'Hara, the new security supervisor."

Roberta was a stocky woman in her mid-sixties with callused hands and graying hair caught in an untidy bun. She gave O'Hara a first cursory nod and then a second, more appraising and definitely more appreciative stare. If the man wasn't handsome, he did have a certain battered masculinity that might appeal to some women. He had a high, broad forehead and thick straight brows. His nose, once high-bridged and aquiline, had been broken, several times with enthusiasm, each time in a different direction. An old scar split his right eyebrow, and his hair was a tight cap of black curls. His mouth was wide and expressive and his chin was very square and very firm, and his skin was such a warm, healthy brown that I felt anemic by comparison.

O'Hara bore up calmly beneath her appraisal, and Roberta turned to me finally and said, "I heard about the Luddite, Star. Are you okay?"

"I am just dandy," I said.

Roberta gave me a compassionate look that made me want to scream and with conspicuous tact changed the subject by handing me something. I took it automatically. "Look at this."

It was a terracotta tile, dark red in color, half a cylinder in shape. It was the kind of tile you could see lining half the roofs of the surrounding subdivision and most of New Mexico. It wasn't really terracotta, of course, the real stuff would have been prohibitive in lift costs from Terra. "What's wrong with it?" I said.

"Feel how much it weighs?"

I hefted the piece experimentally in my hand. "So?"

"So, feel how heavy this one is."

The second sample, although much the same in appearance, was considerably lighter in weight, and I raised one eyebrow at Roberta. She nodded. "The heavier one is from the second batch. The walls would need flying buttresses to hold up a roof full of these, Star. And you'll like this." She took the heavy sample from me and let it fall. It shattered on impact into a hundred pieces. I dropped the other. It bounced several times and remained intact.

"More brittle, too," I observed. Like Simon says, nothing gets by me.

"You said it. The ceramics people have pulled this crap before, Star. Remember when George fiddled around with the formula for the piping in the sewage treatment plants and the waste bacteria ate right through it?"

Did I ever, and I shuddered. "Only too well."

"Will you talk to him? I think he's at STP One today."

"Right away."

"Thanks."

She went back to work, and O'Hara's eyes followed her. "She wears brown."

"All construction personnel wear brown."

He looked at his own red jumpsuit, and from it to the gold one I was wearing. "Why the difference in color?"

"Helps sometimes to tell the different departments at a glance. There's blue for computer and life sciences, red for engineering and security, gold for administration, and so on."

"Color coding."

"*Star Trek*. Tradition is all. Would you like to see the inside of one of the homes?" He nodded and I showed him through the one nearest the aircar, which had three bedrooms, a family room, and two baths. It had the same smell all new houses do, even back on Terra, part sawdust although nothing on Ellfive was made of wood, part glue, and part clean, the edgy kind of clean that dares you to track in a single grain of dirt. The rooms

were airy and spacious, with a window in each looking out on
a patio of generous size filled in with a neat level of pulverized
LIMSH waiting to be bullied into life. As we looked a ray of
sun shifted and poured through the open roof in a golden
stream.

"Very nice," O'Hara said.

"Yeah, the new owners can plant whatever they want, grass
or gardens. Or they can brick it over if they aren't big on yard
work. The family room is framed for a viewport that looks
outside, as well as for an airlock, either of which can be
installed on request."

"They have to pay for it?"

"That'll be something for the colonists to decide among
themselves. I would say the airlocks will probably be installed
at need, at least at first, depending where the new owners
work, inside or out."

We emerged from the house to stand blinking in the sunlight.
"Is this where I'll be living?"

I stared at him. "Where have you been sleeping this last
week?"

"In my office."

"No," I said, shaking my head.

"Yes, I have."

"No, I meant that I try to discourage sleeping over the shop
on Ellfive."

"Why?"

I stopped and faced him. "You already live on the job. All
the department heads are on call twenty-four hours a day.
Archy can locate you immediately through this." I tapped the
communit strapped to his left arm.

"Archy?"

"Ellfive's in-house computer and binary brat."

"I heard that!"

"Archy, I thought I turned you off."

"I recognize the voice," O'Hara said.

"You should, you gave him a voiceprint and he confirmed
your identity when you came on board. He runs the joint, and
you'll need him to help run your department. Have you given
the security file an address yet?" The big man looked an
inquiry and I said, "Really a personal password. Each depart-

ment head has their own voice-keyed operating program. For example, mine is Archy. Ellfive's medical library and personnel files are keyed under Blackwell—"

"It would be useful if security had access to the medical files," he said. "Do we?"

"If you speak Tagalog."

"Pardon?"

"Charlie—Dr. Quijance—is very firm about doctor-patient confidentiality. However, if she can be convinced that whatever information you want is necessary to Ellfive's security, she will spring for information in English."

"If she can be convinced."

"You're catching on. And if you're at all interested in computers—"

"Who isn't!"

"Put a lid on it, Archy—if you're interested in computers, the compsci program can be found under 'Frank.'" The big man looked puzzled and I said, "For Frankenstein. Look, the point I'm trying to make is that once you have a password, Archy can find you anywhere. From that moment on, believe me, you're going to need a place separate from your office to go after work hours. People tend to be more wary of disturbing you after you've gone home for the night." I reflected, and added, "At least they'll hesitate all of one or two minutes before they put the call through, and maybe in that time they can figure out the answer to their question themselves."

"Anyone can call me, anytime?"

"Anyone, anytime," I said firmly. "Call signs are listed on Archy's directory, and besides your communit there are viewscreens about every ten meters all over the place. It is essential that all my section chiefs provide instant accessibility to everyone. We're a team here, from me right down to the newest rigger. Nobody has to go through channels to get to me or to anyone else."

He nodded thoughtfully. I didn't see any resistance to the idea, which took a load off my mind. Some of those Harvard Business School types we got at first were big on chain of command and weekly departmental meetings and goal orientation. They had done enough damage to morale before I managed to weed out the last of them and I wasn't about to go through that again.

"So," he said, "I could move in here if I wanted to."

"Here or anywhere you like, as long as you don't dispossess someone already in residence. As security supervisor you have certain privileges, although—" I hesitated.

"What?"

"I would think one of these homes would be a bit large for a single man."

"I like the patio."

"Oh? You a gardener?"

And he utterly confounded me by saying, "I raise orchids."

"Oh," I said. He grinned, and it was a wide grin that lit his face with warmth and intelligence. I was immediately on my guard. "Orchids?" I said. "You grow orchids?"

"Yes."

"I thought I saw—yes, Archy said you went over the personal baggage limit by fifty-five kays. Orchid stuff?"

"Orchid stuff," he confirmed.

"Orchids grow in New South Africa, do they?"

"Orchids grow everywhere."

"Oh," I said again. "We'd better get back in the air if we're going to finish this tour before midnight."

We'd been cruising for five minutes when he said, "Where have I seen you before? I know you from somewhere, and not just from that garbage they put out over the trivee, either."

"We've never met," I replied with exactitude.

"That's not what I said. I know we've never met. I would remember." I said nothing and he said slowly, "I'll find out, you know. I always do."

"That's your job," I agreed. Star Svensdotter, Woman of Mystery. It was a silly game, but I enjoyed the edge it gave me over the big man all the same.

We passed over two more housing developments and a wide, shallow stream. We were approaching a less finished-looking area of Valley One, planted with slender birch trees and low blueberry bushes just beginning to leaf out. Paths led through the forested area, and I could see a layer of soft moss appearing on some of the lunar boulders the landscaper had placed for artistic effect. The aircar thudded to a halt. O'Hara felt his jaw gingerly. "I think I chipped a tooth."

"Welcome to Heinlein Park."

Setting a grubby collection of clippings to one side with tender hands, Roger hurried toward us through the new green leaves. He was a thin, gangling man who always looked as if he were about to break into a run or burst into tears or both. "What's wrong, Star?"

Roger never greeted me any other way. Murphy wrote his law and Roger lived it. When the oak saplings made it up from Terra intact, Roger worried over whether they would take hold. When they took hold, Roger worried if we had enough water to keep them going. When the H_2O shipment made it in from Luna in time, Roger worried if the solar windows let in the proper amount of light for healthy photosynthesis. If the sun shone down uninterrupted, Roger worried over the CO_2 count. When the meteorologist pronounced the atmosphere in perfect balance, Roger took to worrying over the next shipment of seeds to be coddled into life.

On the other hand Roger, immersed in the mysteries of deep-space progagation of *Solanum tuberosum* and *Coffea arabica*, would never concern himself over something as unimportant as the casual disposal of the odd Luddite. If I'd spaced something with leaves, it would have been a different story.

"Nothing's wrong, Roger," I said patiently, because above all else dealing with Roger required patience. "I'd like you to meet Caleb O'Hara, our new security supervisor. Roger Lindbergh, our chief agronomist."

They shook hands, Roger first wiping his palm down the already filthy leg of his green jumpsuit. "Nice to meet you," O'Hara said. "Perhaps you could help me with my orchids."

Roger's lugubrious expression changed, decreasing in gloom from acute depression all the way to mere dismay. "Dear me, yes, *Orchidaceae*. Epiphytes?"

"I think I'd better leave the trees to themselves," O'Hara said with a smile, "now that you've got them off to such a good start."

"Dear me, yes, what was I thinking of," Roger murmured,

going pink. "Saprophytes it is. You'll need to talk to the
sewage treatment people for compost. Any particular family?"

"*Cattleya labiata. Phalenopsis.* Nothing very exotic."

"But such lovely colors, dear me, yes," Roger said. "You
might like to see a planter we've got that provides up to a
hundred square feet of indoor growing space." O'Hara looked
interested and Roger grew positively loquacious. "It's made of
individual but connected pockets that hang together on a flat,
vertical surface. Roberta McInerny and I designed it to fit on
the average Ellfive living-room wall," he added proudly.

The big man was obviously impressed. "I would like to see
it. I was concerned with available gardening space."

All this was fine but it wasn't getting the job any forrader.
"How's the work coming, Roger?" I said.

Roger's face lapsed into its usual tragic lines. "We're still
having problems with the mameys in the Farthest Doughnut."

I groaned. "What's the matter with them now?"

"We don't know exactly. All the growth seems to be going
toward the roots instead of the leaves and buds."

"That happened once with a new species of orchid I was
trying to grow," O'Hara said unexpectedly.

I raised my eyebrows at him but Roger, not so much of a
snob, said eagerly, "Yes?"

"I was giving it too much fertilizer. I cut back on feedings by
half and had blooms all over the place."

Maybe he really did grow orchids, I thought, but Roger
shook his head and said with regret, "We tried that. All the
leaves fell off."

"So what are we going to do now?" I said.

"We could phase out the mameys entirely," Roger suggested.

I thought. "I can't remember for sure, but wouldn't that put
us below seven hundred on the edible plant list?"

He called up Demeter on his communit. They conferred.
"Yes, it would."

I shook my head. "Then no. We want maximum diversity of
fruits and vegetables. It's going to be hard enough to accustom
people to eating meat and drinking milk out of the vats. The
least we can do is offer alternatives." I thought it over,

frowning. "Listen, Roger, why don't you call the University of Cuba in Havana? The mamey is the Cuban national fruit, isn't it? Maybe they'll have some ideas. What else?"

"We still haven't received our shipment of *Triticum durum* from Omaha Seed."

"That's the stuff they make pasta out of, isn't it?" He nodded. "Fear not, Roger. I get nasty without my fettucini. I'll call Colony Control and have that seed shipped up on the next Express."

Relieved, he trotted back into the bushes as we lifted off. "A nice man," O'Hara said, and I replied, "A genius in his field. He was a student of Richard Bradfield, the scientist who invented multiple cropping and double planting."

"Multiple cropping? Double planting?"

"And you call yourself a gardener. Multiple cropping means that the farming toroids will be growing two crops in every field. Double planting means overlapping one growth cycle with another."

"In other words, planting the next crop before the first one is harvested."

"Exactly."

"Will Ellfive itself be doing any farming?"

I shook my head. "Very little at first, and when the population is up to maximum none at all. For Bradfield's projected four crops per year we'd have to keep the atmosphere low in oxygen and the ambient temperature at something like a constant ninety-five degrees."

"Sounds fine to me," O'Hara said, and I remembered where he was from.

"Not to me," I said fervently. "I was born in Alaska, and I'm allergic to anything above fifty degrees."

From Heinlein Park we went to the oyster farm, where Elmo and Drake were having problems with the hardness of the oyster shells. They explained to me that the shells had to be precisely the right consistency or they would gum up the grinder that would be crunching them into fertilizer after we harvested the oysters. We talked it over and agreed to try a lower water temperature before calling in the genetechs. Why is nothing ever easy? O'Hara inquired hopefully after the possibility of harvesting some of the oysters then and there, and was obviously heartbroken to learn that the oysters had six months to go before they would be edible.

Back in the air O'Hara was distracted, as if he were mentally working out a difficult problem. After a few moments he smiled proudly and cleared his throat.

> "Shellfish were along for the space ride,
> But no bivalves were ready to be fried.
> The Walrus said, 'What?
> No oysters to be got?'
> And the Carpenter was fit to be tied."

He waited with a hopeful expression on his dark face. I maintained a dignified silence, but it was a struggle. He heaved a sad sigh and asked, "Does Ellfive have any lakes strictly for swimming and like that?"

"Nothing is strictly for one purpose on Ellfive, but we do have a swimming lake." I pointed. "Valley Two. That long skinny blue streak on our upper left. Loch Ness."

His eyes followed my pointing finger and he said, "Oh, I see. I—oh." His sigh was long, drawn-out, and reverent. I smiled to myself.

The South Cap sported rakish mountains three thousand meters high, rough-peaked. They marched around the South Cap in uneven rings, and they looked as if they had been old when the world was young. They were in fact just three years of age, planted with various species of fir and dotted with tiny lakes. I discovered I still enjoyed the expression on someone's face when he was seeing them for the first time.

When he spoke O'Hara's voice was awed. "Where the hell did you find the material?"

I tried hard to keep the proprietary pride out of my voice, but I had to admit that I sometimes felt as if I personally had put the Big Rock Candy Mountains together a stone at a time. "Some from Luna. Some from meteoroids and asteroids. Some from the remains of the comets."

"The remains of the what?"

"Comets. We trapped half a dozen or so ten years into the

project. The trap burned out on the seventh try or we would have trapped more."

"Uh-huh," he said. "You trapped comets. You want to tell me how?"

"I would if I could."

"What, is it a secret?"

I made a rude noise. "No way. There's none of that top-secret crap on Ellfive. No, the comet trap was born of a brainstorming session between a Brazilian theoretical engineer, a Japanese mechanical engineer, an astronomer and an astrophysicist, both French, a Virginian architect who specialized in the design of zerogee structures, and Simon. I was there, too; I didn't understand one word in ten, but I was in there pushing."

"So?"

"So I didn't understand one word in ten. The engineers called it an electromagnetic pseudo-gravitation broom star deception device. I called it a comet trap."

"I begin to see," the big man murmured.

"Yeah, they tried to explain it to me twice, both times in polysyllables. After the second try I said the hell with it, other than to thank God we had unlimited power from the paraboloidal mirror off the South Cap when we tried it."

"I can imagine. Or I can't, because I'm not an engineer, but I suppose given enough power you can solve any engineering problem."

"So they tell me." Our eyes met and we exchanged our first real smiles in a conspiratorial amusement over the universal damn-the-torpedoes, can-do, Tom-Swiftiness spirit of all engineers. "I guess we haven't come that far, have we, from the days of the old Saturn V rockets, which at five gallons to the inch were slightly less than fuel efficient?"

"Thorstein Veblen, where are you now?"

"Ah, well. Truthfully, I don't much care how they pulled it off, they filled an urgent material need for water and hydrogen and the Rock Candy Mountains. That was all that was really important." I fingered the diamond in my right earlobe from habit.

"I figure that to be a full carat," he said.

I dropped my hand and looked at him.

"Well, I am from New South Africa," he pointed out.

"So you are."

"It's nice. At a guess, I'd call it a flawless. Where'd you get it?"

"It's a bonus from the comet trap. We mined diamonds out of the nuclei of the comets."

"No kidding?"

"No kidding. Everyone on the comet trap team got one." I grinned at him. "I wear mine to remind myself to ignore theoretical physicists who insist a thing is physically impossible." I pointed again. "See that opening? No, up farther, at the center of the endcap, surrounded by the peaks."

"That circular hole?"

"That's the zero-gravity corridor."

"What does it connect to?"

"Nothing yet, it isn't finished. When it is, it will link Ellfive to the zero-gravity industries module and the farming toroids, aka the Frisbee, the Nearest Doughnut, and the Farthest Doughnut. When Ellfive is commissioned that will be the way to work for most Fivers."

He looked from the valley floor to the endcap. "How will they get there from there?"

"Look up. No, straight up, over our heads. That's one way."

"What are those? Hang gliders?"

"Some of them. Others wear just plain wings."

He snapped his fingers. "How could I forget—the Zerogee Club! I remember seeing something about it on the trivee."

"I should think so. It's one of our best recruiting incentives. Your belt fastened? Hang on and don't burp or the zero gee will make you fart."

"I have yet to be sick in zero gravity."

"Is that so?" I said politely. "And how many times before the trip upstairs have you experienced zero gravity?"

"I went to Mitchell Observatory two days ago by scooter," he replied, looking wounded.

"I don't call a half-hour trip out to the Warehouse Ring experiencing zero gravity. How many times altogether?"

He made a production out of counting on his fingers. He

caught me looking and grinned suddenly. "So, okay, today will
be the third time."

"Congratulations. You're holding up remarkably well," I
said, and pulled back on the yoke to hitch a fast ride on a
thermal layer up to twenty-four hundred meters. He barely had
time to swallow. Sometimes I think I am not a nice person.

The farther we got from the rim, the more our gravity
decreased, until at the axis there was none at all and our bodies
started tugging at the seat harness. The increasing low gee
made it easy to climb the Big Rock Candy Mountains, even
carrying nine kays worth of plastigraph wings and straps and
stirrups on your back. It was even easier to launch yourself into
the air, and flyers were launching themselves into the air in
record numbers that afternoon. "Oh Ellfive we say one flyer in
the air is recreation, two is a race, and three is an airshow," I
said. "This looks like Oshkosh in August."

"They must have heard I was coming," O'Hara murmured.
I stole a sideways look at his rapt expression and held my
peace.

I had seen that expression before. Axial flying at Ellfive was
the dream come true of every child from six to sixty, manned
flight under manned power, no propellers, no pressure plates,
no fairy dust, just flyers and their wings and the deep blue of
the sky. There was nothing like it anywhere else in the solar
system, except perhaps the Bat's Cave, the cavern they had
sealed over on Luna. Unless the Russians had started jumping
off Nix Olympica on Mars. We watched flyer after flyer launch
from the two ledges, taking turns jumping from Orville to
Wilbur and back again, soon afterward to glide by the aircar on
their colorful graphite-and-plastic wings. A few of them
waggled their wings in greeting. Most of them cursed us for
being in their way. Flyers are no respecters of authority when
it interferes with their glide path.

"You know, I remember after the Beetlejuice Message," the
big man said finally, "how all the crazies came crawling out of
the cracks. They had bug-eyed monsters on the cover of
Scientific American and little green men chasing each other
across the news on every trivee screen on Terra. Liberals were

ready to welcome the new and no doubt superior race with open arms—"

"—and conservatives speculated darkly over the intentions of what was undoubtedly an invasion force," I said, getting into the spirit of the thing. "We were no longer alone in the universe. But what did the Bettlejuicers look like?"

"And what did they eat?"

"And did they have separate sexes?"

O'Hara dropped his voice and said in a tone one step up from the tomb, "Did they have sex?"

We looked at each other and smiled. It was getting easier to do, and it made me nervous. "That was a time."

He nodded, looking back at the flyers. "It was that. Funny how Frank Sartre turned all that into an afternoon on the wing for these folks."

"All Frank said was what he'd been saying for the previous twenty years." I quoted, " 'The surest road to the stars is to build self-supporting habitats in orbit about the earth, colonies that will pay for themselves with solar power and zero-gravity industries as well as provide bases for further exploration and exploitation of the stars.' But after the Beetlejuice Message everyone decided he was a prophet and swore him in as chairman of the Habitat Commission."

"He design this?" O'Hara waved an all-inclusive hand.

"God, no. Frank proposed a small, enclosed sphere maybe two kilometers in diameter. It was Congress who decided to go for broke and build the largest of all the O'Neill habitat designs. One of the structural engineers told me there was more margin for error that way." I hesitated, wondering if he would understand. "The Beetlejuice Message was like the spark from heaven, and afterward there were no light half-believers of casual creeds left. I don't think Frank expected the response that followed the Message. Not a tenth of it."

"It was one hell of a spark," O'Hara agreed. "Where do I get my wings?"

I was admiring the style of one woman in a pair of bright blue Wright Flyers. She would beat up almost to zerogee, until she couldn't quite grab air anymore, and then sideslip a hundred meters down on one gentle swoop, until gravity began

to tug her down, only to climb again. "Talk to Anitra
Kvasnikof at Daedalus. She'll arrange for you to be fitted and
have the cost of the wings deducted from your salary."

"How much?"

I turned to measure his impressive frame with my eyes.
"What you have left over from your first paycheck after the
freight on the orchid stuff ought to just about cover it."

We watched the airshow for a while longer. "What's the
worst I can expect on the job?" he said, suddenly serious.
"Bottom line. You could start with this Luddite movement that
keeps kidnapping astronomers on Terra."

Back to business. "Obviously the Luddite group has stepped
up its activities—"

"Obviously?"

I sighed. He wanted chapter and verse. Well, if I were the new
security supervisor, so would I. "Do you know who they are?"

"I know a little about what they represent. A rabid antitech-
nology terrorist group, aren't they? Started about two hundred
years ago back in the English part of the European Common-
wealth, when guildsmen thought the mechanization of the
industrial revolution was going to put them out of work. The
group we're talking about now was formed more recently.
They've got around two thousand hardcore members and
another fifty thousand dilettantes who merely dabble in de-
struction. Ideologically, the group opposes space exploration
and colonization on the grounds that if Terra was good enough
for their fathers, it's good enough for them."

Put like that, the Luddite demon shrank to a much more
exorcisable size. "That's them." I rubbed my forearm. The
shamskin had long since fallen off and the teeth marks were
almost invisible. "You must understand, O'Hara, that when
you accepted the job of security supervisor, you took over
the—the—you inherited the duty of—of—well, you get to
space the next guy who tries to blow me up."

"Uh-huh," he said absently.

He wouldn't have been so goddam nonchalant the week
before. I struggled to match his calm. "Have you been briefed
on my no-weapons policy?"

"Yes."

"Do you agree?"

"No." He smiled at my expression and said, "But you're the boss."

I nodded. "Yes, I am, but I expected more argument out of a security supervisor who once fought a revolution and wound up responsible for the defense of an entire Terran nation." I waited hopefully but he said nothing more and I went on. "The closer it gets to commissioning, the more frantic the Luddites will get to prevent it happening, and the more alert we have to be for sabotage. I want you to concentrate your efforts in preventing a repeat of last week."

"All right," he said equably.

I was insensibly comforted by that deep-voiced reassurance, pronounced in an interesting amalgam of African sibilants and eastern seaboard A's. Next to a cat's purr my favorite noise is English spoken with an accent. "Sometimes we have trouble with liberty parties from Orientale, but in general the Patrol MPs manage them pretty well. For the rest, discipline is enforced through the director's mast for punishments and rewards. You settle the petty cases and save the Solomons for me. Most of the supervisors handle their own departments, which is why there have been only one hundred and seventeen masts in the last fifteen years."

"I think it might have a little to do with the swift and speedy execution of justice on the part of the director. I like your style, Star."

"Other than sabotage—"

"I like the way you blush, too." One forefinger investigated the opening of my collar. "How far down does it go?"

I moved out of reach, or tried to. An aircar is not what anyone could call roomy. "Theft here isn't as bad as some projects I've worked on. Of course there aren't many places four hundred thousand klicks from Terra to hide a D-9 StarCat."

"No."

I knew he was laughing at me and I went on doggedly, "The problems here aren't all that different from the problems on any large construction project anywhere on Terra. Ellfive welders are just as thirsty as any 798er out of Tulsa, Oklahoma, and the

operators are even more horny than their union brothers
downstairs, if that's possible. There are a few illegal stills. Two
years ago we had a couple of hookers posing as biotechs show
up and sell over half a million Alliance dollars in magazine
subscriptions until Kate found out and alerted the Magdalene
Guild. That's about as exciting as it gets. I don't have any
problem with drinking or doping as long as blood and urine are
clear on the job, especially zerogee and EVA. There isn't much
anyone has to import to have fun."

"What happened to the last security supervisor?"

"Nobody knows." He stared at me, startled out of his
placidity, and I nodded once for emphasis. "There was trouble
with one of the silicon techs in the Frisbee. She was a hell of
a tech and he wasn't much of a supervisor, so I was fixing to
fire him when she came to me and asked me not to. A few days
later he went EVA for a safety inspection. He didn't come
back, and no one's seen him since."

"You think—"

I held up a cautionary hand. "I've told you exactly what I
know happened firsthand. Anything else is speculation, no
more, nor less."

"And she was a hell of a tech," he said.

"Yeah. She signed on the first mining expedition to the
Trojans. I was sorry to see her go."

He shook his head. "Right. Tour over?"

I nodded, and said, "You might want to spend the rest of the
afternoon choosing a home."

"Question."

"Go ahead."

"Where do you live?"

I made a vague gesture that encompassed the entire South
Cap. "I've got a place a couple thousand feet below Orville and
Wilbur, about halfway down the mountains."

He peered over the side. "I don't see it."

"It's a little house, and it's the only one there."

He looked back at me. "Sounds lonely."

"Sometimes," I said, trying to be honest. "Sometimes just
alone. I like it that way."

"Yeah." He didn't sound convinced. He raised one hand and

touched my cheek. "Soft," he said. He tucked a wisp of my hair back behind an ear. "Pretty."

My communit started wailing the emergency call and I keyed it to receive. I kicked in the throttle and had the aircar in a steep, diving turn back toward the North Cap almost before Archy bellowed, "Star, Patrolman trouble at Kate's! Rex says get there soonest!"

"On my way, and I've got the security supervisor with me." I leveled off at three hundred and let the throttle out, although an aircar at flank speed would have trouble keeping up with a snail with a limp.

"What's up?" O'Hara said, loosing his death grip on the side of the aircar and raising his voice to be heard over the sound of air rushing by.

"Sounds like trouble with the liberty party from Orientale. Archy? What's happening now? Let me talk to Rex."

"He's not answering his communit, Star. Kate says they're heading for their shuttle and to go directly to the hangarlock."

Twenty minutes later, most of which I spent mentally composing a speech to Daedalus on the advisability of upgrading aircar performance, we were at O'Neill. I was at the hangarlock in ten minutes flat, an Ellfive record, rolled into the barrel lock, and rolled out the other side into the middle of what seemed to be World War IV.

Half the combatants were Ellfive longshoremen and the rest were Patrolmen, with a few Ellfive security guards standing out like red bees at an ant convention. Rex was one of them, and as I watched, a man in the black and silver of the Space Patrol braced himself against a joist and brought a fist down hard just behind Rex's left ear. O'Hara winced and clicked his tongue. Rex's eyes rolled up and his body went limp and the force of the blow knocked him literally into a spin across the hangar toward us. O'Hara fielded him with one hand, unhooked a bungee cord with another, and fastened Rex to a cargo sling safely out of the line of scrimmage.

The fight would have caused the Marquis of Queensberry considerable anguish and Buster Keaton nothing but pure, unadulterated joy. Fortunately the walls of the transitional hatch were heavily padded; we had had too much experience with green hands pulling a little too hard on a load that was a little too large to handle once it got moving. The rules of inertia and mass don't change just because the rule of gravity no longer applies. The longshoremen had an edge in home ground and weapons and were laying vigorously about themselves with boathooks and fenders, where the Patrolmen had only their fists. An unconscious longshoreman tumbled across the cargo bay, bounced off a bulkhead, caromed off an extinguisher rack, and for all I know may be tumbling still. I saw a Patrolman take a swing at one longshoreman, miss completely, and continue around in a pirouette that brought him in an increasingly lazy circle to the center of the lock, where he tangled with a cargo net. The longshoreman hooked his feet into a toehold, snagged the net with a boathook and gave the net and the Patrolman a firm nudge toward the opposite bulkhead. The net and the Patrolman picked up speed, the Patrolman smashed into the wall, fifty kays of net smashed into him, and the lights were out for that representative of zerogee law enforcement.

Something scratched at my sleeve and I looked down to see someone's front tooth, the root bloody, bump into my forearm. A globule of blood promptly attached itself to my sleeve and spread into a dime-sized stain. I looked up. There wasn't a Patrol MP in sight. I cursed and turned to pull myself out of the way and ran up against—who else? Caleb Mbele O'Hara. I glowered at him. "You are more underfoot than a litter of kittens."

He jerked his head toward the melee and inquired serenely, "You want me to break that up?"

"And just how would you go about it, pray tell?"

He thought it over, surveying the scene as he dangled one-handed from a wall grip. "Could we turn the gravity back on?" he suggested. In spite of myself I almost laughed, and O'Hara saw it and grinned, a white slash in his dark face. "That's better. Is there a P.A. around here somewhere?"

"Over by the p-suit locker," I said, pointing. "See the control panel?"

"Got it." He reversed neatly and began pulling himself swiftly from one wall grip to another. I followed, noticing that he was a quick learner, because he bore no resemblance to the guy grabbing for sky all across the hangarlock the previous week.

We got to the control panel and I pulled the mike and thumbed the switch for the loudspeaker. "Crank it up to full volume," O'Hara said, tucking his toes beneath a locker and cupping the mike in both hands, "and plug your ears."

I did both and nodded that I was ready.

I saw his chest expand as he took a deep breath, another, and then the entire hangarlock was filled with a shrill, high-pitched shriek that escalated into a kind of ululation that sounded like deranged laughter. The sound echoed from bulkhead to bulkhead and the vibration bounced me around worse than my worst aircar landing. Whenever the sound seemed to be dying down O'Hara filled his lungs and brought it back to life. The fight slowed up right away, as the brawlers broke off fighting to jam their fists in their ears instead of each other's faces. It turned out there wasn't a thousand to each side, but more like ten or twelve.

When the activity had slowed enough to suit him O'Hara gave the bulkhead behind him a gentle kick that had him running out of steam in almost the exact center of the hangarlock. "All right," he said, still into the mike clipped to his collar, "break it up. You"—he pointed to a Patrolman with stripes on his sleeve—"and you"—he pointed to Rex, who had regained consciousness and was fighting his way free of the bungee cord—"follow me. The rest of you stay put, and Duffy"—this to the lead longshoreman—"you see to it they do." He turned and sent the mike tumbling toward me end over end. I caught it, snapped it back into the wall socket, and followed the three of them through the barrel lock.

"I want to call Orientale," the Patrolman said immediately.

Rex was almost, but not quite, too angry to speak. "This started at Kate's, Star. They gang-raped one of her girls."

Charlie's brown eyes looked tired when she came back into the dispensary. "She was able to identify her assailants before I sedated her. I pulled the visas filed with security when the party checked in and printed out pictures. Name, rank, med

file, and serial number on the back of each. DNA matches the
semen samples." She shoved them at me. "Here. Get them
away from me."

"How is she?"

"Multiple contusions, concussion, loss of blood, nightstick
fracture right ulna, retinal damage to left eye, shock, no front
teeth left, and that's just the physical damage." Charlie shook
her head. "I don't even want to talk about her mental state.
She's angry now, but that'll wear off, and when it does . . ."
Her voice trailed away, and she shook her head again.

"What does she say happened?"

"She says one of the Patrolmen—that one—wanted to buy
an hour. She didn't like his attitude, so she said no. When he
got obnoxious about it she left. He followed her upstairs and
insisted, with help from his three shipmates. She fought. A
customer next door heard the commotion and came in to check
and they jumped him and made him watch." Charlie tugged at
the collar of her jumpsuit. "That's all she remembers. She
passed out when they started taking turns." She was silent for
a moment, and then said, "I'd forgotten this kind of thing still
happens, Star. I just—I guess—I didn't believe it could happen
here, on Ellfive. Want to see her?"

"If it will help," I said steadily.

She gave a tired shrug. "It can't hurt."

When I got back to Kate's my control was hanging by a
thread. Kate, her bartender, three of Kate's other girls, and the
customer—a longshoreman who had called in his friends and
forced the Patrolmen into a retreat to the hangarlock and their
shuttle—confirmed the victim's story. The Space Patrol sergeant in charge of this liberty party, his face waxen, repeated
the only thing he had said so far, "I want to call Orientale."

"You don't cooperate with this investigation and you'll be
lucky if you ever see Orientale again," I told him.

"She was only a whore," he said. There was a murmur of
agreement from his comrades in arms, grouped in back of him
in a stiff line with their hands bound behind their backs.

We were standing in the middle of the shambles of what had
been a friendly neighborhood bar with a little casino in the
back. The second story was full of rooms with beds in them

that took up almost all the floor space of each room. Variously bruised and bandaged and all of them white and shaken, Kate's staff was sweeping up broken glass and stacking pieces of broken tables and chairs in a big pile. Kate herself, a large, normally ebullient woman with sharp black eyes and a nose like a bran muffin, was straddling a chair on my left, smoking a slender cigar with her little finger crooked as if she were drinking tea with King William. Her black eyes squinted against the smoke, fixing on the sergeant's face in an unwavering stare.

I looked at Kate looking at the sergeant, and I thought of that battered girl, and I knew a momentary impulse to take Rex and Caleb back to my office to inventory the paper clip supply. We could return in an hour or so with mops, to clean up all that would be left of the liberty party. I controlled myself. The boss is paid to control herself. I was goddam tired of being boss. "She isn't *only* anything," I said to the sergeant. "She is a Fiver, with all the rights and privileges implied therein. She said no. Everyone here heard her, including you. You couldn't buy her because she wasn't selling, so you took. You don't 'take' on Ellfive."

Kate puffed out a large cloud of smoke. It drifted into the sergeant's vicinity. "Or you don't and live," she added gently.

The sergeant closed up like a clam. "We're Patrolmen. You can't do anything to us. I demand to call my commanding officer on Orientale."

"You sure about that? At least four of your people as trained warriors are guilty of assault with a deadly weapon, and of rape, and the rest of you are guilty of conspiracy of silence in the action of a felony. The penalty for any one of those offenses is the same on Luna as it is on Ellfive."

He maintained a stubborn silence. O'Hara motioned to me and we moved to the other side of the room. "Who is their commanding officer?"

"Commodore Grayson Cabot Lodge, CSPOB, Luna."

He whistled. "The Fourth?"

"The same."

"What's the problem? Turn 'em over. Lodge is a fine

soldier, and from all I've heard a responsible and even an honorable one. He's not going to condone this kind of behavior in troops under his command." I remained silent. He said, "You'll have to turn them over sooner or later." I said nothing, and he added, "Unless you want me to space them here and now?"

I blew out a breath. "Where's your viewer, Kate?"

She jerked a thumb over her shoulder, her eyes never leaving the Patrolmen. I picked my way through the debris around the bar. The viewer was miraculously undamaged. "Archy, get Lodge."

He kept me waiting for fifteen minutes. When finally the screen dissolved to Space Patrol Headquarters on Luna, his bright brown gaze was steady and guileless. Only the very best liars can meet your eyes with that kind of candor.

"What can I do for you, Star?"

The sergeant must have heard and recognized Lodge's voice for he let out a yell. O'Hara promptly and efficiently gagged him. I told Lodge what had happened in flat monosyllables. His face had darkened by the time I finished, but all he said was, "My men?"

I stared at him. "Your men are fine, Grays. Not a scratch on any of them."

"Well, ship them on back to Luna, along with any evidence you have." When I would have protested he raised one hand and said, "They will be punished under the law, Star, I will see to it personally. You have my word."

Somewhat to my surprise I saw that he meant it, that he was furious beneath his calm. "Too little, too late, Grays," I said, more mildly now. "This is the second riot started by a Patrol liberty party in two months. We were lucky last time, nobody got hurt. This time, your people go back to taking liberty at GEO base." He started to say something and I raised my voice. "I imagine Kate will be sending you a bill for damages. The girl's unconscious now, but when she wakes up I'll encourage her to file suit in the System Courts for actual and punitive damages, medical expenses, and wages lost. I imagine the Magdalene Guild will be contacting you as well."

"You imagine correctly," Kate said over my shoulder.

Lodge's lips compressed into a thin line, but he gave a curt nod and I cleared my screen and turned to O'Hara. "Take them back to Orientale restrained and under guard. Archy."

"I'm here, boss," Archy said, sounding more sober than I would have believed possible.

"Tell Daedalus to assign an Ellfive pilot to the Patrol shuttle. Caleb? Stay at Orientale just long enough to land and turn over your cargo and no longer. Don't sit down to eat with those sonsabitches, don't accept so much as the offer of a drink, and don't stay the night. Rex? Take the security scout and go with him to bring him back, and be careful, damn it. Go."

The liberty party marched out, escorted by Rex and Caleb. Almost on the inward swing of the door Paddy materialized with the inevitable squeebee. I grabbed it and downed three gulps before I remembered what it was I was swallowing. I coughed and said, "And what did you do in the war, Mommy?"

"Wasn't it a good thing I was after finishing up the punch card on the hangarlock?" she said soothingly. "I wouldn't have been so close with the tay as I was otherwise."

"We could have used some help."

" 'Tis a lover and not a fighter I am, Star Svensdotter, as well you know. And wasn't I listening in to the donnybrook on the gadget, now?" Gadget was Paddy's word for any technological device newer than the plow, and in this case meant her communit, which for once was on her wrist.

I took another gulp of poteen. "Just one damn thing after another, Paddy. Just one damn thing after another."

"Sure, and I haven't had this much fun since the Maze in '97," she observed. She reclaimed her squeebee and held it out to Kate, who refused the offer with less tact than speed and headed for the bar. Paddy vanished.

Responsibility is a fine thing; when you take on a lot of it for someone else, they give you a big house with a wet bar, and only last Christmas Frank Sartre sent me a crate of Glenlivet, most of which was still there. I went home to both.

—3—

Just One Damn Thing After Another

A man who is always ready to believe what is told him will never do well.

—Petronius

I sleep hard and wake up surly. You would think, then, that Archy could have found some more appropriate way of waking me up than by blaring the *1812 Overture* over the ceiling pickup. On the other hand, I have to admit that sometimes nothing less will get the job done.

I groaned. " 'Kay, Arch. Gimme minute." I rolled over and sat up as Hotstuff protested loudly from the foot of the bed. A series of indignant squeaks indicated that her five daughters and two sons were not amused, either. Archy had a lot to answer for. "S'matter?" I said thickly. "Flare alert?"

"No, it's Helen. She's waiting for you onscreen."

I knuckled my eyes and heaved myself to my feet, wrapped

myself in the sheet—Hotstuff's progeny protesting at this further disruption of their breakfast—and staggered into the office to flop down in front of the viewscreen. Helen's gray eyes looked out at me. "Good morning, Star."

I looked at the chronometer blinking red in one corner of the screen. Five o'clock. "Yeah, the hillside's dew-pearled. What's so important it couldn't wait another hour?"

"Bad news travels fast. There's a *Time* reporter at GEO Base. She's coming up to Ellfive on Monday's shuttle."

On the whole I would have preferred the flare alert. I took a deep, calming breath, counted to ten, and said carefully, "You got me up in the middle of the night to tell me that?"

Helen's tiny smile came and went. She looked in excellent spirits, which would have made me suspicious right from the start if my ganglia had been closer to on than off. "No. Remember the Russian gentleman we were discussing? He's ready to come over."

I sat up, suddenly wide awake. "Vitaly Viskov? The silicon polymer specialist?"

"Yes."

I whistled. "How did you put that together so fast?"

Even from a distance of four hundred thousand kilometers the smugness of Helen's expression was unmistakable. "His wife defected in Paris two days ago. They haven't seen each other since he was posted to Tsiolkovsky Base. He asked us if we could smuggle her to Luna since his own people wouldn't do it. I informed him that if he cared to transfer his place of employment, they could both have jobs on Ellfive."

I shook my head sadly. "Helen."

"Yes?"

"You are such a ballbreaker."

"I am, aren't I," she said, not without pride.

She was in Sartre's study, and the good doctor stuck his head into pickup view. "Tell me about it, Star."

"How are you, Frank?"

"My balls remain intact thus far."

I congratulated him. "Viskov arrived at Copernicus Base last night, your time," Helen said, ignoring us in a manner that indicated at least one of the three of us was a grown-up. "As soon as you can find him a place, Jorge will ship him over."

"I don't have to find him a place, he's got a job as of yesterday with Jerry Pauling's bunch in the Frisbee. What's his wife's specialty?"

"Frank said she's a botanist." She turned to look at her husband and he said something I didn't catch. "Says her name's Yelena Bugolubova."

"Yelena Boogie-what?"

Helen spelled it for me. "I'll put her on the TAVliner for GEO Base today." She paused. "I'll reserve her a seat on the Express next to the *Time* reporter."

I brightened. "Helen, that's an inspired idea. 'Red Lovers Seek Refuge in the Sky.' What reporter worth her Gothic typeface wouldn't go for a byline under a headline like that?" And leave me alone in the process. "A botanist, huh?" I thought. "Roger will take her on like a shot. We could use some fresh blood in the farming toroids. Maybe she knows something about mameys." Helen didn't respond or sign off, just sat there looking expectant, waiting for me to ask, so I sighed and said, "Okay, Helen. I'll bite. What else?"

The flickering smile waxed and waned. "Dr. Viskov's opening bid for our services was a copy of a rather intriguing message from Gagarin City to Baikonur. It seems the Russians on Mars have intercepted a transmission from Betelgeuse."

Was that all? I sat back in my chair and tried not to snicker out loud. "Another one?"

Since the original 1992 message everyone from ham operators in Sri Lanka to BBC listeners in London, along with Project META, Arecibo, and the James Clerk Maxwell Telescope on Hawaii had been interpreting submillimeter spectrum readings, magnetic distortions, and solar flares as messages from the Beetlejuicers. The messages, freely translated, ranged from plans for an eminent attack on Terra to excerpts from "Emily Post's Guide to Extraterrestrial Etiquette," and usually provided most or all of the light relief in the *Ellfive Gazette*.

So I snickered, or tried not to, and Helen said, "They haven't translated it yet, because it seems it's coded differently than the '92 message, but they do say they intercepted the information by tapping into Odysseus II's daily transmissions to JPL."

I harrumphed and rearranged my face into a frown, fixing my boss with a stern stare. "What have you and Frank been up to, Helen?"

"Nothing, Star, on my honor," she assured me.

"What have you and Helen been up to, Frank?" I said.

He craned his neck to put his head back in range of the pickup and said around his pipe stem, "She's telling the truth, Star. For a change."

"Uh-huh," I said. "Archy, go to secure scramble, ears only, hush both ends and do not record. Although I should record this for posterity," I added for Helen's benefit. She stared back at me, unblinking. Her face was unlined, with regular, unremarkable features, except for her hair, which stood up around her head like a dust mop in zerogeé and made her look like a cross between Albert Einstein and the Bride of Frankenstein, and her eyes. Those eyes got to me every time, an intense, passionate, hypnotic gray that saw everything without giving anything away themselves. Those eyes said that Helen Ricadonna, like J. Moore, was on a mission from God. Whenever I wondered what the hell I was doing at Ellfive, something that had been occurring more often of late, I remembered those eyes and stopped wondering, but today I would not be overawed. "Helen," I said, slowly and carefully, as one addresses a backward child, "wherever that message came from, it didn't come from Betelgeuse."

The good doctor stuck his head back into range. "I know that, Star, and Helen knows that, and you know that." He gave me a smile I would have called impish on someone less jealous of his personal dignity. "But the Martians don't know that."

"All right then, assuming I believe you, which I don't, where did it come from?"

Helen shrugged. "Where do any of them come from? The Martians probably misinterpreted some of the probe data." Her fleeting little smile reappeared. "They sounded a little, well, frantic, shall we say."

"I'll bet they did," I said dryly. "This month anyone inbound for Terra by way of Odysseus II has to pass through Mars's orbit to get there. I'll just bet they're nervous."

"I wanted you to know before the news broke. Especially with the *Time* reporter on her way up."

"What's her name?"

Helen smiled and somehow I knew she'd been waiting for that question since the beginning of her call. "Emily Holbrook Castellano. I believe you have met before."

We had, and Helen knew we had. Castellano was Dewayne Nierbog Jr.'s unofficial press agent and a certified Luddite sympathizer, if not a card-carrying member of the organization's public relations arm. "I had to space a Luddite the day I got back, Helen."

"I know."

"I can't take much more of this shit and Castellano, too."

"That's why we sent you O'Hara."

"So you say. He doesn't seem to be doing much but follow me around."

"How nice for you."

"Up yours, Ricadonna," I said. "Is this guy really any good?"

"You tell me," she said sweetly, and in the background I heard Frank's hoarse guffaw.

"Helen," I said, and I wasn't smiling.

She sobered and said seriously, "He's the best there is, Star. You couldn't do better if you had him made to order."

"He says you hired him last month," I said. "He says because he isn't an Alliance national it took a while for the visa and the green card to come through."

"That is correct."

"Uh-huh. What's O'Hara really doing on Ellfive, Helen?"

"Caleb Mbele O'Hara, son of Sean O'Hara, mercenary, and Uhura Mbele, chief," Helen recited. "Father died in the New South African revolution. Mother is now minister without portfolio for the New South African Tribal Congress. Enrolled at Dartmouth, studied history, dropped out to serve in the War of Independence in his father's unit, and later in the Diamond Rebellion. NSA Cross of Freedom with bar, Medal of Valor—"

"Yeah, yeah, and enough ribbon to trim a ball gown," I said. "Saw post-war service as a special security adviser to the new president, set up the New South African equivalent of the Secret Service, security consultant to various international organizations and events including the Winter Olympics in Anchorage, application to emigrate has been on file at Colony Control for five years, never been married, no known offspring. I read his file, too."

"I liked the caution of that last entry," Helen said.

Exercising great restraint, I said, as calmly as I could, "Helen. What I want to know is why someone who stands to practically inherit an entire nation on Terra chose to space instead."

She said blandly, "Why would someone who was running offshore oil drilling operations for practically the entire West Coast of the American Alliance choose to space instead?" I had an answer for that but she jumped in before I could voice it. "How is the work coming? Any major problems?"

I spluttered for a while. "Oh, the hell with it. If you won't talk, you won't. Simon says we're on schedule, except for personnel housing, but that should be up to speed by the time the first colonists arrive. We've taken a few meteorite hits but they're so tiny and we're so big that pressure isn't affected before we have time to slap a patch on it. The alarm system Simon worked out with Archy is performing perfectly—"

"Thanks, Star!"

"Quiet, Archy," I said, "and I mean it this time. The flowers are blooming, Helen. The trees are leafing out. My front lawn needs mowing. The first crop of wheat was harvested from the Nearest Doughnut last week and the last batch of biobeef out of the vats tested Grade A. You can send up that first load of pioneers as planned." She was silent. "Helen?"

"I heard you." Her tiny smile came and went. "We're going to do it. We're really going to do it."

"Just like you said we would. Unless the Beetlejuicers get here first." She stared out at me from the viewer, the picture of outraged innocence, and I laughed, my first real belly laugh in far too long. "How is the colonist selection process coming?"

She grimaced. "Everybody wants to be the first one on board the *Mayflower*. No one is willing to wait a year or even a month to emigrate, no matter how high up they are on the approved list. I would find their enthusiasm encouraging if I didn't suspect that panic was an even stronger motivating factor."

"I can't blame them."

"Neither can I. As you saw for yourself last month, things are getting more than a little crowded down here, and what with the North American drought and the African famine, not to mention the conventional wars breaking out like an epidemic of measles now that we're using nuclear warheads for rocket fuel instead of peacekeepers—"

"This blessed plot, this earth, this realm," I said. "Another couple of weeks, Helen, and we can start to take some of the pressure off."

Her face cleared a little. "And you, Star? What are you going to do when it starts getting crowded up there?"

"Move to Mars," I said lightly. "The Russians should be glad to see a new face by now. By the way, have you checked the Hewies lately?"

"No. What's up?"

"There's some activity in area 378, Monitor Seven." She said nothing. "I was considering going to standby flare alert."

"Star, how many times do I have to tell you," she said. "It wasn't your fault."

I shifted beneath her steady gray gaze. "Yeah." It didn't change the fact that thirty-two people had died, and died horribly, while I was in charge.

"Don't overreact to a little solar activity," she was saying. "You were the guiding light behind the installation of the Hewies; you should know better than anyone how well they work."

I gave a reluctant nod and was about to say good-bye when she raised her hand, halting me. "One more thing."

"Yes?"

"What has the Space Patrol been up to lately?"

I looked at her sharply but I could detect no change in her expression, not that I ever could if she didn't want me to. She was as enigmatic to me now as when we were roommates at Stanford. "Plenty," I admitted, and told her about the rape and the subsequent riot, and added as an afterthought the docking screwup with the *Taylor*.

Helen was silent.

"Is there something I should know, Helen?"

Our eyes met. "Nothing I can prove, Star. Just—keep your eyes open, all right?"

"It's the best way I know of to get around." I cleared my screen, laced my fingers behind my head, and turned to look out the window, straight down Valley One to the North Cap, barely visible through the clouds. I thought about the Space Patrol, and the fight in the hangar, and from there my thoughts proceeded naturally enough to the new security supervisor. Since the cures for cancer and diabetes and Alzheimer's had been discovered, human life expectancy was well over a hundred and women were remaining fertile into their seventies. Terra's population was booming in spite of the forced contra-ception programs in places like India and Bolivaria. Caleb Mbele O'Hara looked like a man who needed elbow room. Maybe that was all there was to it.

Maybe. "Archy?"

"I'm here, boss."

"What's the population of New South Africa?"

"Sixty million, give or take a hundred thousand."

"Land area?"

"After the Diamond War, about the size of Alaska."

"So what's the population density work out to? About a hundred and twenty per square mile?"

"About."

Crowded enough for me to shake the dust of Terra and never look back. "Thanks, Arch."

"No sweat, boss. Want to hear about his royal dryness, old king tut?"

"Not right now, Archy."

Archy sounded aggrieved. "You never listen to my jokes anymore, boss. I suppose now I have to go help Helen and Simon play with perfect numbers."

"I suppose." And then I said, "Archy, load Frank."

"Loaded."

"Run. Flag for messages. Simon, what have you been doing

to Archy? He gets more human every day. I don't think I like it. At least tell him he can't sound off during director's mast with cracks about getting out my blindfold and scales. Love Star, end run, exit Frank."

"Aw, boss—"

"Exit Frank, Archy."

Was that a sigh, or my imagination? "Done, boss."

I wondered how all those flatlanders were going to take the news of a second message from Betelgeuse. Perhaps this time Terrans would be able to take a confirmation of extraterrestrial life more in their stride, and the geocentrism that was such a pervasive factor of Terran life would begin to ease. But I doubted it.

I knew most Fivers, myself included, had a hard time not figuratively as well as literally looking down on our contemporaries on Terra. From our lordly distance they seemed like so many sheep, so easily panicked, so compliantly led, so effortlessly roused over trifles. All too ready to make a firebreak for a backyard burnoff with a company of flamethrowers and in consequence burning down the entire neighborhood. The American Alliance and the Union of Eurasian Republics were constantly testing each other's military prowess, taking sides in contests that took place anywhere but on either's native soil.

The Mediterranean Conflict was a good example, flaring up in fits and starts since Rehoboam inherited his throne from Solomon. The latest fracas between Israel and Egypt bid fair to lay waste to the entire southwestern coast of the Mediterranean Sea, and then what? Libya was already gone, a lifeless monument to a mad dictator. Perhaps Cyrus II of Persia, formerly the individual countries of Syria, Iraq, and Iran, would step in with a firm hand and a reasonable solution. His namesake had placed the Israelis in charge of their homeland of Palestine and respected their religion. Of course that was around 500 B.C.

I tried to imagine peace in a united Middle East, under a Moslem ruler, no less, and failed miserably.

There was no place for that kind of divisive chauvinistic nonsense on Ellfive. At the very least, the harsh dictates of vacuum provided for a courteous environment. I placed a call to S. Bolivar Blanca, who was editor of the *Ellfive Gazette* as well as head of communications and traffic control, and told him of the projected visit of Emily Holbrook Castellano. Bolly greeted the news with a snarl and a decorative curse on my grandchildren.

So much for courtesy. I cleared my screen and looked at the chronometer. Today I had to check personally on progress in the farming toroids and the zero-gravity industries modules, and that meant I was going EVA. If I had to fight my way in and out of a p-suit I needed all the extra time I could get. I regretfully put thoughts of my warm bed out of my mind and got to my feet.

"You've got your martyr's expression on, Star," Archy said.

"The hell you say." Then, startled, I said, "How can you tell?"

"Didn't you know?" Archy sounded surprised, but it could have been my imagination. "Simon created a new program, Image Interpretation and Analysis. Your 'Martyr' look is filed between 'Mad' and 'Myopic.' "

"My eyesight is perfect," I said indignantly.

"I don't think that's what he meant."

I didn't think so either.

"Now you look kinda pissed off, Star."

I looked at the viewer, half expecting to see the face of a cockroach in a derby hat peering back at me. "Who's been teaching you that kind of language? Never mind, I don't want to know."

"Okay," Archy said agreeably. "Want to hear about mehitabel's extensive past?"

I gave in. "Sure, and put the coffee on while you're at it."

I know it is theoretically possible for a computer to mimic the behavior of anything, but the trick is in defining the "anything" to the extent that the computer has an unlimited number of responses to any given situation. Most computer personalities I had encountered since the revolution in parallel processing began in the 1990s were wooden and repetitive, if thoroughly competent, in response. Archy was more original than most, but that was because Simon was a more original programmer than most. He never

stopped tinkering with Archy's personality. I remembered coming
back from one trip to Terra to find Archy talking like Charlie
Chan's Number One son and sticking "honorable mother" on the
front and back of everything he said to me. When Simon started
fooling around with Blackwell's voice, Charlie taught her medical
log to speak Tagalog, which effectively shut out Simon's direct
access, if not Archy's.

So I drank coffee and listened indulgently to Simon's
brainchild. When I was on my second cup and Archy his third
story someone thumped on the front door. I opened it and
found a sprite on my doorstep. She was a beautiful sprite,
slender and faerylike, with an inky black fall of hair, enormous
brown eyes slanted up over high elfin cheekbones, and ears
that came almost to a point. At my feet Hotstuff meowed and
jumped straight into the sprite's arms. They touched noses
gravely and Hotstuff started purring loud enough to be heard at
O'Neill.

The sprite looked up at me. *Hello.*

"Hello, Elizabeth. How did you get here?"

I stole the aircar.

I rolled my eyes and said, "Great. Your parents know?"

'Course not. If they knew, it wouldn't be stealing.

"Of course not," I agreed. "I don't know what I was
thinking of."

You wouldn't come to me, Auntie, so I had to come to you.

"So I see."

The mountain to Mohammed. She smiled, a fey, mischie-
vous expression that chased across her face like sunlight
through a prism, and suddenly I was very glad she was there.
*You're supposed to come to dinner tonight. Seventeen hundred,
and Mom says you don't have to bring anything except
yourself, but Dad says you could bring some of Frank's
Christmas present if you want.*

"I'll be there."

You're going EVA today.

"Yes."

Without me?

I opened the door wider. "Apparently not. Have you had
breakfast?"

Is Archy making muffins?

"Blueberry."

Then I haven't had breakfast. She bounced inside. *And I need you to help me with a paper Emaa wants me to write.*

"Omigod." I sat down and fortified myself with coffee. "Okay, kid, lay it on me. What's your grandmother up to now?"

You know how she teaches history with socio-anthropological datelines?

"She taught your mother and me before she started in on you, Elizabeth," I said. "Believe me, I know how she teaches. What's your assignment?"

Well, we were studying twentieth-century American history, and I asked her how come there were so few women running things back then. I mean, there was Thatcher and Meir and Gandhi and Bhutto, but most countries and businesses and everything else downstairs were run by men. Upstairs, it's the other way around.

"And you want me to tell you why?"

Well. You're kind of an original source reference, Auntie Star. You hired most of the women on Ellfive. And Helen's your boss.

"Helen and Frank, Elizabeth," I said. "They run Colony Control together." Elizabeth raised one very skeptical eyebrow in my direction. She looked far older than her ten years and a lot like her mother when she did that. "Okay, okay, never mind that now," I said hastily.

Elizabeth set her communit to record and I cleared my throat and prepared to be preserved for posterity. "At the end of the twentieth century, the majority of Terran societies persisted in perpetuating themselves as patriarchal entities. This even as women, liberated by equal rights movements in every country—you remember, Terra was split into a couple of hundred countries back then, not half a dozen hegemonies the way it is today?" Elizabeth nodded. "Okay. Where was I?"

Equal rights movements.

"Right. So, in spite of the equal rights efforts, women felt their movement into the patriarchal structures of government

and business was too slow, plus half the time they got only half
the salaries men were making in the same jobs."

Weird.

"Very."

Then what?

"Well, when the Beetlejuice Message shook up everyone
downstairs and space exploration and colonization became a
reality, capable, ambitious women chose to move off planet.
Men were doing fine where they were, they had less incentive
to move. So it was only reasonable, even statistically probable,
to expect that a majority of extra-Terran leaders in every field
would be women. And so it has proved."

Elizabeth thought it over. *Sounds too easy.*

"Everybody's a critic," I said.

On the point of leaving, we were delayed by a call from
Conchata and the first words out of her mouth were, "The
son-of-a-bitching *bees*, Star, the son-of-a-bitching *bees*!" The
third—or was it the fourth now?—set of beehives had been
boosted direct from Onizuka Spaceport to the Nearest Doughnut at full gee. The entire crew of the specially modified
TAVliner got flightsick and stuck both hands out for hazardous
duty compensation. Due to careless handling one hive got
loose in the hangarlock; they swarmed and stung a longshoreman into anaphylactic shock. I called Charlie and she said it
was touch and go whether the guy would live. I called Bookie
in Payroll and found out the guy had a wife and seven kids in
Kalamazoo, Michigan. "Let's get out of here before the ASW
union calls, Elizabeth," I said.

We were in the aircar speeding to O'Neill forthwith and the
first person we stumbled over in Airlock OC-3 was Caleb
Mbele O'Hara. The man really was twins.

"I hear you're going EVA today," he said cheerfully. "I'd
like to go along, if you don't mind."

I fell back a pace, and said, "What the hell was that sound
you were making the other day? The one you used to stop the
fight in the hangarlock?"

He said offhandedly, "It's how we call hyenas down home."

"Oh." Now who in their right mind would want to call a

hyena? Without much hope I said, "I suppose you have been checked out on pressure suits?"

His face remained perfectly sober but his eyes were laughing at me. "Yes. I was cleared for EVA Wednesday and assigned a suit. I soloed to the capsule catcher. You can check with Daedalus if you like," he added helpfully.

"That won't be necessary," I said, trying to sound less like Grumpy. "Good job Monday, by the way," I added.

"Thank you."

"Did you hear how it turned out on Luna?"

"No."

"Lodge executed the four rapists yesterday afternoon, and sentenced the rest of them to life in Luna Maximum."

"A good man and true," O'Hara observed, and looked at Elizabeth. "And this is?"

"My niece, Elizabeth Quijance-Turgenev. Elizabeth, this is Caleb Mbele O'Hara, the new security supervisor."

He looked down at her and said, "Simon's daughter."

"You've met Simon, then," I said.

"In a manner of speaking," he said, still looking at Elizabeth.

Hello, Caleb, she said, her fingers flashing.

"She says hello," I told him.

He looked at me. "She doesn't talk?"

"She talks all the time, nonstop," I said, and Elizabeth looked indignant. "She just doesn't talk out loud."

"Doesn't, or can't?"

I looked at Elizabeth and said, "Won't," and had to laugh at Elizabeth's affronted expression.

Elizabeth signed hello to me from her crib at seven months. When by the age of two Elizabeth had yet to say "mama" or "chocolate" Charlie threw the not inconsiderable resources of the entire Ellfive medical department behind an effort to find out why. She never did. Elizabeth's larynx was fine and so was everything else. Elizabeth just didn't use them. Charlie, who lived to put Humpty-Dumpty together again, almost died of chagrin when she discovered she was helpless to reassemble her own daughter. This might have meant that nothing was broken in the first place, I pointed out, and for my pains didn't get a home-cooked meal for a month.

Please don't talk about me as if I weren't in the room, Elizabeth said with quaint dignity.

"I beg your pardon, Elizabeth," O'Hara said, extending one hand in apology to engulf her tiny palm in his enormous paw.

Auntie Star doesn't like spacing people, she said, as usual coming right to the point. *Even Luddites.*

I translated, the way I always do for laggards who have yet to learn how to sign. O'Hara's eyes lifted from Elizabeth's hands to meet my gaze for a brief, expressionless moment. "I know," he said.

Do you do that now?

"Yes."

Good. Elizabeth gave a single, sharp characteristic nod of approval, and dismissed the subject. *Is Mbele a Masai name?*

He smiled, squatting on his heels to bring himself down to Elizabeth's eye level. "No, Zulu. I'm from New South Africa. The Masai live up around Kenya way."

Did you have to kill a lion before they'd let you grow up?

He laughed. "No. The only lions left in Africa are in zoos, and if you kill one of those they throw you in jail."

Oh. She thought it over. *Archy says you make up limericks.*

I groaned and O'Hara laughed again. "Yes."

Can you make up one about me?

He looked up at the ceiling for inspiration. We waited. After a few minutes he nodded. "I think I've got it.

> "At Ellfive the resident elf,
> Put her gravity one day on the shelf.
> In a single bound
> She reached the speed of sound,
> And inertia ran away with her self."

That's really awful, Elizabeth said sternly, trying not to smile. *Am I the elf?*

"Yes."

Why?

"You know who the elves are? The High Elven?"

She nodded vigorously. After Rivendell and Lothlorien, Elizabeth knew all about elves.

O'Hara smiled into her inquisitive brown eyes. "Then you'll remember Arwen Evenstar. 'Queenly she looked, and thought and knowledge were in her glance.' "

Elizabeth was enchanted. So was I, damn it.

The littlest, skinniest person in the orchestra always plays the tuba, and the largest, hardest-to-fit people always work EVA. These are the philosophical truths by which we live our lives. Even normal-sized people in pressure suits look like a cross between the Michelin Man and the Pillsbury Doughboy, and in spite of fifty years of engineering progress, wearing one is still like wrestling with an octopus from the inside of an inflated balloon. The suits are so expensive in fabrication and maintenance that even my elevated status would not have got me one with my name on it. My size did, though, which meant I didn't have to smell anyone's sweat but my own. I sweat a lot and it wasn't much consolation.

As I stood in the airlock, hunched over so my helmet wouldn't scrape the ceiling, I punched the lock cycle and said, "Archy? Can you hear me?" I rubbed my head against the inside of my helmet to push the commlink more securely into my ear.

"Yo."

"When does Paddy say the zerogee corridor will be open?"

He consulted Keystone, the structural engineering program, and looked up the construction schedule. "She says before the colonists arrive."

"That's not good enough. Tell that Irish bootlegger I'm tired of having to go EVA every time I want to visit the Doughnuts or the Frisbee."

"Yesterday's report says they're having trouble with the bearings in the rotating joints."

"Tell them to roust out that Brown and Root architect who dreamed up those damn joints in the first place—what's his name, Fullenwider?"

"Fullenwider? You mean Ellensweig?"

"That's the guy—I knew it was something like Fullenwider. Can't Paddy get him on it?"

There was a brief pause. "Charlie told Blackwell he went space-happy. She certified him unfit for employment and he invalided out."

I swore. The hatch popped open and I stepped into space, with nothing showing through my chin window but my own white boots. I grabbed a handhold and steadied myself against Ellfive's rotation. "Okay, get Keystone to find Craig Bechtel. Tell him he and his crew are reassigned as of now to work exclusively with Paddy on the zeegee corridor until it's open. Tell them that I expect it to be open by Monday at the latest."

"Gotcha, boss. I bet Paddy teaches me some new words when she hears that."

So that was who he'd been talking to. I might have known.

"What kind of a computer is Archy anyway?" O'Hara said, popping out of the hatch in his turn.

"The Amazing Grace Model II."

"Amazing Grace?"

"That's right."

There was a brief silence. "After the Navy admiral? The first one to call computer glitches 'bugs'?"

"The very same," I said, trying not to sound surprised.

"I just wanted you to know that I knew who she was," O'Hara said, sounding satisfied. "Still doesn't tell me anything, about Archy, I mean."

"All right." I sounded deceptively mild. "He—it is a new-age parallel processor uniting smart-power chips made of silicon with the Seitz Cosmic Cube Model 12 handling over a thousand volts on integrated circuits that aren't hard-wired."

"Oh."

O'Hara sounded deflated and I relented. "Or something like that. I never know what the hell Simon is talking about when he's speaking binary." I grabbed my way across ten feet of Ellfive's exterior to a storage rack that held a dozen jetpacks. I had myself strapped in by the time O'Hara was all the way out of the lock and was able to help him into his jetpack, which gave me a nice little glow of superiority until I realized he was perfectly capable of assisting himself. He didn't chase his tail

at all. The first time I tried it I made more RPMs than Ellfive.
"You seem to have picked up the hang of this pretty fast," I
observed, "for someone with EVA time still in single digits."

"I am pretty quick, aren't I?"

I stifled a laugh at the self-congratulation in his voice.
"Ready?" I said, after we had double-checked each other's
gear.

I couldn't really see his face through the mask but he
sounded a little breathless, which made me feel better. "Green
lights across the board."

"Elizabeth, key your communit to my receiver."

After a moment I heard the familiar tinkle of Elizabeth's
code. *Punch it, Auntie!*

I had to grin, even though she couldn't see it.

"She can talk to you from her suit?" O'Hara asked.

"Archy made up a code and Daedalus fixed her up with a
special glove with a keypad in it. Archy'll translate for you."

Elizabeth waved the squared-off gauntlet on her right hand at
Caleb and her code tinkled. After a moment I heard O'Hara
laugh. He gave her a thumbs-up.

"Okay," I said, "on me, on three. One, two—"

On three I kicked out of the foothold and fired my verniers
to jet away from Ellfive's surface. Riggers and mechanics
worked in p-suits in vacuum all day every day. They got so
good at EVA maneuvers that they could let go from the
centrally located valley locks at exactly the right moment so as
to use Ellfive's 644-kph rotation to sling them to their work
area. They used the verniers on their jetpacks for direction and
braking, almost never for propulsion. Not me. I was always
afraid that if I tried it I'd wind up in orbit around Tau Ceti, a
gift to the galaxy with love from Ellfive.

We came up over the edge of the North Cap, dropped our
polarizers against Sol's glare, and sped down the length of the
cylinder three hundred meters above the surface. "First stop
today is Farming Toroid Two, or FT-2 for short."

"Also known as the Farthest Doughnut," O'Hara said.

"Right. In order, attached to the South Cap from the outside
in are the paraboloidal solar collector, the power station, the
farming toroids, and the zero-gravity industries module."

I could almost hear him squinting against Sol's rays to make out the shapes in front of us. "All the facilities have the same diameter as the Ellfive cylinder?"

"Yes, six and a half kilometers, but only the doughnuts rotate to provide gravity to the agricultural areas."

"Why is that?"

"Plants are like us, they grow best with something to pull against. The solar collector and the power station are stationary because they are designed for zero gravity—no moving parts, no friction, no wear and tear—and the zero-gravity module is here specifically for industry to take advantage of zerogee and vacuum manufacturing."

We matched orbits with the main airlock on the Farthest Doughnut, a fat gray toroid with a wide belt of solar windows that looked like a line of silvery icing, and told Archy to let Roger know I had come to see and conquer.

And sweat, Elizabeth said.

"That too," I said, and cycled the lock.

Roger took my helmet as I struggled out of my p-suit, and handed me a towel. "I'll bet hell isn't as hot as this place," I said, mopping my sweating face. Knowing what to expect I had dressed for the trip in shorts and a thin shirt, but as always I felt like a miner fresh from the creeks, dog-dirty and loaded for bear.

Persis Nehru, another agronomist, paid close attention as O'Hara emerged from his p-suit. When he stood up she caught my eye in a deeply appreciative, purely feminine glance that was easily interpreted as a subvocal "Wow."

I grinned and O'Hara caught me at it. Persis quickly passed out extra breathers. O'Hara watched as Elizabeth and I clipped the tube to one nostril and the O_2 pack to our belts. "The CO_2 count in the farming toroids is high," she explained, "which is good for the plants and great for inducing headaches in the farmers." He nodded and clipped on his own breather, and we stepped from the airlock into the warm, moist air of Farming Toroid Two.

I was raised on an arctic coast, surrounded by green mountains and blue sea, and the tangled jungle of the Farthest Doughnut made me claustrophobic. The side of the toroid curved up in back of us, overhead, in front of us, and down around beneath our feet again, and extended in concentric arcs to our left and right. The vegetation was so thick it was hard to detect the curve in the walls. It was like being inside of Terra, a Terra drained of oceans and shorn of mountains and turned outside in like a pillowcase. The only relief to this sea of living, grasping green was the belt of solar windows, open to the reflectors outside, which poured in a steady, unceasing stream of Sol's rays. Nowhere else in the planned stations and colonies of space, not even in FT-1, had I ever encountered such an undisciplined-looking habitat. I knew, intellectually, that this disorder was appearance only. I knew, intellectually, that FT-2 was an efficiently balanced ecosystem designed to produce maximum food with minimum fuss. But each time I entered the Farthest Doughnut I clutched instinctively for a machete, and when I left I always had the crawly feeling that there was something alive inside my p-suit besides me.

In contrast to the groves of fruit-bearing trees, which seemed ready to march in conquest on the rest of the arable land at any given moment, the cultivated fields looked as though they had their backs to the photosynthetic wall. One slip, one corner overrun, one furrow lost to an encroaching carambola tree and it would be all over. A pair of hummingbirds whizzed by our heads and I saw the flash of a rabbit's tail. We walked down a path to a small orchard of trees bowed under the weight of bunches of small, reddish bananas. "Go bind thou up young dangling apricocks," I said, pointing.

"Red Orinocos," Persis corrected me, and picked one for each of us. The skin was thin, the meat firm and tasty. I nodded my appreciation with my mouth full. She read the glint in my eyes correctly and picked me another. "The lazy man's fruit," she said. "A little fertilizer, a lot of water, almost no cutting back or thinning, and violà! Dessert."

I said through a mouthful of banana, "What are those?"

"*Theobroma cacao*. For chocolate."

Yum, Elizabeth said. *How can they get enough sun, planted under the banana trees like that?*

"*Theobroma cacao* is a very prima donnish kind of plant," Persis said, putting on her UCLA lecturer's voice. Elizabeth smiled at me behind Persis's back. "Full tropical sun will kill it. On Terra it is subject to all kinds of fungi and bacteria, so it has always been grown beneath the shade of banana and rubber trees. That way, if the cacao tree died, the farmer's income was guaranteed from another source."

"Sensible." I inspected the cacao pods, which looked like furry, oversize footballs. "If Helen Ricadonna had told me when she yanked me off a drilling platform in the Navarin Basin that this job would make me a jackleg botanist, I would have laughed in her face. Which reminds me. Can you use another botanist, Roger?"

Roger looked at me with his usual sorrowful expression. "Do you even have to ask?"

"You ever hear of Yelena Bugolubovo?"

Roger stared at me, arrested in full moan. "Z. Y. Bugolubovo? The 'On the Hydroponic Propagation of Food Grains in Zero Gravity' Bugolubovo?"

"The very same." I had had Archy look up the love of Vitaly Viskov's life in *Who's Who in Science*. "So, can you give her a job?"

"Christ!" Roger said. I blinked. "Do you know who she is?" he asked Persis. "Do you know what she does?" he asked Elizabeth. "Do you realize who we're talking about here?" he asked O'Hara, who had yet to say a word. Before any of us could respond he looked around the tangled green surroundings of FT-2, threw up his hands, and shouted, "This place is a mess! What's she going to think?" He broke into a trot in the general direction of the experimental station buildings, dictating rapidly into his communit as he went.

I looked at Persis. "Do you think he can find her a job?"

Persis was laughing, too. "You might need someone to do Roger's job after she gets here."

"I was going to ask him if he was having any more problems that I could help with, but I think I'll have to settle for you. How are the mameys doing?"

"We talked to the University of Cuba, as you suggested, and their School of Agriculture gave us a few tips. The dean hit me up for a job. He and his family have their applications in for immigration."

"Good."

"One thing, Star. The humidity in here is still too low for really maximum productivity. We need some more hydrogen."

"You want it wetter?" I passed the back of my hand across my forehead. It came away dripping.

Persis nodded, not smiling.

I shook my head in disbelief. "I'll get on the horn to Helen. We might have to preempt the next seed shipment, though. Roger will love that; he already thinks we dedicate far too much Express tonnage to inessentials like machinery and people as it is."

"Do it quick and he'll be so caught up with la Bugolubovo he won't even notice."

"You're getting as devious as Helen these days, Persis," I said severely. "I'll get on it as soon as I get back to my office." I wiped my forehead again, and said with a gloom to rival Roger's, "Wetter."

"Look on the bright side, Star. You can't beat Ellfive agriculture for trouble-free propagation. No bugs, no fungi, no nematodes, no viruses. And no one hoofing it over the back fence with your best peaches."

"Yet," I said, and the image of some kid in patched overalls, freckles, and uncontrollable hair sneaking into FT-2 to commit grand theft fruit was cheering enough to banish the woe caused by Doughnuts' insatiable demands for water and more water.

The visit to FT-1 was a relief, cooler and dryer, although O_2 breathers were still necessary. We climbed up to the coffee plantation, where the beans looked ready to pick. I could hardly wait; finally we were going to be able to dump that hydrox stuff from Colombia, which looked like cocaine and tasted like pine tree sap and had a lift cost second only to that of hand tools.

One section of the Nearest Doughnut was blocked off for the vats, where we conducted the mycoprotein cultivation of meats and the fixed-bed-enzyme synthesis of milk. Sol's rays poured unchecked into the tanks to stimulate the yeast cultures; outside the tanks it frosted twice each year for the benefit of the apples and the pumpkins and the potatoes. The ducks were as messy and noisy as ever, the chicken farm smelled like a chicken farm and the hogs smelled even worse because, so Greta Hochleitner frigidly informed me, some gottverdammt fool had mixed a bushel or so of rhubarb leaves in with the corn and sweet potato cuttings that made up their feed.

"That could have happened on a farm on Terra," I observed, my spirits insensibly lightened to hear of a problem there was nothing I could do to resolve.

"Not on my farm on Terra," Greta said, her face carved whole out of disapproving Minnesota granite.

I agreed meekly. I wondered what had happened to the gottverdammt fool. I decided on the whole it was better not to ask. He or she was probably pushing up wheat germ or worse, permanently assigned to the pigs.

The zero-gravity industries module had been the first facility to begin construction and was the first to be completed. Frank and Helen believed, wisely, that the sooner a return could be shown on the space habitat investment, the sooner the nay-saying Nierbogs and Chandras in the Alliance Congress would be pacified. The Frisbee was carved like a nautilus shell into spiral wedges, the only common denominator being the 180-meter depth, divided in two. Each cubicle had direct access to vacuum and each had unlimited power, courtesy of Ellfive's solar power station. There any similarities from one cubicle to the next came to a screeching halt.

We had held an ad hoc executive meeting twelve years before, Helen and Frank and I. Over the vociferous protests of the Habitat Commission we decreed that Ellfive would charge no rent for Frisbee space, oh dear me no. Ellfive accepted applications for prospective leaseholders, vetted the proposed projects of thousands of scientists, inventors, and business-men, paid their way to Ellfive, housed them comfortably, fed them superbly, provided a laissez-faire atmosphere and ade-quate facilities for pleasurable leisure time activities, and waited patiently until each entrepreneur developed a market-able product.

Then Ellfive took twenty-five percent of the gross, before expenses and before taxes and before anyone else they were in hock to got so much as a penny. Helen wanted forty and Frank sixty-five but I beat them down. I wanted the Frisbee healthy and prosperous; now that it was self-supporting and showing a small but steadily increasing profit I was toying with the idea of cutting back our percentage. It was time to spread some of the fiscal responsibility around, or did I mean share the wealth? I've never been strong in economics. But I might run it by the Frisbee Council, I thought, listening with half an ear to Jerry Pauling describe the latest semimiraculous long-chain polymer his group was synthesizing for a graphite-based starship hull material, the first such to be completely manufactured in space.

"Sounds like it's going to do everything but take out the garbage," O'Hara commented as we were suiting up. "Are all the Frisbeeites this charged up about their work?"

"Actually, Jerry's one of our calmer researchers," I said, holding Elizabeth's gauntlet for her.

"And they're all making money?"

"Oh, well, we've got a few wide-eyed dreamers who believe in research for research's sake, who shun the crass commercialism of their peers, and that's fine. Pure research has its place, and R&D always pays off." I reflected, and added, "If not always in a way the researcher expects."

"So you're willing to put up with a certain amount of exploration into the sex life of snails," O'Hara said solemnly, but with a smile in his green eyes.

"I suppose so. There's not a lot I have to put up with. Most of the Frisbee's leaseholders are as interested in making a buck as we are. If their product also happens to be good for mankind, that's fine, too, but it's only a bonus. Profits are what make the Frisbee rock and roll." In that spirit Colgate/Lilly and Bristol-Myers had constructed labs on site as soon as atmosphere was established and had begun shipping drugs downstairs within the year. Here, four hundred thousand kilometers from diseased, infected Terra, were the perfect conditions for distilling insulin for those diabetics still in remission, interlukem for the last of the cancer victims, and the hormonoids that were extending the life and fertility of every man, woman, and child in the system. Late in the previous year Lever Brothers had developed a vaccine against the common cold virus and was mass producing it at Ellfive, and the profit projections made my mouth water.

Elizabeth looked up from her helmet, twinkling at me. *The Frisbee offends Mom's humanitarian instincts. She says it's like selling typhoid vaccine for top dollar in the middle of a plague.*

"Yes, well, your father, who has no humanitarian instincts, is already designing a computer program to put the Lever process on automatic. For a small fee, natch."

Natch. And then they'll all want one, especially Revlon.

"Revlon?" O'Hara said, half laughing. "The powder puff people?"

Elizabeth shook her head at him. *Don't you sneer at the powder puff people, Caleb. The starstone was discovered in an accident in the Revlon lab.*

O'Hara's expression changed from amusement to respect, and so it should have. Clear as a diamond, as glowing as an emerald, as fiery as a ruby, the starstone was a crystal that began life in a vacuum petrie from a slopped-over mixture of facial masque and wrinkle eraser, with an organic catalytic agent Revlon was understandably keeping very hush-hush. The gem was actually alive when harvested, and interacted with individual body chemistry to change hues according to the mood of the wearer. The longer it was worn the more brilliant it grew, and the manufacturing tax on the starstone alone accounted for an eight percent correction in the balance of payments deficit Ellfive had with the American Alliance. I prayed nightly for the health and well-being of the Terran nouveau riche.

It was late that afternoon when we finally finished all three tours of inspection. I was exhausted from struggling in and out of jetpack and p-suit seven times in eight hours and I was not looking forward to an eighth ordeal, even if it was the last of the day. I took my time going home and Elizabeth and O'Hara made no objection.

And why should they? The view was spectacular. Sol was at our backs, and on our right silvery Luna was being pursued by a hunting pack of stars. On our left hung the spidery lattice-work that was the spare skeletal beginnings of Island Two. Three hundred meters below our feet Ellfive was a glittering, spinning cylinder, and 322,000 klicks beyond it was the steady glow of GEO Base and a string of solar power stations, a sparkling necklace clasped to Terra's blue-white throat.

She looked, at this distance, so various, so beautiful, so new. Lovely Terra, where in some places the Chernobyl- and Seabrook-tainted air smelled worse than the inside of my p-suit. Beautiful Terra, where in other places a Remington scattergun was more common to hand than a toothbrush, and more necessary. Blissful Terra, where it still rained and snowed when it would and where it would. Oh, to be in England, my ass.

I spread my arms, embracing the Big Blue Marble. My hands spanned the equator easily. As always, I looked for Denali. As always, I couldn't find it. If I shifted my right hand I could throw the entire eastern seaboard into a manual eclipse.

Tell O'Hara about "The Day Star Went Nova," Elizabeth said.

I mumbled something, and O'Hara said, "What?"

"Elizabeth wants me to tell you about my first trip EVA," I said. Elizabeth giggled and of course then I had to tell him.

Extra-vehicular activity had not always been such a fine careless rapture. My duty at Luna Base had been so frantic with activity that I had had no time for the esthetics and so when I first went spacewalking at Ellfive I was agog with anticipation, thrilled at the prospect of occupying the all-time front row seat. I, Star Svensdotter, Mrs. Svensdotter's little girl from the wrong side of Kachemak Bay, would have the universe at my feet and, moreover, someone was actually paying me to look. I might even write a poem in celebration of the event, dedicated to my father in elegant prose.

"On First Looking Into the Face of the Universe" (heroic couplets, I thought, or perhaps an Italian sonnet) would have to wait. I spent most of my first EVA dodging space cranes, reaction tugs, honeycomb clusters of thirty-thousand-kilogram steel-and-aluminum external fuel tanks from the first STS shuttles, half-finished solar cells, and free-floating stockpiles of LIMSH. True, it was all left motionless relative to the orbit of Ellfive. What weren't motionless were approximately one thousand solarscooters which, zipping through the maze with happy abandon, took turns trying to run me down. I ducked

one that came back for a sporting second try and a torqueless
wrench set in motion by a careless rigger tumbled so close to
my visor that my first EVA was very nearly my last. "I felt like
I'd wandered into the middle of a vidgame," I told O'Hara,
"and after I made it back inside alive and changed my shorts I
told a few people how I felt, and I fired a few others, just to get
their attention."

*Dad said you couldn't have done anything better to endear
yourself to the average Ellfive working stiff than to pin the ears
back on a few jet jockeys,* Elizabeth said.

"I wasn't trying to be endearing, Elizabeth, I just wanted to
survive my next EVA."

"That must have been when you set up the Warehouse
Ring," O'Hara said.

"Yeah, I moved all construction materials to an orbit sixteen
klicks out from Ellfive's axial equator. Then I restricted scooter
traffic to twenty-four klicks an hour within that ring and set
minimum altitude at three hundred meters above Ellfive's
surface. I pulled a reaction tug from the Lagrange–Luna route
and rededicated it full-time to moving materials at minimum
speed from the Warehouse Ring to Ellfive proper on a strictly
need-to-use-*now* basis. The logisticians squawked but I could
pretty much do what I wanted to back then."

So what's different now?

"Quiet, brat. And then Simon worked up a traffic control
program to monitor and police all traffic, jetpack, scooter, tug,
shuttle, TAVliner, Express, mass driver capsules, before I
went EVA again."

And then Paddy wrote "The Day Star Went Nova."

"What," O'Hara said, "is that a poem?"

A song, Elizabeth told him, *and a good one, too.*

I hoped she hadn't heard the same version I had. It was all
history anyway now, eleven years back, before Ellfive had
atmosphere or spin or even the real shape of what it was to be,
before Archy was, or Elizabeth. We were all living in a
translucent geodesic dome stuck to bare scaffolding like a wart
on a robot's broken nose. Water and calories without even a
token resemblance to food were strictly rationed and our
surroundings were, to say the least, utilitarian. The only up

was in relation to Terra until I had a roustabout paint in a dark floor and a blue-white ceiling. I thought longingly of dinner at Charlie's and afterward my bed in my cottage in my Big Rock Candy Mountains, and I leaned back into the arms of my jetpack and triggered the verniers. "Come on, Elizabeth. Race you to the lock."

There was no corresponding kick or acceleration. I frowned and thumbed the switch a second time.

My visor went black, as black as space without stars. It was either that or I had gone suddenly blind. "Elizabeth?"

There was no reply.

"O'Hara? Are you there?"

Silence.

This was silly. Keeping my voice as calm as I could, I said, "Archy? Archy, are you there?"

But my voice made no sound.

And then I began to see the voices.

But no, they weren't voices. There were no words, no sentences, no sound. Or yes, there was sound, though I couldn't hear it. There were pictures, too, pictures I couldn't see. I was bereft, and cried with frustration, but no tears slid down my face.

And then I was staggered, and then soothed, by the touch of something, some force that felt me, felt through me, slid through my skin and stroked the veins in my limbs, the cells in those veins, the very atoms in those cells. I was flooded with a dark force so bright it would have blinded me but that I had no eyes to see. I felt my mind begin to speak a language of imagery and shape and delicate grace, without my willing it and yet, not against my will. It was an invasion so visceral it was almost sexual.

And there was something else, someone else, not just nibbling at the periphery of my consciousness but occupying the next seat over from my cerebral cortex and reading with dedicated interest the record of my whole life, my hopes, aspirations, dreams, desires, wants, needs. Each experience was removed from its place in my memory, thoroughly examined, and replaced. It was as if a curious, methodical child were playing with a completed jigsaw puzzle, taking out a piece at a time, in exact order, to examine the shape and texture and even the taste of each piece individually, then looking at the puzzle without the piece, and then replacing the piece to view the picture the puzzle made whole and intact.

I was not forced, I was led. I was not invaded, I was visited. I felt a curiosity so intense it drowned out the clamoring of my own will, but the curiosity was my own. I felt a hunger so fierce, so terrible in its need that it consumed every other impulse and instinct. I would never know everything I wanted to know, and I despaired. I had an eternity in which to learn, and I rejoiced. I knew that eternity was far too little time, and I raged.

At last, at last, I opened my eyes to the sight of Elizabeth's p-suit floating outside Airlock OC-3, the one closest to my office, the one through which the late unlamented J. Moore had made his final inelegant exit. The digital readout in the corner of my visor blinked at me, its tiny red figures counting down in a placid and inexorable manner. It told me that less than a second had passed since the blackout had begun over thirty kilometers away. Fuddled, I thought, I would be justified in throwing myself off Ellfive for traveling at that speed. It was another moment before I realized that I had never traveled that fast, that no one ever had.

Over the commlink O'Hara sounded old. "Star?"

I turned my head inside my helmet and saw him floating on my left. "Yes." I was slightly surprised to hear my own voice, weak but in working condition.

"Are you all right?"

"Yes. I think so. Elizabeth?"

There was a brief, heart-stopping pause, before I heard the familiar tinkle of notes in my communit. *I'm all right, Auntie Star. What was that?*

"I don't know, sweetheart." It was a moment, several, before I could even make a move toward the lock, and the way I felt it would take me hours to get out of my p-suit.

"Star?" I heard O'Hara speak from a great distance, his voice thin and tinny.

"Yes?"

"I'm hungry."

"Yes."

"No, I mean I'm really *hungry*. My gut feels like it's chewing on the end of my windpipe."

"I know. So does mine." Actually it felt as if my stomach was crawling up my esophagus. It was either hunger or nausea and could be both. "Elizabeth?"

Me, too, Auntie. I'm starving.

"Take your fructose tablets, Elizabeth. Both of you. They should have enough calories to get us inside and out of these suits."

O'Hara's voice was rusty, exhausted, joyless, and totally without conviction. "Someone has finally invented something more fun than sex."

— 4 —

A Little Night Music

It is in the long run essential to the growth of any new and high civilization that small groups of men can escape from their neighbors and from their governments to go and live as they please in the wilderness.

—Freeman Dyson

We ransacked the commissary for something to contain our ravenous appetites until dinner. The aircar journey to Valley Two was quick and quiet. All too soon we were on the ground next to the white cottage that stood on a small rise at the north end of Loch Ness. I got out to take a look at the water mark. When all else fails, routine.

Loch Ness was still below minimum capacity. "Damn it," I muttered. "That settles it. I've got to go to Luna."

O'Hara stood next to me and looked up the loch. "How long is it?"

"About three klicks," I said, "and one klick wide."

"Where did it all come from?"

"Some from the comet trap, and more from Terra. Roughly half of it came from Luna."

"I didn't realize there was this much water on Luna."

"Polar probes in the early nineties discovered large quantities of oxygen and hydrogen. Copernicus Base ships it over by mass driver."

"Mass driver?"

"Sort of an electromagnetic slingshot. There's a mass catcher sixteen klicks out in the warehouse orbit. We crack the capsules there and reaction tugs bring the cargo the rest of the way in." I fell silent, watching Sol set in the reflective ripples of the loch. "O'Hara—"

"My name," he said, enunciating his words carefully, "is Caleb."

I paused. "Okay," I said at last, "Caleb. You could have written your own ticket in New South Africa. Why didn't you?"

"Maybe I wasn't ready to join the family firm." His voice was half serious, half mocking. "Why are you here? Why does Star Svensdotter run a space habitat?"

"I wanted a Roc's egg." He looked blank, and I said, "Robert Heinlein in *Glory Road*." I quoted, " 'What did I want? I wanted a Roc's egg. . . . I wanted raw red gold in nuggets the size of your fist and feed that lousy claim jumper to the huskies! . . . I wanted to float down the Mississippi on a raft and elude a mob in company with the Duke of Bilgewater and the Lost Dauphin.' "

"Heinlein," he said, frowning thoughtfully. "Like the park?"

I closed my eyes and shook my head. "Yes. Heinlein, like the park."

"So," he said. "A Roc's egg. That the only reason?"

"My father was a king crab fisherman in the Gulf of Alaska. When I was little he would take me out on the *Aleutian Princess* now and then, so I would know how he made our living." I smiled in memory. "Charlie was going to be a doctor from age two. Dad knew I was his only hope to take over the *Princess*."

"But you didn't."

"No."

"What happened?"

Dusk deepened to twilight and with the dying of the light I looked up, straining to see through the blue-tinted solar windows. Caleb and Elizabeth stood on either side of me, their faces lifted, too. "Have you ever been on a boat anchored in Kamishak Bay, in the middle of an Alaskan November? I have. No city lights, no other boats, just Dad and me on the *Princess*. All Dad had was a pair of binoculars, but he would take me up on the flying bridge and show me nebulas and red giants and white dwarfs. One time we saw a globular cluster, real low on the horizon. He showed me the constellations and told me the names of their stars and taught me how to use them to get home if the compass broke. One night I couldn't sleep, so I went out on deck and looked up. And there were all these stars, streaking across the sky, enough shooting stars to keep me in wishes the rest of my life. I was scared to death. I ran and got Dad up and told him the sky was falling." I laughed a little. "He told me it was the Leonid meteor shower. I asked him where they came from. From outer space, he said." I looked at Caleb. "It wasn't that I didn't believe him. It was just that I wanted to see for myself. That's all, really."

Caleb smiled at me. It was a quiet, appreciative, unchallenging sort of smile. I said urgently, "No one in your department felt anything? No blackouts? No fainting spells? No visions? Nothing?"

His smile disappeared. "No." His voice was flat and unemotional.

Nothing at all? Elizabeth asked plaintively, and he shook his head.

"Vacuum dreams," I said unconvincingly. "It wouldn't be the first time someone's imagination ran off with them after they spent too long EVA in a pressure suit."

It's the first time it has ever happened to you, she said. *And you don't have much of an imagination, Auntie Star.*

"Thanks a lot, kid," I said. "What did they feel like to you?"

She thought about it for a few moments, her little face grave and still, and then she looked up at me and smiled. *O joy, O rapture, O bountiful Jehovah.* I must have gaped at her because she added, *You know. Like Toad in the motor car.*

"You thought it was fun?" I said, just to make sure, and she nodded, looking at me expectantly.

Nothing less than the truth would do for Elizabeth, so I gave it to her. "It unnerved me, Elizabeth. Whatever it was, it left me tired and hungry. I want to eat, and sleep, and take some time to think it all over, and wait and see if—" I broke off.

If it happens again?

"God forbid," Caleb said.

Elizabeth was dismayed. *You didn't think it was fun?*

"No, Elizabeth," he said, apologetically but firmly, "I'm afraid I did not think it was fun. I just felt like I'd been walking around my whole life with my fly open. Embarrassing."

Oh. Oh, dear, she said, and added, *we better not tell Mom and Dad. We don't have any explanations, and it would only worry them.*

I had to smile. At times Elizabeth seemed more like a fifty-year-old matron than a ten-year-old girl. "Elizabeth, sometimes you scare me."

Without warning she dived into my arms, fiercely hugging as much of me as she could reach around. Her fervor startled me; she wasn't normally a demonstrative child. "What's all this?" I said, rocking back on my heels. I held her close.

I love you.

"I love you, too."

I know.

We were silent then for a long time, Elizabeth in my arms and Caleb at my side, standing at the head of a long blue lake reflecting more blue from the windowed sky above. "Well," Caleb said at last, "Joan of Arc heard voices, too."

"Yeah, and look what happened to her," I said, and felt Elizabeth's shoulders shake in a silent laugh. "But why am I not afraid?"

Or me?

"I am." He bit off the words, and I realized with something of a shock that beneath his stoic exterior Caleb Mbele O'Hara was quietly enraged. "I don't like being turned on and off like a trivee in somebody's living room. I felt like I was the subject of the latest "Interplanetary Geographic Special," going up against *Space Doctor* on Channel 5 and *Galactic Bandstand* on Channel 11. I'm scared, all right."

"I'm not," I said. It was the truth, and it puzzled me. "I don't know why not."

Me, either.

His hand slid over mine and squeezed. "Oh, hell. Maybe it was just the Beetlejuicers, paying their respects."

Elizabeth looked at me, an eyebrow raised, but before we could say anything we heard Simon's basso profundo behind us. "What are you doing, standing around out here?"

"Just admiring the view," I said, turning.

"Just checking on the water level, you mean," Simon said. "Give it a rest, Star, at least for tonight." He grinned at Caleb.

"Caleb O'Hara, meet Ellfive's compsci department and my second in command, Simon Turgenev."

Simon's grin widened. "Hello, Caleb."

"Hello, Simon."

"You know each other?" I said, unnecessarily, as the two men were already embracing, thumping each other on the back and calling each other names. Men are very strange; sometimes I think they belong to an entirely different species. If at first sight after a long separation I addressed Charlie as "you old fartknocker," poked her in the gut, and said she'd gotten as fat as a hyena at an elephant feast, she would deck me, or try to.

Simon, giving O'Hara a last thump, said, "Before you drafted me, Star, I built and sold a computer system to the New South African Ministry of Defense. They insisted I see to the installation personally. Caleb was my trusty native guide."

I said automatically, "I did not draft you. You volunteered."

Simon snorted and said to his daughter, "Squirt, you are in serious trouble."

Elizabeth was the picture of innocence. *I left messages with Frank and Blackwell.*

"Leaving a note explaining you have stolen the aircar your mother needs to get to work doesn't get you out of a gang-tickle. Attack!" He scooped Elizabeth up into his arms, growling fiercely, and she squealed and giggled all the way to the house.

It was a duplicate of five hundred others scattered in varying stages of construction around the edge of Loch Ness, with cherry and maple saplings filling up the empty spaces in between. When Shepard Subdivision filled up, Loch Ness would be next in line for the colonists. What Charlie missed most on Terra was water, large bodies of it, with ceilings of amber and pavements of pearl. So Simon convinced Roberta McInerny to finish one cottage on Loch Ness two years ahead of schedule, complete with chemical toilet since the Valley Two sewage treatment plant had yet to come on line. By a strange coincidence Morgan, the architect's computer program, now had illegal downlinks to the in-house data bases of every major architectural firm on Terra, and another, even more illegal link to the Greek's Betting Palace in Las Vegas, which was as close as Roberta, born in Kentucky and raised on a stud farm, was going to get to a horse on Ellfive.

Inside the door, Caleb looked around at the pillow furniture in primary colors, the sagging bookshelves, the corners filled to overflowing with green plants, the large picture window overlooking the Loch. "Nice." He turned, about to ask Simon a question, and Charlie came out of the kitchen patting perspiration from her brow with the edge of a ruffled apron.

"Charlie, this is Caleb. Caleb, my wife, Dr. Carlotta Quijance, head of medical services."

I'm like Dad, blond, blue-eyed, and all squarehead. Charlie is like Mother and they both look as if they have just stepped down from a Tahitian travel poster—you can hear the rustle of the grass skirt and smell the frangipani in the lei when either one walks by. Charlie had black hair all one length falling from a central part to her waist, her eyes were tilted and merry, and her mouth was wide and never very far away from a smile. I compensate by being thirty centimeters taller, which annoys her, which breaks my heart.

Charlie gave Caleb her hand, smiled sweetly up into his smitten green eyes, and murmured, "I'm taken."

O'Hara got his eyes back into their sockets and his jaw returned to a workable position and said with flattering regret, "I know."

She fluttered her eyelashes. O'Hara, that hairy twin of King

Kong, looked faint. I wanted to puke. Charlie, the best general practitioner upstairs or down, was also the biggest flirt on two planets, one moon, and half a dozen habitats. "My little sister isn't," she purred.

"Charlie," her little sister said lovingly, "you really should have been detongued at birth."

Simon looked interested. "Was it an option?"

Charlie tucked her arm into Caleb's and drew him farther into the house. "I've heard a lot about you, Caleb," she said, lowering her voice so he'd have to lean closer to hear her, "but since it all happened before Simon and I were married I suppose it's covered by the statute of limitations."

My ears pricked up. O'Hara looked at Simon and said reprovingly, "My reputation, Iago, my reputation!"

Simon looked smug and said, "Let me introduce you the rest of the way around. Elmo and Drake, marine biologists."

Elmo lifted his arm from around Drake's shoulders in a gesture of greeting. The other man smiled at Caleb over the rim of his glass. "We've met."

"Crippen Young, one of the first pilots for Space Transportation Services, now an Express pilot. Roger Lindbergh you know. Bolly Blanca, editor of the *Ellfive Gazette* and our chief of communications. Petra Strongheart, our meteorologist." The dark woman with the solemn face rose to shake hands. She was thick through the shoulders and neck and had the massive arms of one who flew for a living.

"Meteorologist?" Caleb said. "I would think weather was about the last thing Ellfive had to worry about."

Petra smiled one of her quiet smiles. "Weather, no. But someone has to watch the humidity, keep an eye on the atmosphere mix, help monitor the Helios Satellites, and make it rain."

"Oh," Caleb said, and gave his charming smile. "My mistake."

"And this is Paddy O'Malley," Simon said. "Paddy, this is Caleb O'Hara, the new security chief."

The stocky redhead stuck out a square hand, giving Caleb a broad grin and a blatant inspection. "O'Hara, is it now? Sure, and isn't that the finest tan I ever saw on an Irishman?"

"Paddy is a structural engineer," Simon explained. "Don't pay too much attention to her, she spends most of her time EVA in a p-suit and we think it's finally getting to her. You can see how shy she is."

I left Simon to play host and followed Charlie into the kitchen, where she was shaking paprika into the chicken adobo with a lavish hand. I glanced over her shoulder and sniffed appreciatively. "Eye of newt, toe of frog. What do you know about Caleb that I don't?"

"Didn't Simon tell you about him?"

"Nobody will tell me anything about him," I said. "When I ask Helen she just stares at me with those eyes of hers, and when I ask Frank he starts reliving the good old days on the veldt filming *Universe*. Even Archy says he can't find anything but what's on Caleb's personnel file. So what do you know about him?"

"I know he makes your wees kneak."

My sister is pragmatic and supremely unromantic. She isn't at Ellfive to explore new frontiers or for the excitement of adventuring into the unknown or to boldly go where no one has gone before. Charlie is at Ellfive because thirteen years previously, two years into actual construction, I made a special trip to Seldovia, Alaska, and begged her on my knees to leave her free clinic to keep me company four hundred thousand kilometers from home. She thought it over, carefully and methodically, making a list of pros and cons and checking each item off one at a time, starting with assigning me the task of finding a replacement to run her clinic. She spent three months with DOS's flight surgeons learning the ins and outs of practicing medicine in space. She wangled, I still don't know how, another three months at the Soviet Space Hospital in Temirtau. She spent a week assimilating data before she decided yes, she could do the job. After which she held me up for a salary that would have made Henry Morgan blush for shame and a budget that would have made John D. Rockefeller blanch. She waited impassively until I signed off on both before she said yes, she would do the job. No, not a romantic, my sister. That didn't stop her meddling in my love life.

"Caleb," Charlie said, slapping my hand as I reached for a

piece of pineapple. "He makes your wees kneak. Nobody's made your wees kneak since Grays." She stirred the adobo. "Why Grays, anyway? I never did understand the attraction. Stuffy isn't your type."

I said, equally enough around a mouthful of pineapple, "Probably because he's the first man ever to walk into a room with both of us in it and look at me first." She made a face. "It's over, anyway. He screwed me to get closer to Ellfive. I'm not the first woman that's happened to, and I won't be the last."

Charlie dropped her spoon and turned to glare at me with her hands on her hips. "My, aren't we positively platonic today? So calm, so broad-minded, so matter-of-fact, so—"

"Tolerant?" Charlie made a gagging sound and, annoyed, I said, "Charlie, is there something you want to say to me?"

"For only about ten years," she said. "Grays is a soldier, Star. He defines strength in traditional military terms. How many troops does he have to deploy. How many guns does he have to shoot. How many bombs does he have to drop. And how much more of all those things does he have than the other guy?" She waved the spoon at me. "You, on the other hand, are striving to create a peaceful, self-sufficient community that finds its security through economic strength. Entrepreneurs, not troops. Dollars, not guns. Profit margins, not bombs. And who cares what the other guy is doing as long as your bottom line is in the black?"

"So I was a military objective?"

"Among other things," she said dryly, beginning to stir again.

"And this lecture on Grays and my basic incompatibility is in aid of what?"

She stopped stirring and spoke in forceful tones. "You're still mad because Grays took advantage and you fell for it, and the person you're maddest at is yourself. What are you, omniscient, omnipotent, you know all, you see all? He's a charmer, I grant you, it would have been a miracle if you hadn't fallen for him once he turned it on. The minute you saw where it was going, you walked away. Give yourself a little credit, sister mine. You give everyone else on Ellfive a second chance. Why not yourself?" She fixed me with a hard stare. "And why not Caleb, while we're at it?"

The worst thing about Charlie was that I couldn't slug someone that much shorter than I was and look myself in the mirror the next morning. I began to feel that it might be something I could overcome, given time.

Reaching for a cutting board, she took another, closer look at me, and paused with the knife poised over a green pepper. "You look exhausted, Star. What's really worrying you?"

If I told Charlie about the blackout she would have Elizabeth, Caleb, and me strapped to a table in her surgery in five minutes flat, stuck with a lot of uncomfortable probes, and forced to answer searching questions about our diet for the last month. So I said, "Caleb is worrying me."

Her gaze sharpened. Charlie might be determined to get me laid, she might tell me with a straight face that it was essential to my continued good health, she might even go so far as to handpick a candidate, but the one thing that superseded Hippocrates's oath with Dr. Carlotta Quijance was a ferocious familial loyalty. It was that loyalty that permitted Charlie, dedicated to protecting and preserving human life, to stand aside while I ended the life of a terrorist who had threatened mine. If you were Charlie, it all made perfect sense. Bristling with suspicion, she demanded, "What exactly do you mean by that?"

"He's too well qualified for the job of security supervisor at Ellfive, for starters, especially for so short a term. When we commission, and remember commissioning is less than a month away, his job is finished. He doesn't strike me as the kind of man to stay on and run for chief of police. So just what is the heir apparent to New South Africa doing nursemaiding a space colony of less than five thousand people, that will never have a population of more than a million-five?" I added, "He always seems to be somewhere close by me, too. I've felt crowded ever since he got here."

She relaxed and one delicately raised eyebrow told me what she thought of my peevish tone. "I suppose the obvious explanation won't do." I shook my head. "Of course not." Her voice was mocking. "Why don't you just ask him why he's here?"

"I did. He said he wasn't interested in going into the family firm."

"The family firm being the government of New South Africa." I nodded. "Well, maybe he was telling the truth."

"Maybe he was," I said. "But there is something he isn't telling me. I don't know what it is yet, but there is something. It's a hunch, Charlie," I said, stopping her. "I can't shake it, and I won't ignore it."

"So you're going to wait before—"

"Yes. Before."

She made a face. "Don't let the romance of the situation run away with you, Star."

"You should talk," I retorted.

Charlie tested the sauce for the sweet-and-sour spareribs. "What do you think?" she said, offering me the spoon.

I smacked my lips judiciously. "Needs more pineapple."

"You always say that," she said, annoyed. "Where did you take Elizabeth today?"

"The Doughnuts and the Frisbee."

"She took off without telling us."

"I told Archy to call you."

"He did," she admitted grudgingly. "But she was supposed to go to the dispensary with me today."

"Ah."

" 'Ah' what, you—"

"How's it coming?" my brother-in-law said cheerfully from behind us. "We've got hungry people about to riot out there." Charlie let him taste the sweet-and-sour sauce, and he said instantly, "Needs more pineapple."

"What did you two do, rehearse?" she said. "Both of you always say that."

"That's because you never put enough pineapple in," Simon pointed out in a maddeningly patient voice. "And what are these, green peppers? You're not going to put those in the spareribs, are you? I hate green peppers in the spareribs."

"Fine," Charlie said. "There will be more for the rest of us."

"I didn't say I didn't want any, I said I didn't like cooked green peppers. I'll eat around the peppers, all right?"

"Hey," I said.

"Fine." Charlie stirred the ribs with unnecessary vigor.

"Good," Simon said. "I'm glad we straightened that out."

"Uh, hey?" I said.

"Fine," Charlie said again, stirring madly.

"Hey!" I said. "Remember what I did the last time you two got into a fight." It wasn't really a question, the outcome spent the day with me EVA. "I've still got a lock on my office door," I added, but I was bluffing, and they knew it.

The hardware doesn't exist that Simon can't take apart, stir in a bowl, and put back together blindfolded, and since he wrote most of the definitive software during the revolution in parallel processing he could take most computers apart down to their bits and bytes. Simon loved to take things apart. He lived to take things apart, in exactly the opposite way Charlie lived to put people together. But at what Simon really excelled, his true vocation in life, his raison d'être, was pissing Charlie off. "And by the way," he added, ignoring me, "you left the aircar battery unplugged again yesterday."

"I left it unplugged? *I* did? Whose daughter had no trouble in disappearing in that same aircar less than twelve hours later?"

"Why is she always my daughter when you're mad at her?"

The wooden spoon was making enough revs to power a skiff. Simon winked at me over Charlie's head and I stole away quietly on little cat feet and told my niece to put the storm flag up.

In spite of the kitchen skirmishing between cook and kibitzer dinner was enormous and excellent. By the time I got myself on the outside of a fourth helping I had decided I might survive. Elizabeth had fifths and Caleb sixths. Charlie didn't so much as raise an eyebrow. I never thought I'd live to see the day I would be grateful that Simon picked a fight with his wife.

As was the custom after one of Charlie's feeds people lay around the living room and groaned and moaned and wished out loud that they'd worn something without a belt. Then someone sang a snatch of song, someone else joined in, and

Simon fetched my guitar from the aircar. I ran through my repertoire of sea chanteys. Elizabeth got out her flute. Charlie plugged in her keyboard, and Simon washed out the adobo pot and provided percussion with a pair of wooden spoons. I reminded myself yet again to talk to Helen about a new set of drums. The four of us jammed on Mozart, Jellyroll Morton, and a few new jazz numbers by Shanghai Wang. I scowled down Elizabeth's suggestion we sing "The Day Star Went Nova." They sang it anyway. As usual Paddy insisted on "The Hills of Connemara," and as usual Crip retaliated with "The Green Hills of Earth."

When the conversation began seriously to interfere with the music we packed the instruments away. Elizabeth set up the Scrabble board and Elmo and Drake sat down to the slaughter, Crip told lies about the early days in NASA, and I hid or tried to from Bolly Blanca.

"—she makes 'stampeded' out of my 'stamp' and your 'stamped' and gets a triple word score on top of it and you think she's cute? I'll show you cute. Gimme some more tiles—"

"—rat turds and monkey shit floating all over the middeck and then the toilet broke down again—"

"I would just like to say, Star, that Emily Holbrook Castellano can take a flying—"

"Orchids? Who does he think he is, Nero Wolfe?"

"We lose a pound of atmosphere every time the man inhales."

"Lighten up, you guys. You say the same thing every time I show up at Mitchell."

"Yes, but, Star, the man makes up limericks!"

"Well, if somebody kills him we'll be able to call it justifiable homicide, won't we?"

"—and you're wanting the zeegee corridor open by Monday, is it now? Sure and we're pedaling as fast as we can, Star, but I'd be grateful knowing if it's good work you're after having done, or what an Orangeman would settle for, which is something else altogether—"

"—theoretical physicists never get the girl."

"Come on!"

"It's a fact. Experimental physicists got sex appeal—"

"—son-of-a-bitchin' *bees*—"

"I hear you held mast at STP-1 three days ago, Star."

"Oh, my God, yes. Mast number one-one-eight. You should have been there, Simon. Dien Pran had to break up a fight Torkelson and Lachailles were having over Nesbitt."

"Her again."

"Yeah, Pran was livid. He said he'd never met anyone who thought with her crotch before—only he didn't say crotch—and if someone had asked him he'd have forgone the privilege, thank you very much."

"How did you find?"

"Why don't you have Archy call up Orestes and read it for yourself? Torkelson and Lachailles wanted to fight a duel. Yes, really, a duel. I told them they could fight it out in the nearest airlock but that they had better settle it quick because in sixty seconds I would blow the lock."

"Jesus."

"Yeah. I was mad. Things calmed down after that. I broke Nesbitt from foreman to tech third class on the charge of inciting to riot, and split Torkelson and Lachailles up between Valley Two and Valley Three plants. Archy told me to spit on my hands and get out the cat-o'-nine-tails. Which reminds me, Simon, about Archy—"

"—and even if they live they can't eat—"

"Unusual activity? Oh, yes, Area 378. Star was asking about it. No, it's more like a controlled burn than a flare. Remarkably steady, actually; there is hardly any fluctuation in proton emissions in Area 378 at all. Very odd in solar atmospherics. Lord, when I think of all that energy going to waste! Passive solar power is all very well—"

"—do realize who we're talking about here? Zoya Yelena Bugolubovo? Author of 'On the Hydroponic Propagation of Food Grains in Zero Gravity'? The first Terran agronomist in space?"

"Isn't she married to the Vitaly Viskov who won the Nobel Prize for his experiments with silicon polymers?"

"Who?"

"—and even if they eat they can't fly—"

"—and then the goddam shuttle hull starts to *glow*—"

"Do you want to hear about freedom of the press, Star?"

"No," I said plaintively.

"I'll tell you about freedom of the press, Star, as we knew it—all two days of it—and loved it in my hometown of Buenos Aires—"

"What do you think they'd been doing up there for twelve months at a whack, studying the military applications of tiddlywinks in zero gravity? They were planning how to survive a seventy-eight-million kilometer voyage in a weight-less environment. Every time they went up they plugged part of their ship into their orbiting laboratory and left it there. They even had a couple hundred kids age ten and up living in a cosmonaut city, training to live and work in space. They were going to Mars all right, and the even money said they were on their way before 2000." Crip snorted. "They beat that by four years. And we were stuck with a space truck that couldn't make it past low earth orbit and half the time couldn't even get off the goddam ground, and when it did—" Crip broke off, but we all knew he was thinking of *Challenger* and *Challenger II*.

"So, what are we saying here? That the Soviets—all right, all right, the UER, but by God once a Russian always a Russian—you're saying the Russians put us where we are today?"

"Russians, hell! The Russians were broke, even broker than us. We didn't need another Red scare, we needed a—a sixties' sense of mission, or at least that same kind of clarity of purpose. What we really needed was a cause, like Sputnik. We needed an Oregon Trail to the stars."

"And we couldn't find one ourselves?"

Crip, drink forgotten in one hand and well away on his favorite hobbyhorse, said, "The Oregon Trail offered the excitement and adventure of exploring and colonizing an unknown. Whereas the Terran scientific community was a little too clever for our own good from about 1950 on. Venera, Viking, Voyager, Vega, they were all far too reliable and efficient. The average citizen of the 1980s knew more about Chryse on Mars than did the average American pioneer about the Mojave in California. The bottom line is, both Chryse and the Mojave are deserts. So we all knew beyond any doubt that there weren't any move-overs on Venus or any thoats on Barsoom and a lot of the romance went out of the solar system. And what is exploring a new frontier, without romance?"

There was a brief silence, which Paddy broke. "What was it Mark Twain was after writing about the Mississippi? When it was a riverboat pilot he became? 'Now when I had mastered the language of this water, and had come to know every trifling feature that bordered the great river as familiarly as I knew the letters of the alphabet, I had made a valuable acquisition. But I had lost something, too. I had lost something which could never be restored to me while I lived. All the grace, the beauty, the poetry, had gone out of the majestic river. . . .'"

" 'All the value any feature of it had for me now was the amount of usefulness it could furnish toward compassing the safe piloting of a steamboat,' Caleb finished up, smiling at her. The African sibilants following hard on the heels of the Irish brogue sounded very strange, but strangely right. I wished Caleb would stop surprising me.

"So, what you're saying, Crip, is that we needed the Beetlejuice Message to provide an impetus to space."

"Yes, that is what I am saying. And we're damn lucky we got it, because you and I would still be flatlanders if we hadn't."

Tori Agoot waved a dismissive hand. "One lousy message and not one word since."

"Caleb O'Hara, Tori Agoot, star gazer over at Mitchell."

"Glad to meet you, Caleb. Personally I think that linguist Sartre married has him seeing messages in his Cheerios. And the time factor—"

"It's stopping right there you'll be," Paddy said firmly. "Talk of wormholes is one thing I'll not be putting up with after dinner. It's dizzy thinking about time travel always makes me. Talking about it makes me fair seasick."

"You don't believe in E.T., Tori?" Crip said. "Shame on you. Next you'll be saying there are no Vulcans."

"Personally, I chose spacing because I hoped I'd meet a Wookie out here someday," Ariadne added, grinning. She held out a hand to Caleb. "Ariadne Papadopoulos. I do all the work at Mitchell while Tori takes the credit."

"I think it is reasonable to believe that intelligent life might, I say *might* exist on other planets," Tori said obstinately, "but simply believing don't necessarily make it so."

"I'd settle for intelligent life on Terra," I said, and everyone laughed politely at the very old joke. Old and still my favorite.

"That's not the point," Crip said to Tori. "Because we haven't seen them doesn't mean they don't exist. The point is that I don't know for sure that there are no little green men or bug-eyed monsters. I haven't visited every single planet orbiting every single star in every single galaxy in this universe. And since such a voyage is probably impossible—"

"Probably!" said several voices at once.

"For now," Crip said. "For the foreseeable future. Someday, though. Someday." He and Ariadne got these faraway looks in their eyes, as if they were computing parsecs per ECFCPCs.

Elizabeth sat on the floor, leaning against my knee, her eyes bright with interest. *You know, Tori,* she said, *two thousand years ago a lot of people who sounded like you went around saying, "The earth is flat!"*

"Show me," Charlie said simply, unexpectedly entering the lists.

"We can't," Simon replied, naturally coming out for the opposing side.

"Until you show me, I won't believe."

"If more people thought like you, a lot of priests would be out of business," Simon said gently.

"What a pity they don't," I said.

"The devil you say!" Paddy exclaimed.

"No, Paddy, priests," Charlie said impatiently. "Pay attention." She looked at Simon. "There had to be a beginning to the universe. What if we are it?"

There was a slight pause while we all looked at Simon expectantly, Crip excited, Charlie intent, Caleb amused, Paddy red-faced and holding back a belly laugh, Tori a little scornful of the whole subject, and the rest of us waiting for Simon to light the match and the fireworks to begin. Simon gave a rueful grin. He was more at home in binary than in System English, but tonight he wasn't being given a choice.

Simon was difficult, demanding, brilliant, mercenary, curious, judgmental, and ruthless, and he had more hair than a sheepdog. For the first year I knew him I wasn't sure he had eyes. He cut his hair for the wedding and they turned out to be dark and sad, over a long, slightly hooked nose and a chin like a shovel in perpetual need of a shave. He used a standard depilatory and carried a razor with him at all times and Charlie still had whisker burns every morning. He had long, thin, hairy arms and longer, thinner, hairier legs, and his skin was pale, as if he spent all his time in a frame room pulling data cards, which he did. When he wasn't defending Columbian philosophy, that is. He had a voice like Big Ben when by all rights he should have sounded like Daffy Duck. "My vote is for the care and feeding of the human spirit. A belief in extraterrestrial intelligence—"

We are extraterrestrials, Elizabeth stated.

Everyone chuckled and Simon said, "You're quite right, Elizabeth, although from the level displayed here this evening we could call extraterrestrial intelligence as we know it a contradiction in terms." Charlie flushed and her eyes began to sparkle. "But for the purposes of this argument," Simon went on smoothly, "will you allow extraterrestrial intelligence to be limited to what does not originate on Terra?"

Elizabeth gave her father's suggestion careful consideration, and nodded once, decisively.

"Thank you. To continue. Imagination and curiosity are two of the greatest human motivators. For example, the META project, even if we had never intercepted the message from Betelgeuse, was and is a worthwhile project, because it is right and proper for the human race to keep looking into our universe, even if we don't quite know what for."

" 'I would rather be ashes than dust,' " Crip quoted. " 'The proper function of man is to live, not exist.' "

"Exactly. We wouldn't be having this discussion sitting in a space habitat four hundred thousand kilometers from the old home place if the human race had been resting on the laurels of what they knew, say, a thousand years ago. We couldn't. We have to follow our noses. It's a genetic imperative."

"The fault, dear Brutus, lies not in our stars, but in our double helixes," I declaimed in sepulchral tones.

"Nature or nurture?" Charlie said thoughtfully.

"Oh, my God," Simon said, casting up his eyes, "don't let her get started on genetic engineering, please."

Charlie stiffened, her very hair seemed to crackle with outrage, and a lot of people rushed into nervous speech. Petra shouted the rest of us down. "Simon, I was going to ask you if you were working on Archy this afternoon. I got a blip in the readout of Hewie Seven and I couldn't track it down."

"That's odd," Roger said, looking up. "I was accessing Demeter this afternoon and I noticed a hesitation in the data readout myself."

"Hey, that happened to Blackwell, too," Charlie said, momentarily diverted from battle.

"What time?" Caleb and I said with one voice. Elizabeth was leaning forward with wide, inquiring eyes.

"Around eighteen hundred," Petra said, her brow wrinkling as she looked from me to Caleb and back again.

We looked at Roger. "About then," he confirmed, and Charlie nodded.

"What's going on?" Simon said with a frown, and we said, again with a single voice, "Nothing." We were getting a lot of odd looks. "Did you get the message I left in Frank, Simon?" I said. "The one about Archy mouthing off during mast?"

The lines around his mouth deepened. "No, I—"

"Good gracious, Simon," Charlie said, at her sweetest and therefore her most deadly. "Don't tell us Frank forgot to tell you something."

Simon looked like he'd been stabbed. "One of Frank's data bases crunches a terabyte's worth of numbers every nanosecond. Not once has he ever forgotten *anything*."

"Then perhaps there is a design defect in the hardware," Charlie cooed.

"That will do," I said hopefully.

"Uh-oh," someone muttered.

Caleb was watching with amazement. It was the first time he

had ever seen Charlie and Simon in full cry, something I wished I could say.

"Are you insinuating," Simon said, enunciating each word with precision, "that the Amazing Grace Model II is a *kludge*?" The last word was hurled with such passionate loathing that the room burst into laughter.

"Sounds like a personal problem to me," Crip muttered, grinning.

Paddy laughed and said, "Sure, and it was that peaceful this evening I was forgetting where I was."

"Go for it, Simon!" Archy cheered. "Defend my honor! AI forever!"

Caleb transferred his slack-jawed stare to the ceiling pickup, and said wonderingly, "He sounds almost sentient."

Simon heard that, and he broke off the fight just long enough to round on Caleb. "The hell you say. The day that pile of crossed-up circuitry starts talking back is the day I start ripping out his wires."

"I heard that, boss."

"Archy," I said, exasperated, "I've told you before that eavesdroppers never hear anything good about themselves. Now stop tuning into things that don't concern you before I start ripping out wires myself!" There was silence for a moment, and then I looked at Simon and said painfully, "Did I just yell at a computer?"

He nodded, and Charlie said, "Now you see why I keep nagging her to go on R&R?"

"I just spent two weeks downstairs," I protested.

"I don't call that R&R and neither do you," she said triumphantly.

Simon, who I had unwarily reminded of his erring wife's existence, turned back to her and picked up their argument right where it had left off. "There is nothing artificial about intelligence, anyway, Charlie, whether it is generated by living cells or metal chips. Either you're smart or you ain't. Archy is."

Elizabeth heaved a loud sigh and turned to me, disgust writ large upon her countenance. *First they'll fight, and then they'll make up and get all mushy. I don't know which is worse.*

"I know," I said. "It is not a pretty sight."

"Mushy?" Caleb said. "In what context? In my capacity as security supervisor, I have to tell you I get the definite feeling we shouldn't leave these two alone in a room containing any blunt instruments."

By then Simon was going Norbert Wiener and Charlie was returning blow for blow with help from Sigmund Freud. Sigmund Freud? I thought, and saw my mystification mirrored on the faces around me. There is nobody like Freud to clear a room, and the party began to break up. "Don't forget the expedition council meeting tomorrow, Crip," I said. "And maybe you could make it for once in your life, Paddy? Ten hundred hours, people, O'Neill conference room. I've got to go to Luna the day after, so don't miss it, please."

Roger took Caleb back to his office, where he had been bunking in spite of my little homily on living over the store. Crip went home with Paddy, and I watched them climb into Paddy's aircar with my mouth open. Nobody ever tells me anything, and I'm not at my most observant when it comes to personal relationships. The only reason I had known about Charlie and Simon was that in a place as small as the Wart there wasn't much room to throw things and sometimes Simon missed.

I grounded the aircar next to my cottage and sat there, gripping the yoke, looking out over the beauty of Ellfive in the twilight. In spite of the enormous meal I didn't feel remotely sleepy. I felt edgy and restless and unsettled, unable to get the afternoon's close encounter of the first kind—if it wasn't that then I was crazy, and I didn't want to be crazy—out of my mind. I went into the house, changed into my skirt and tights, and slung my skates over one shoulder for the trek up the hill.

Less than half a klick from my homesite was a small lake nestled in a hollow about the size of a hockey rink, frozen solid by submerged refrigeration lines. Hemlocks stood in a small grove at one end of the rink, barely four feet in height, new green in color and smelling of their own sap. The sloping hills rose up around us to form a tiny amphitheater.

I sat down on one of the benches lining the lake and laced up my skates. The white leather boots were grimy and creased but the blades were shiny and sharp, and when I removed the guards and stepped out on the rink they bit into the ice with confidence. The ice was hard and took an edge well, without chipping. The friction between blade and ice at half a gee could be tricky; jumps were higher and turns faster, and absolute, calculated control of feet, ankles, and arms were necessary if you didn't want to build up so much speed that it whirled you right up off the rink. I warmed up with bunny hops and hockey stops, built up speed and did a simple three turn, landing cleanly on my right edge, and extended my left leg up in a backward spiral.

I had had this rink pretty much to myself for more than two years, at whatever time of the day or night the fancy to skate took me. What would it be like when the colonists came? They'll want to organize ice shows, I thought sourly, leaning into a bower. They'll put Snoopy on skates for the kiddies. I tacked sharply, leaped into an axle, hands clenched with the effort, did an Arabian, toe loops, splits, camels, flying camels, a series in a routine I had performed long ago to "When the Saints Go Marching In." I had the ghost of Sonja Henie for company, four hundred thousand meters above the fleecy skies of the globe that gave her birth. I slipped and touched one hand down two thirds of the way through the routine, made a hockey stop, and started over again from the beginning. Talent in a skater is necessary, but discipline and perseverance are what makes talented skaters great.

Discipline was also essential in an environment four hundred thousand kilometers away from Terra and any semblance of her judicial system or its enforcement arm. The alternative to being cribbed, cabined, and confined by rules written to be understood by the lowest common denominator at the lowest common altitude was to trust in the discipline and good sense of your employees. Justice had to be swift and sure and as public as possible without taking everyone away from their jobs and lining them up to watch, and the sentence had to be of sufficient horror to discourage other would-be terrorists. With the majority of the people attracted to space colonization, frontier individualists most of them, object lessons were seldom necessary. Sometimes, however, they were, and I was the boss, so I taught the lesson. But I don't have to like it, and I never have.

The only way to make something foolproof is to keep it away from fools. I think I would have felt better about the little Luddite's death if his life hadn't been such a waste. All he had, all he could have been, his life's very essence, was now scattered abroad to the stars. Nothing in his life became him like his leaving it. I gave myself another mental kick for forgetting my pack and fell out of a triple axle. Grimly, I began again. The hell with J. Moore.

And Grayson Cabot Lodge the Fourth, now that the vulgar expenditure of blood, toil, tears, and sweat in building Ellfive was nearly complete, was making ready to step in and take command, as befit the noblesse oblige of a sixteenth-generation Puritan born and bred to lead, regardless of whether or not anyone was willing to follow. I knew it, I knew it as well as I knew the projections for starstone output for the next thirty days, I could smell Grays's determination and rapacity all across the sixty degrees separating Luna from Ellfive. I nailed the triple axle on my third try. Also the hell with him.

After three hours or so I began to feel tired and leaned into a layback, arms extended and arched, came up into a blur, and waited for the ice to slow my blades before stopping the spin with my right pick. I held it, my arms in second position, motionless, the folds of my tiny skirt coming to rest against my hips.

It had been a long time since I had taken my bow to applause. The sound startled me so that my skates went out from under me and I fell smack dab on my shocking pink fanny. It was Caleb Mbele O'Hara, of course, sitting on the bench next to my discarded shoes. I got up and brushed the ice from my bottom. "How long have you been here?"

In the dim light I could see the flash of his grin. "Anchorage Olympics, right? I told you I'd remember. You skated in the women's singles competition. No medal, though."

I shrugged and skated over to the bench. I sat down and began to unlace my boots. "I was never fast enough on Terra. I'm too big."

"That is a matter of opinion, and, incidentally, not mine."

I slung the skates and stood up. "Why the rendezvous?"

I started down the hill and he fell into step beside me. He bounced a little in the half gee until he got used to it. "I couldn't sleep. I didn't think you'd be able to, either."

I opened my front door and halted, sniffing the air. "What's that smell?"

"I brought you a present," he said. He was so close behind me I could feel his breath stirring the hair at the nape of my neck. "I hope you don't object to a little breaking and entering in a good cause."

I waved on the light. On the coffee table in front of the sofa sat a hollow glass ball with the top sliced off, half-filled with oval glass pebbles and water. In it floated several large, sunset-colored flowers with delicately layered petals. *"Cattleya labiata biensientes,"* Caleb said. "October orchids."

"They are lovely, Caleb," I said around the lump in my throat. "Thank you. How did you get them to bloom so quickly?"

"They were already budding when I brought them up from Terra. And Roger found them some fertilizer."

I picked one out of the bowl and cradled the glowing thing in my hand. Behind me Caleb said softly, "On Terra, orchids grow from sea level to altitudes of four thousand meters, from the tropics to above the tree line in the Andes, even in the Arctic. They are hearty as well as beautiful. And sexy." He took the bloom out of my hand and stroked it down my cheek. "They remind me of you."

I met his eyes. "Hearty?" I said.

He did not smile. "Hearty, h-e-a-r-t-y, an adjective meaning 'characterized by warmth and sincerity, strongly felt, vigorous, abundant, nourishing,'" he said. "And beautiful. And sexy."

"This is trite," I said. "Where's the box of candy? Flowers, for God's sake."

"Are they working?"

"Yes," I said, and hoped my voice didn't sound as shaky as I felt.

"Good. That's all that matters." Caleb dropped the glowing bloom back in the bowl. "I'm lonely and I'm scared and I'm tired, and I need to make love to you tonight," he said. He waited, making no attempt to touch me.

I reminded myself of my conversation with Charlie earlier that evening. "So you're going to wait?" she had asked with evident disapproval. "Yes," I had replied firmly.

The hell with it. Woman's at best a contradiction still. "I wanted you the day you walked into my office," I said with my usual subtlety.

"I know you did, so why the song and dance?"

Three or four answers presented themselves, and I said finally, "I've been alone a long time." It was the truth, if not the whole truth.

"So have I," he said. "Together is better."

I smiled at him, and he smiled back. "Let's find out," I said over the thudding of my heart, and took his hand.

On the way into my bedroom we tripped over his duffel bag. Caleb Mbele O'Hara was always very sure of himself.

— 5 —

Thinking Big

There is nothing more difficult to take
in hand, more perilous to conduct, or
more uncertain in its success, than to
take the lead in the introduction of
a new order of things.
                —**Niccoló Machiavelli**

Why did the *Mayflower* cross the Atlantic?

To get to the other side.

We're always going somewhere, up from Africa into Eurasia, across the Alaskan land bridge into North America, from Tahiti to Hawaii, from Plymouth to Plymouth Rock, from Terra to Ellfive. Simon's genetic imperative in action.

Now we're heading for the Asteroid Belt.

The proper term for the individual objects orbiting between Mars and Jupiter is "minor planet." Asteroid means "starlike," which asteroids are anything but. Some frustrated astronomers went so far as to refer to the small, rocky bodies gyrating around Sol between the orbits of Mars and Jupiter as "the vermin of the sky." Their disgust and frustration rose from the fact that to accurately predict asteroidal orbits it is necessary to calculate the gravitational attraction of each of the major planets on each asteroid, and then the perturbing effects each asteroid has on the other.

This massive compilation of data proved so exhausting that there were serious proposals to abandon study of the minor planets altogether. No such luck. By now we know that Mars's gravitational pull determines the inner edge of the Belt, more or less, and Jupiter's pull defines the outside edge, more or less. The Belt is somewhat toroidal, like the Doughnuts, and is as wide as the distance from Sol to Terra. More or less.

Here's the deal: The only rule of size, shape, orbit, inclination, or composition of individual asteroids is that there isn't one. Tiny Hidalgo has an orbital period of nearly fourteen years and has howdied with Saturn. In 1937 Hermes came within 760,000 kilometers of Terra. Icarus has an orbital period of thirteen months, but there are other rocks that take even longer than Jupiter to make a 360 around Sol. The bulk of the asteroid belt is only somewhat inclined to the plane of the ecliptic in which the planets revolve, but Feodosia has an orbital inclination of over fifty-three degrees.

See what I mean? Albedo readings indicate compositions varying from carbonaceous chondrites to nickel-iron metal, and while Ceres with less than a third the diameter of Luna is dense enough to provide a surface gravity strong enough to keep your food and your feet down, provided your food and feet start out that way, the combined mass of *all* asteroids including Ceres has been calculated at not more than ten percent of Luna's, which has less than a quarter the diameter of Terra.

There are almost as many theories about the formation of the minor planets as there are minor planets. The original theory was that a planet broke up, with four variations on the major theme: 1) that the breakup was caused by an explosion, origin unknown; 2) that a too-rapid rotation caused a deterioration and eventual disintegration; 3) that a tidal disruption did same; 4) that a collision between two planets did same. Later telescopic studies advanced the notion that the planetismals developed along with the rest of the solar system from a swirling nebula of gas and dust that gradually agglomerated into larger and larger bodies. Some astronomers speculate that Chiron was once an asteroid; others consider the Trojans, orbiting sixty degrees ahead of and behind Jupiter, and incidentally the site of the first uranium finds in the late twentieth century, to be lost satellites of Jupiter and not asteroids at all. Phobos and Deimos look like asteroids; Io, Europa, Ganymede, and the rest of Jupiter's satellites could have been asteroids transformed into moons by the red giant's gravitational pull.

With the help of Mitchell Observatory in orbit next to Ellfive the Belt had become more familiar territory, and more provocative, and independent prospectors as well as geologists sponsored by each and every Terran government were sniffing around the Trojans. Before long news of monster uranium strikes was commonplace on the cube. Rumor and speculation took their place right next to truth in these reports, due in part to the spectacular imaginative capabilities of Belt miners.

Now, the average Belter is not that great a liar; he is simply unable to tell the precise truth. This seems unnecessary; the Belt lends itself to exaggeration anyway, but Mohammed Bahktiar made the first discovery on Achilles and his subsequent actions set the standard for behavior ever after. He shook a kilogram of almost pure U-235 out of one cubic meter of his claim. This was better than anyone had ever done in the history of mankind, but he was unable to resist gilding the lily. He said he took out five. Nobody believed him and there was a lot of snickering before and behind. On a bet K. C. Kennecott filled a breaker box with a couple of shovelfuls from his claim next door just to prove the lie, and panned out two kays to the c/m. A couple of klicks over Smokey Stover swore his claim would produce a thousand Alliance dollars to the half meter and sold it to Olga Chernenko, who pulled fifteen hundred per cubic centimeter, to Smokey's great and vocal disgust. And that's the way it went—the Belters continued to lie valiantly, and their claims kept outrunning their lies.

The most significant and the one unassailable proven fact is this: The Belt is 167 million miles or 270 million kilometers or 1.8 astronomical units out from Terra, take your pick, so none of these mining finds would have been possible without safe, swift, and economical space travel, which even in the 1980s still seemed decades away. Then in 1992 the first message from the Beetlejuicers came in via the Odysseus II Space Probe and Project META, and the resulting scramble to acquire high-ground acreage to extend the hand of friendship to our alien brothers, or to provide a line of defense against alien invaders, take your pick, left no Terran nation capable of inventing, buying, or stealing space travel earthbound.

The United States, with a space program crippled by the *Challenger* explosion and three decades of an unwise special-ization in manned space travel, dusted off an old plan by General Atomic to build a nuclear starship. Project Orion was a nuclear bomb-powered rocket ship planned in 1958 to have them shining their shoes on Saturn's rings by 1970. When you consider that one B-53 thermonuclear bomb had an explosive yield of 9 million tons of TNT or 750 Little Boys or 30 MX missile warheads, this was not such a farfetched idea. Then the Test Ban Treaty of 1963 prohibited atmospheric testing of atomic bombs, and the final blow came when Wernher Von Braun's chemical rockets were chosen to carry out the Apollo program. Project Orion was relegated to a dusty file and the occasional nostalgic mention in *Scientific American*.

You could say that Project Orion went out with a whimper and came back with a bang. The leaders of the newly formed American Alliance—then only the United States, Canada, and Japan—were agitated by a populace hysterical over the Bee-tlejuice Message. After the announcement of the Mars expe-dition, they were understandably nervous that the United Eurasian Republic—still only the USSR—was going to beat them skyward yet again. So they negotiated the historic SALT VII agreements.

SALT VII banned nuclear power in all but transportation and generation fields and provided for watertight verification. The ink on the treaty (for which Frank Sartre as key scientific adviser won his first Nobel) was hardly dry before the American Alliance handed a blank check to the newly created Department of Space and told them to solve the fallout problem in the Orion's exhaust and get it operational as in yesterday. They did, and LEO Base, GEO Base, and Copernicus Base came in ahead of schedule and under budget, at which time Frank won his unprecedented second Nobel, this time sharing it with Helen Ricadonna.

The Orion starship was powered by the controlled velocity distribution of nuclear explosions. DOS called them "pulse units," the Space Patrol called them "charge propellant systems," and Colony Control called them "Express-class freight carrier propellant charges" but they were nothing more or less than nuclear bombs modified into nuclear fuel after SALT VII. Nuclear bombs were made with plutonium, which was bred from uranium. There are two kinds of uranium—uranium-235, the only naturally occurring fission fuel for the making of nuclear energy, and uranium-238, which is not naturally fissionable. U-235 was rare on Terra and virtually nonexistent on Luna, and if the Martians had found any significant deposits they weren't saying. U-238 had been plentiful on Terra at one time and breeder reactors can convert it to plutonium-239, which is fissionable and therefore suitable for building the bombs that powered the Orion starship that would get us to the Belt where we could find more uranium to build more bombs to fuel more ships.

All of which was partly why I was determined on an Ellfive-sponsored Belt expedition, but only partly.

Island One of the Ellfive habitat project was almost complete. The bulk of material to construct Island One had come from Luna. But Luna was growing in population herself, and we were already hearing noises about cutbacks in supply once the existing contracts for Island One were filled. Island Two was a mere skeleton, and to flesh out that skeleton we might have to find other sources of supply for essential life elements such as oxygen, hydrogen, nitrogen, et cetera, et al., not to mention the ores we needed for manufacturing. So someone had come up with the obvious solution of mounting an expedition to exploit the Asteroid Belt, and to man that expedition we were tapping into the Ellfive work force, five thousand strong, some of whom said decidedly they had gone far enough. But there were others, still driven by Simon's genetic imperative, who wanted to keep on going. After commissioning the entire matter would be taken out of our hands, but I was determined that Island Two was not going to be strapped for material through shortsightedness and a lack of planning on our part.

I walked into the staff meeting the following Monday and into the middle of a discussion on Terra's slow, painful move toward a unified planetary government, delayed, according to a sardonic Crip, mainly by those who still believed the Trilateral Commission was poised to take over life as we know it.

"Does no one read history anymore?" Whitney Burkette said, looking disdainful.

"I heard that," Sam Holbrook said emphatically. "If the Russians thought Afghanistan was a bad dream, running France after the post-SALT VII invasion was pure nightmare. The Trilateral Commission, even if it existed, running all of Terra? Give me a break."

There was a chorus of agreement, which I silenced by rapping my knuckles on the table. "Order, children, please, order," I said. "We don't give a damn how they do it downstairs, remember? Let's get down to the business at hand. At the end of the last meeting we had some questions on just what this expedition would be shipping in from the Belt. I've got a few answers for you. Ready? Okay." I sat down and called up my notes on the viewer in front of me. Charlie passed down a steaming cup of coffee and I fortified myself with a long swallow before wading in.

"We're planning this expedition to ship raw materials back to Ellfive for the construction of Island Two, but shipping raw rock is only the beginning," I said, looking around the table. "It is always cheaper to ship a finished product than it is raw material. That's why there are oil and gas separation centers on the Arctic slope, pineapple canneries on Maui—"

"The Frisbee on Ellfive," Simon pointed out.

"Exactly. Obviously this expedition will not start out ready to refine and ship pure ore, but we need to develop an interim plan, a compromise between raw rock and pure ore."

"We got that far last week, Star," Whitney Burkette said.

"By way of introduction, Whitney," I said. "May I continue?" He inclined his head graciously. "Thank you," I said, and Charlie rolled her eyes at me. "Shipping ore raw, partially processed or as a finished product—all these have different values to us, to the miners, and to Ellfive. For example, it would be cheap for us to ship the rock raw forever, but eventually not worth the effort of refining on arrival at Ellfive. So the trick is to develop a cheap, quick, in-transit method of processing, using parts of the asteroid itself for propulsion but leaving the essential minerals in place. To put it simply, the idea is to start at the Belt end with a chunk of mixed matter and to finish in Terran orbit with a mass of more or less refined ore, or at least a mass with a reduced amount of slag, to speed up extraction on the Ellfive end. The process may be automated, it may have to be manned."

"If we do come up with this process, and if it does have to be manned, who do we hire?" This from a dark, heavyset man with jowls that wriggled when he spoke, who did not seem so much skeptical as intent on nailing down every loose end. "We're only going out there with two hundred and fifty people, Star, and we'll need every one of them."

"It's Mike, right? Mike Cowper? Exogeologist?" I waved my hand toward the general direction of the Belt. "How many prospectors out there do you think have struck out repeatedly in the last five years, Mike, and are by now looking for a free ride downstairs? We train them, set them up in stores and showtapes, and send them on their way."

"What's to stop them from goofing off the whole trip?"

"Simple greed. We signal ahead to Ellfive, giving them the composition of the rock and the expected delivery percentages. The supercargo is reimbursed on arrival by a prearranged fee per metric ton of refined ore. And," I added, "if that doesn't work, they either space the sumbitch or let him work off his passage in one of the sewage treatment plants, and we make sure the story gets around."

He grunted. There was silence for a moment, until Sam Holbrook, who always looked as if he were trying to remember if he'd left the telescope on when he left Mitchell, said dreamily, "You know, if you mix methane with ammonia and pass electricity through it you can form organic matter?"

I said cautiously, "So?"

"So Jupiter's just lousy with methane and ammonia."

"Oh." There was another silence.

"But," Sam admitted sorrowfully, "Jupiter also produces twice as much heat as it receives from Sol. I've heard estimates of an interior temperature of ten thousand degrees absolute plus. That'd kill anything organic."

"How unfortunate," I said solemnly, and he nodded in sad agreement. We paused for a moment in silent memoriam to Jupiter's—for now—forfeited resources. Sam dreamed a good dream when he put his mind to it.

"We're still going to have to supply the expedition, no matter how self-supporting we make it," Simon observed. "We can use the return trip for some refined ores, like silicon, and any others we need most."

"Good idea," Crip said, "it frosts me to think of eating either end of the transportation cost."

I smiled at him. "So maybe we should think of something to take up space, in case we have any left over."

He examined my smile with suspicion. "Like what?"

"Well." I paused. "On the trip out, like tourists, for example."

There was a stunned silence, broken at last by Crip. "Are you out of your mind?"

"What is this, Star, public relations or reality?" Simon chimed in. "Space is for professionals, not passengers."

"Unless they're paying passengers," I retorted. "Simon, if we're going to sell this idea to Colony Control and the Habitat Commission, not to mention the American Alliance, we've got to explore every possibility to make both the trip out and the trip back pay. Tourism is an obvious option. Just think about it, all right? I'm not asking you to guide tours, for God's sake. If it comes to that, it will only be a very few, very well-heeled passengers. The captain can wine them and dine them—"

"Thanks a whole bunch, Star," Crip said crisply.

I sighed. "Which reminds me. Have you found us a manager for flight operations yet?"

He nodded. "Perry Austin."

I whistled. "I don't know whether to curtsy or just genuflect and get it over with. I thought she was pretty well settled with Space Services."

"She told me she'd been feeling crowded lately. Said she wanted some elbow room."

"We can promise her plenty of that."

"Maybe not for long," Charlie said. "I saw on the trivee last night that a private outfit named Mayflower, Inc. is taking applications for homesteaders for a future flight to the Belt on one of the new fusion ships. If they ever work the bugs out of the drive."

"The Oklahoma Land Rush," I said. "Well, we'd better do our best to beat them to it and stake out the best claims. Now. Personnel. Listen up, take notes, this is important. I want you to make sure everyone who applies to go on the Belt Expedition understands that this trip is in the proposal stages only, no guarantees that it's actually going to happen. However"—I transfixed the table with what Charlie called my Medusa stare—"I want you to make equally certain that each and every prospective employee understands that we are dead serious about the quality of personnel we want for this hypothetical trip. And when I say quality, I mean everybody we hire is capable of wearing at least two hats."

"Specifically?"

"Specifically, when we hire on a geotech I want him or her trained in hydroponics or spacemed or solar power maintenance as well. I'll expect department heads to review the personnel roster daily, on the lookout for anyone who shows an aptitude for their department's line of work. It goes without saying that any applicant's chances improve a hundred percent if they have a background in vacuum construction."

I hesitated, and said carefully, "And although I don't wish to limit anyone in making his or her personnel selections, do keep in mind that brute force doesn't mean diddly in zerogee, that women consume less food and less oxygen than men, and that women are more radiation resistant than men. Generally speaking women also mass less and are cheaper to transport." I patted the air with my hands. "Okay, okay, I'm not

overlooking the need for a sexually balanced crew that far from
home. Just keep it in mind, okay?"

Whitney Burkette made a neat note on a pad lined up
precisely at the edge of the table in front of him. He was an
Englishman with a walrus mustache, bulging, walruslike eyes,
and a walruslike capacity for the female sex. If I'd said I
wanted the Belt crew all women except for him he would have
sacrificed a chicken to the gods in my name. He was a genius
at zerogee construction or I wouldn't have put up with him and
his clammy hands for a minute. "Any other caveats, Star?"

"Only one. Please, please, please, let's keep the sociologists
out of the planning loop this trip. If I have to debate the
long-term ramifications of space exploration and colonization
on the human race one more time, I will vomit. Same for the
psychiatrists and the anthropologists. Space travel should be
routine enough by now that we can get by without their dubious
help."

"No intellectuals need apply," Charlie murmured.

"That's not what I said, Charlie."

"No, but that's what you meant, Star."

"If you mean I don't want to waste time butting heads with
someone who has never been able to understand the industrial
revolution," I retorted, "much less accept it, you are correct."

"Depends on where you saw it from, whether you thought it
was a good idea," Simon said. He caught my eye and added,
"The industrial revolution. Whether you saw it from London or
Bangkok."

"Ethiopia or Ellfive," Charlie said, enjoying herself, and I
saw Caleb choke back a laugh behind one square hand.

"Well, on Ellfive," I said, staring my sister down, "you'll
be giving classes in tooth extraction and emergency appendec-
tomies and zerogee CPR. We've already signed on seventy
people for this expedition and I want to keep them busy. Enid,
as soon as you can start instruction in food management, waste
management—"

"And packing," Enid said. "Packing things into a spaceship
is an art in itself."

"How true," Crip murmured.

"What else?" I said. "Ah—look for backgrounds in exogeology, seismology, photography, assaying and opticom systems, and oh, everyone, whether they hold a valid certification or not, shines up on their EVA procedures."

"Don't let your enthusiasm turn our students into drones," Crip drawled.

"Okay," I said agreeably. "You're a graduate of that monster astronaut training program with DOS, you can follow behind me and monitor the course schedule. If you find a class you feel is redundant, cut it. If the lab time is too tight, change it." I smiled at Crip. "From this moment, you are the student representative to the board of regents."

"Thanks a whole bunch," he said again, with even less enthusiasm. "Man can't even make a passing comment around here."

"I can start a course in basic hydroponics techniques right away, Star," Enid said.

"And I'll work out a teaching plan in fiberoptics for intraship communications and suprasonics for extraship," Bolly Blanca said. "And we'd better have some elementary instruction in how to read and maintain an Express's inertial-measurement unit."

"A what?"

"An IMU, a space compass," he explained.

"I've stolen a couple of pressure-suit techs away from Daedalus Flight Service," I said, "and scheduled them for classes in hundred-hour p-suit maintenance checkups. I've got some powertechs standing by to instruct us in the manufacture of electricity and water from oxygen and hydrogen through the use of fuel cells. And some waste management technicians to give lessons in how to flush the toilets and how to change the canisters of lithium hydroxide that purify cabin atmosphere and how to vacuum filter screens on the air-conditioning system."

"Whew," Simon said, wiping imaginary sweat away from his brow. "You've been busy. All I've done is line up some drive engineers to teach a comprehensive course in ship propulsion, from construction and maintenance to detonation. They assure me that then they're done, there won't be one of us who can't dropkick an Express." He grinned. "Theoretically, anyway."

"I've set up a ferry schedule between Ellfive and Mitchell Observatory," Sam Holbrook said, "and I'm prepared to begin tutoring everyone—by appointment only, please!—in star sighting and astrogation." He gave me a sideways look. "I've already test-drove the program on Star, here, and I'm pleased to say she's doing well."

"Sure," I said, "I did fine once I stopped mistaking Hercules for Orion."

"I wouldn't go that far," Sam said immediately. "You got a little cocky there for a while."

"Which you cured by logging a simulated IMU failure and letting my imaginary Express run out of fuel trying to find the Pleiades." Everyone laughed, but it had not been a fun sim. I hate being lost almost as much as I fear solar flares. "So has everyone got enough to go on with?"

"More than enough I would think, Star," Whitney Burkette pronounced after judicious thought.

"Yeah, could we slow to sublight now?" Bolly pleaded. "Tell us how your trip downstairs went."

"If I never again smell the inside of a high school gymnasium, I will die a happy woman," I said. I stood up and stretched, and wandered over to the window. Behind me I heard people pushing their chairs back, pouring and passing cups full of coffee, and propping their feet up on the table. The sun poured in through the windows and glinted off a receding aircar. There was a horde of tiny figures swarming over Owens Arena about a klick down Valley One, making all ready for orientation of the first load of colonists in two weeks. God, it looked good out there, and how I wished I were out in it.

I turned back. "I'm sorry to say the news from downstairs ain't good. Standard Oil and Solar is making noises around the Alliance Congress about how the Ellfive Corporation will soon be a major exporter of goods and services, and how that makes Ellfive security a concern of the American Alliance, and why its administration should be removed from the hands of mere civilians."

There was a short silence. "Lodge is moving in for the kill," Simon said at last.

"It looks that way," I agreed. "He's been disrupting or

trying to disrupt hangarlock service. And either by turning a blind eye or by outright advocation of violence, he has encouraged Patrol liberty parties to cause as much trouble as they can here, which he knows can only lower morale and slow construction."

"You think he was behind that rape?" Bolly asked me directly.

Caleb uttered an inarticulate protest, and I said, "Behind the rape itself, no. He executed the rapists, had you all heard?" There were approving nods around the table, and I said, "I think he meant them to make trouble, and I think they knew that, and I think it got out of hand."

"How is—?"

"No name," I said sharply. "She can go public if she wants to, but until she does we maintain at least an illusion of privacy for the kid."

Charlie said to Enid, "Physically she is recuperating. Mentally—" Charlie paused. "Mentally, she's a wreck. Nightmares, guilt, shame, rage, depression, you name it, she's feeling it." She turned to me. "You really think Lodge is ready to make a move?"

"I don't know. I don't know how he could convince himself that five thousand Fivers are just going to roll over as he rolls in." I rubbed my forehead. "It is a fact, however, that Space Patrol Commodore Grayson Cabot Lodge the Fourth is the cousin of Senator Dewayne Nierbog, Jr., as well as the nephew of Charleton Cabot Winthrop, chairman of the board of SOS. I also hear tell how Commodore Lodge is bored with monitoring SDI satellites at GEO Base, and even more bored with watching Commissar Korolov at Tsiolkovsky Base watch him. And I myself am pretty well acquainted with the size of Commodore Lodge's personal ambition, which may be slightly smaller than his ego, although I wouldn't bet any serious money on it."

There was a murmur of comment. "I was just wondering," Charlie said at last in a soft voice pitched for my ears alone.

"What?" I said.

"How much of the animosity he shows toward Ellfive is personal," she said, and our eyes met.

"Why should it be, after all this time? I don't have any toward him," I said, and could feel my face redden when she raised an eyebrow.

"Of course you don't," my sister said, still in that deceptively soft voice in which she makes all her best points. "You left him, not the other way around. Understanding and forgiveness for you is easy, even obligatory. But Grayson's kind don't know how to lose. At anything."

I fiddled with the viewer controls. "What do you suggest I do about it?"

She made a face. "Nothing you can do, except wait for him to move. You can't take action until he does."

I rubbed my eyes. "Charlie," I said, raising my voice, "if life were a Greek tragedy, you'd be the chorus, every time."

Simon laughed a little, and Charlie glared first at him and then at me. "And maybe," she snapped, "just maybe, you shouldn't have been so adamant in keeping weapons off Ellfive. Knowing Grays is on the prowl, I'd feel a lot safer if we had a few laser pistols of our own in reserve."

The room became very still. I folded my hands on top of the table and regarded them intently. "Charlie," I said softly to my hands, "are you quite happy in your job?" I lifted my eyes and regarded her with my eyebrows raised. I heard Simon take a deep breath, and hold it.

Charlie's face flushed a deep, dark red. "Yes, Star," she said steadily.

"Then you feel that you can continue to live and work under the established rules and conditions currently governing our lives here at Ellfive?"

"Yes, Star," she said again, her voice still steady and her face still red.

"I am happy to hear it," I said, and I smiled at her. "I'd have a hard time replacing such a competent medical supervisor, and one so thoroughly integrated into the project."

A big sigh went around the room, and I leaned back in my chair. We didn't broadcast the fact that Charlie and I were sisters, something made easier when Charlie took Mother's maiden name, and at times like this I was glad of it. "However, Charlie, you're quite right in thinking we've caught the

Alliance on the jump. We put this project together in two-thirds
the time the Habitat Commission projected, those who expected it to be completed at all. The first colonists are arriving
in less than two weeks and Ellfive is about to pay off in a big
way. The Frisbee is already supporting itself." I laughed
shortly. "The prize is tempting, and I'd be lying if I said I
wasn't worried over Grays's intentions. He can always point to
Ellfour as a security risk."

"Ellfour doesn't even have spin yet."

I shook my head. "You haven't been downstairs in years,
Sam. It doesn't just smell down there anymore, it stinks. Hell,
why not, after Seabrook and with the greenhouse effect the
air's almost toxic. There's never been enough to eat, they can't
or won't come up with a global, mandatory birth-control plan
so there's barely enough room to sleep, and if there are only
five governments running Terra now instead of a hundred and
fifty, that still doesn't mean they can agree on a common
problem, forget a solution. The way the American Alliance
looks at it, the United Eurasian Republic may have a base on
Luna and a colony on Mars but they're way behind in habitat
development. In the not-too-distant future these habitats are
going to be, if not supporting Terra, then at the very least a
vital factor in her survival. What better way to catch up than
simply to move in on Ellfive? The fact that the UER would be
appropriating someone else's property has never stopped them
before, as the honorable senator from Wisconsin has pointed
out on numerous occasions."

Simon grunted. "Red baiter."

"Smile when you say that, pardner. I only know what I see
on the trivee."

Nobody said anything for a while, and then I said, "If Lodge
makes a move, it will be before the colonists arrive. There are
only a thousand Patrolmen at Orientale, less than two hundred
at GEO Base, and about fifty on LEO."

"Gideon only needed three hundred," Caleb said.

"Grays isn't Gideon, and he sure as hell isn't carrying the
sword of the Lord. With our five-thousand-man crew, even
without weapons, I think we can hold off the Space Patrol. You

can only shoot so many in a crowd before the crowd runs over you."

"Is this crowd going to stand up to be shot at?" Caleb said, and I looked at him in some surprise.

"Of course."

"You're very sure."

"Of course," I said again.

Caleb looked at Simon, who looked at Charlie, who examined me with a slight smile on her face. "Tell me, Star, are you sticking around to nurse this Utopian child once you get her born?"

I laughed, sort of, and said, "Let's just get her born, okay? There'll be time and more to worry about my future afterward."

"You know, Star," Whitney Burkette said, frowning down at his precisely placed notebook, "if they have the Alliance Congress behind them, a Space Patrol takeover might be legal."

"The Habitat Act of 1993 specifically grants autonomy to each individual habitat, providing Ellfive makes full restitution of debt plus interest to the American Alliance," I said sharply.

"Acts can be repealed," he pointed out, calmly enough, but with that trace of self-righteous assurance in his manner that always annoyed me.

"He's right, Star," Simon said. "No, now, just hold on a minute. We could offer to up the interest. Make it too profitable for them to take us over."

"Why would the Alliance settle for a piece of the action if they think they can have it all? Besides, I won't have Ellfive held hostage to Terran greed."

He grinned suddenly. "Well, we could always ask the Beetlejuicers for help," he said, and Charlie giggled.

I looked at Simon, unsmiling. "Since the first and only message we've ever received from our friends on Betelgeuse was over fifteen years ago, and since the linguists say the message itself wasn't much more than an interception of a routine ship-to-ship transmission that indicated no awareness whatever of Terra's existence, I don't think we should hold our breath waiting for them to bail us out, do you?"

"I suppose not," Simon said solemnly. Charlie giggled again, sounding exactly like Elizabeth. Caleb looked puzzled, but no one was paying any attention to him, and to my surprise and relief he didn't ask any questions.

The meeting broke up and I called Simon to one side. "Simon, if anything happens to me, no, let me finish. If anything does happen to me, and if Lodge tries something on, I want you to call Jorge Velasquez at Copernicus Base and tell him I said to fill you in on Plan A."

He smiled slowly. "Plan A?"

I didn't. "Yes, Plan A."

He sobered and said, "Why don't you tell me about it, right now?"

"Because we might not need it, and if we don't, it's better that as few people as is practical know about it." His eyebrows rose and I said, "I'm sorry. It sounds like something on *The Galactic Overlord*, doesn't it? But don't forget, okay? Plan A. It's important."

He regarded me with an impassive expression. "I won't forget."

Caleb and I got back to my office just in time to find that the Bugolubovo and Viskov dog-and-pony show had arrived. Roger and Jerry Pauling were dancing attendance on their new protégés and did everything but send up rockets to indicate how welcome another pair of hands was going to be in their respective work places. Viskov, dark and stocky and stolid, held hands with his wife, who was fair and stocky and stolid. Neither of them spoke English, but that was all right since Jerry was speaking to Viskov in silicon and Roger was speaking to Bugolubovo in botanic. Everyone seemed happy except for Emily Holbrook Castellano, who didn't speak Russian or silicon or botany or, I sometimes suspected, System English either.

Notwithstanding the language barrier, it was evident that nothing less than a hacksaw was going to separate Emily from the sources of *Time*'s next cover story. Red baiting hasn't changed much in the last fifty years, more's the pity. She did graciously spare a minute of her valuable time to say to me,

"Of course you will make yourself available for a tour and an interview later on in the week."

It was difficult to keep the dismay out of my voice, so I didn't try. "You're going to be here a whole week? We are rather busy right now, Emily. I've got to go to Luna for a couple of days and commissioning is less than two weeks away."

"If you commission," she said.

I looked at her. She had mousy brown hair slicked back in a severe bun, a style she fondly imagined made her look like Tatiana Romanova of the Bolshoi Ballet but that really made her look like a diamondback in molt, only not as cute. "Are you trying to tell me something, Emily?"

I was taller than she was so it was more of a strain for her to maintain eye contact. She shoved her chin up as far as it would go and said pugnaciously, "The public has a right to know about the status of the Ellfive project. Of course, if you can't spare the time—"

"I am tempted to point out," I drawled, "that the American Alliance public is not Ellfive's public." Caleb didn't even twitch. Elizabeth, working out a problem in Boolean algebra at my desk, shot me an apprehensive glance, but then she'd known me longer.

"The American Alliance is bankrolling Ellfive with tax dollars collected from the American Alliance public," Castellano said, her lips curled in a sneer that made me think a forked tongue would dart out between them at any moment. She was hell on sneering, was Emily Holbrook Castellano, even if she did have trouble with simple declarative sentences. "It might interest them to know there have been airlock executions without benefit of trial taking place without discrimination since Ellfive pressured up." She sneered some more. "The last one taking place two weeks ago and not a kilometer from your office."

There had been airlock executions going on without benefit of trial since before Copernicus Base had been completed, but I didn't say so. I wondered how she had picked that up in the two hours she had been on board. "Spend some time at

Orientale before you went to GEO Base, Emily?" I said, taking
a guess. "Maybe have dinner with the commodore?"

My guess was right on, I could see it in the quickly
suppressed flash of surprise across Emily's face, and suddenly
I was angry, so angry I was trembling with it. I don't know
what my face looked like but Elizabeth dropped her pencil and
started around the desk as if to stop whatever she thought I was
going to do. Emily paled but to her credit stood her ground.

I was proud of myself. I didn't take her into the john and jam
her down the head. I said, "Elizabeth? Come here." Elizabeth
came to stand beside me, looking from me to Emily with wide
eyes. "Observe closely, Elizabeth," I said, resting one hand on
her shoulder. "This is a specimen that has not come your way
before. Emily, although she will claim all the outward impar-
tiality of any member of the press, is a Luddite sympathizer
who would like nothing so much to happen as for Ellfive to
wobble out of orbit and spiral into Sol or Terra, always
providing there was time for man-on-the-street interviews on
the way down. It is politically expedient for her to speak
favorably of us at the moment, but I would advise you to watch
your back as you grow up here."

Emily Holbrook Castellano flushed a dull purple right up to
the roots of her bun. "One story," she said softly, through her
teeth, "one story, Star, and I could have your job and discredit
the entire colony project."

"She also suffers from delusions of grandeur," I said to
Elizabeth. "Making threats before lunch, Emily? How very
uncivilized of you." I smiled, and Elizabeth winced. Caleb
was examining his cuticles with intense interest. "Well, go
ahead, give it a try. It would, after all, be something of an
about-face from the progressive theme you usually preach.
Five years ago it went something like this, and I quote:

> "If you can believe the eulogies of Star Svensdotter,
> Ellfive is the hybrid of a brave new world and the next
> life. Svensdotter is following in the footsteps of Magellan
> and Cook, Lewis and Clark, Armstrong and Aldrin. Like
> all pioneers she is driven by a messianic sense of mission
> and a love of adventure, as well as a clear and enthusiastic

view of the future of mankind that is as contagious as it is optimistic.

"I believe you'll recognize the hyperbole," I told Emily. "I always thought your mother was frightened by a Victorian novelist when she was carrying you, but I admit that story was good for a few free meals. Did I ever thank you?"

Her color slowly fading back to normal, Emily turned her back on me and gave Viskov and Bugolubovo an insincere smile. I couldn't see it but I saw Bugolubovo smile back and I knew Emily. For the first edition, the banner headline could read "Ellfive Despot Repeals First Amendment." For the final I rather liked "Truth, Justice, and the American Way Suborned."

I said, "Jerry, Roger, I'm placing Zoya and Vitaly in your care. Give them a day to settle in and then show them to their work areas. If the zeegee corridor isn't open by then make sure Daedalus checks them out in p-suits." I smiled at the Russian couple. They stared stolidly back. Emily had probably promised them a special on *Time Marches On*, Sunday night at nine. Souls have been sold for less. Why should these two be any different? "Archy?"

"Yes, boss?"

"Stand by for voiceprints of Vitaly Viskov and Zoya Yelena Bugolubovo."

"Has the Red Menace arrived?"

"Stop being such a smartass," I said sharply. Archy did not reply. I didn't know if he was squelched or sulking. Whichever it was, Simon was going to do some extensive recoding of Archy's personality cards before any of us were very much older. Roger and Jerry bowed their charges out, with Emily in tow. I relaxed, or tried to.

Caleb said, "Little rough on her, weren't you, Star?"

"Tact is something I leave for diplomats," I said shortly.

"I noticed," he said. "You should pick your fights with more care. She can still do damage, no matter how far along the project is."

I shot him a fulminating look and Elizabeth said hastily, *If that lady is a Luddite, Auntie Star, why did she write such nice things about you?*

"Honey, because Emily writes nice things about me doesn't mean she has to believe them. She doesn't like me, she never has, not since Luna and Grays—" I barely caught myself, and carefully avoided looking at Caleb.

Elizabeth's brow furrowed. *How can she say one thing, do another, and think something completely different?*

"Maybe she's ambidextrous." My niece gave me a reproving look and I said, "Elizabeth, Emily is a journalist. Remember when we were reading Thomas Wolfe? Remember 'the pious hypocrisy of the press with its swift-forgotten prayers for our improvement, the editorial moaning while the front page gloats'?"

Elizabeth digested this in silence. *Does that mean she is going to write bad things about you now?*

I gave a short laugh. "Emily Holbrook Castellano is a vicious, unprincipled bitch with no feel for the future, but she's not stupid. She knows Terra's present mood better than anyone, and the majority of Terrans believe and want to read that space is he last, best hope of mankind. Emily is not about to bite the hand that feeds her." I ruffled Elizabeth's hair. "Even if she does harbor the private belief that I'm the illegitimate daughter of Ming the Merciless, instead of the heir apparent to Flash Gordon and Dale Arden she once claimed. Now, I've got an appointment, and no, you can't come with me." Caleb started to make a noise and I said firmly, "Either of you." I stalked out of the office.

Charlie's clinic was a short hop by aircar, a one-story, cream-colored building halfway between Owens Arena and McAuliffe School, surrounded by oak and maple saplings and a green lawn between flagged paths. Her office was just inside the front door. She eyed me warily as I came in. I was still stalking.

"I need an implant," I barked.

"What kind of an implant?"

"Contraceptive."

Her mouth dropped open and she regarded me fixedly for a few moments. Blackwell beeped impatiently and she turned to write data to a chartdisk. She pulled the disk and filed it, and turned back to me. "How was that again?"

"You heard me," I said, trying not to sound defensive. "I need a contraceptive implant. Get on with it."

"Fine, fine," she said soothingly, "anything for a quiet life." She left the room and returned with a syringe and a smirk. I scowled at her and she straightened out her face. "Timed release, one-year duration," she said, all business. "Same as you had on Luna. That do?"

"Fine." I got up, dropped my jumpsuit, and grabbed the arms of the chair. Charlie smacked the implant home with unnecessary relish and I hauled my uniform back on and ran the zip up to where the tab almost choked me. Charlie pulled my disk and, wrote the prescription to my file, humming Mozart to herself. When she was done, she picked up a red-and-white capsule and tossed it in my direction. By a miracle I caught it. "What's this?"

"A morning-after pill, I'm sure you need it," she said, and laughed when I threw a file at her.

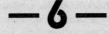

The Calm Before

There is one glory of the sun, and
another glory of the moon . . .
　　　　　　　—1 Corinthians 15:41

When I woke up the next morning Caleb was still there. "Oh,
good," I said. "You weren't a dream."

"No," he said, reaching for me. "You don't do this a lot, do
you?" he said later.

I wondered if I should feel insulted, and decided it wasn't
worth the effort. "No."

"Why not?"

I stretched out against his warm length. "There was someone on Luna. It didn't work out."

"You left Luna eleven years ago. What about here?"

"I've been busy." I could feel his skepticism and said, "It's
true. I wanted to do the job, and it took everything I had to do

125

it well. Something had to suffer." I turned my face into his shoulder. "But mostly it's because if the boss sleeps with one of the help, others who have not been so honored get bitchy and resentful and after a while it begins to interfere with their work."

I felt him smile against my hair. "That's the first time I've ever heard a manager count sex as a factor in productivity."

"Only the very best managers do. Especially when they've got Whitney Burkette measuring them for a black silk negligee."

"Don't tell me that pompous old fart tried it on?"

"That pompous old fart thinks he's Casanova and Don Juan and Jack Kennedy all rolled into one. It's amazing how many women he has convinced he is."

"But not you."

"No. Not me."

He kissed me. "Thanks for preserving at least one of the few illusions I have left."

"Caleb," I said, raising up on one elbow, "I don't like crowds, or lines. The rest I figure we can make up as we go along."

"Actually, I was thinking marriage and children, in that order."

"So it isn't going to be that easy."

"Doesn't look like it," he said, tracing my lips with one finger.

"You don't seem too worried about it."

"No," he agreed. He sniffed the air. "Someone's cooking sausage. Who is in your kitchen?"

"We could ask Archy."

"We could get dressed and find out for ourselves."

"We could do that."

Hunger eventually drove us to it.

You look tired, Elizabeth said to Caleb as he tilted back from the breakfast table with Mungojerrie and Rumpelteazer in his lap.

"Your aunt is a tiring woman," Caleb replied lazily, tickling one kitten behind its ears.

"Don't you want to see your birthday present, Elizabeth?" I said, glowering at Caleb.

She pounced on the package and ripped it open. *You finished it!*

"Yes. I visited Paddy's aunt in Brooklyn while I was downstairs and she gave me some more bainin. Like it?"

She pulled the Aran sweater on over her head and rolled up the cuffs. *It's beautiful. Thank you, Auntie Star. I'll wear it forever.*

I stroked her hair. "Don't grow too fast and you'll be able to wear it for at least a year. I'm going to Luna today, want to come along?"

Why do you think I'm here? Are we staying the night? Can we have dinner at Jorge's?

"I guessed that was why, yes, and I feel certain Jorge will insist on it."

"Me, too?" Caleb said in a plaintive voice that didn't fool either of us for a minute.

I raised my eyebrows. "What do you think, Elizabeth?"

She thought it over with a concentrated frown. *If he tells us why he's really here, here on Ellfive I mean, he can come,* she said.

The front legs of Caleb's chair came down with what was meant to be a thud but bounced gently in the half gee of my home. I warded him off with an upraised hand. "Not me, I didn't say a word to her. Elizabeth picks up on these things all by herself."

He looked at Elizabeth, half in exasperation and half in amusement. "Why does everyone I meet on Ellfive think I have some ulterior motive in coming here?"

Because you do, Elizabeth said firmly.

"Okay. All right. I give up. Star, Helen and Frank hired me to be your bodyguard."

Before I thought I said, "So I was right! You were hovering!"

Caleb was watching me with wary eyes and I realized he expected me to be angry. I wondered if I was. I had been prepared to find out that he was the Space Patrol's advance guard, or that he was a spy for Senator Nierbog, or the

Luddites, or both, or maybe even a fugitive on the losing side of a power struggle in New South Africa. But a bodyguard? "When did they decide this was necessary?" I said in a mild tone. "I've been guarding this body pretty successfully all by myself for forty-one years."

"When your p-suit was sabotaged last October."

"I see."

"What I told you about the family firm was true, as far as I went. I've always been more interested in spacing than in building another Terran empire." He sent me a private smile. "I wanted a Roc's egg, too."

"Why did it take you so long to get here? Why didn't you apply sooner?" I thought of the three security supervisors prior to Caleb—one dead of REM exposure, the second through sheer carelessness, and the third vanished without a trace—and said with a sigh, "We could have used you. I could have used you."

"Until lately I couldn't be spared from what I was doing," he said with a bald recognition of his own worth that reminded me of Simon at his most arrogant. "Then when I could, the American Alliance's local hire laws got in the way—Helen had to call in some pretty high markers to get my application processed through the Habitat Commission as fast as it was. When the last security supervisor disappeared she stopped saying please."

"So you knew about that?"

"Yes. I figured you'd think it was strange if I didn't ask."

"You were right," I said. "But I still don't understand. Why all the secrecy?"

He smiled a little. "Pride."

I stared at him. "Pride?"

"Not their pride," he explained, "yours. They were afraid you wouldn't go for it if you knew I was here primarily to ensure your safety, not Ellfive's."

I could tell he was afraid I wouldn't, either, but he had more reason. "I admit I don't like being maneuvered, but that's something I will take up with Helen. And I'm willing to do you the credit of believing the last few days haven't been part of the game plan."

His face lightened and he leaned over to kiss me, pausing when he intercepted Elizabeth's interested gaze.

Go ahead, she told him. *In a few years I'll need to know how.*

When he sat back in his chair Elizabeth said, *Not bad. Dad kisses Mom like that, when they're making up.*

"Lucky Dad," Caleb said, grinning. I kicked him under the table.

Auntie Star?

"What, honey?"

What about Archy?

We both knew instantly what she meant. "You mean that hiccup Petra told us about at the party?"

And Roger, and Mom, too, if what she said about Blackwell was true and not just something to make Dad mad. It happened the same time we saw the voices.

"I know, Elizabeth, we picked up on that, too. But when I asked him, Archy didn't remember anything about it. He said it sounded like indigestion to him, and he'd never felt anything like the Webster's definition in his life."

"And there's no record of it in the maintenance program," Caleb said. "I checked."

"So that's that."

Elizabeth stirred. *I don't like it, Auntie.*

"I don't either, but I thought you were the only one of us to think whatever happened was fun?"

I was, and I did, but there has to be something more.

"What?"

Her small face was perplexed. *I don't know, Auntie. But Archy knows something, even if he doesn't know he knows it. You know?*

Caleb stirred in his chair and, when we looked at him, said, "Well, maybe I was right. Maybe it was the Beetlejuicers saying hello." He chuckled.

I met Elizabeth's eyes. She nodded her sharp, decisive little nod. I drank off the rest of my coffee and went to refill my cup. With my back to him I said, "There aren't any Beetlejuicers, Caleb." I turned to lean against the counter. I blew the steam

off the cup and sipped, once again thinking longingly of the
ripening coffee beans in the Nearest Doughnut.

He looked from me to Elizabeth and back again. "What do
you mean?"

"Exactly what I said. There wasn't any message from
Betelgeuse. It was all a big lie Helen Ricadonna and Frank
Sartre cooked up to put a little juice back into the space
program. Helen is a linguist and a mathematician and she faked
the message. Frank fixed it so the 'message' would be
'intercepted' by the Odysseus II probe and beamed back to
Terra." I grinned. "I don't think either of them expected the
magnitude of the reaction the message got, but I know they're
both very pleased with the results."

He sat back in his chair. "No message?"

"No message."

"So there's nobody out here but us?"

"Nope."

He took it calmly. "Who else knows?"

"On Ellfive? Simon and Charlie. Elizabeth figured it out for
herself." She looked up with a shy smile when I squeezed her
shoulder. "On Terra, Frank and Helen, of course, and there
must be a few people at JPL and the Deep Space Tracking
Network who would need to know or the message would never
have been 'received.' " I spread my hands. "As far as I know,
that's it."

"That woman," Caleb said thoughtfully.

"Helen Ricadonna?"

"Yes."

"What about her?"

"It was her idea, wasn't it?" I said nothing and he said, "She
reminds me of Medusa. Eyes that could turn you to stone."

"Really?" I said. "I hadn't noticed."

Oh, Auntie! Elizabeth said. *And Helen's eyes are not like
Medusa's,* she told Caleb severely. *Helen has eyes like—like
Archy would have, not like somebody who has snakes for hair.
Ugh.*

"Thanks, Elizabeth," Archy said.

"I thought I turned you off, Archy," I said.

"I know all, I see all, boss," he replied.

Caleb raised his eyes to the ceiling, his expression pensive. "There was a young cockroach named Archy," he said at length, and paused.

I gazed at him with my mouth slightly open.

> "Whose boss she could be very starchy.
> When I asked him why,
> He said merely, 'Oh, my,
> Don't upset the Svensdotter monarchy.'"

And the big man looked at me expectantly.

I recovered enough to say, "I thought I was the only person in this century to read Don Marquis."

"Not even the second. My father read me 'archy and mehitabel' for bedtime stories when I was little." Caleb looked at me. "Why did you tell me? About the Beetlejuicers? You didn't have to."

I mumbled something and studied my coffee absorbedly. Elizabeth smiled at him. *Never mind Auntie Star, Caleb. We told you because you're family now,* and she went around the table to give him one of her rare hugs.

We commandeered one of the unpressurized solarscooters, squeezing Elizabeth in her tiny p-suit between us in the front seat. I dispensed with the services of a driver and took the left seat myself. Not since my first EVA had I trusted a solarscooter pilot to drive me anywhere, the majority of whom were by definition certifiably insane. It was a short trip anyway, a mere sixty degrees and two hours from Ellfive, through the Warehouse Ring and past Mitchell Observatory. We buzzed the canopy and Tori waved at us enthusiastically through a viewport. Sam shot us the finger. Elizabeth hung out over Caleb's side of the scooter to watch as we passed over the tiny, sparking jewels of Terra's solar power stations and the larger, multifaceted gem of GEO Base. LEO Base was eclipsed by GEO and barely visible. And then we were landing at Copernicus Base. Terra was rising over the lunar horizon as we settled down into the crater.

Pretty, Elizabeth said, pointing at the blue-white globe.

"From here," I agreed.

We hiked from the landing field to the terminal's airlock. Jorge Velasquez was on the other side of the door and he grabbed for me with both hands when my visor popped. He was shorter than I was, and heavier, with a clean-shaven head, bright brown eyes, and a round, creased face that looked as if it might burst into joyous song at any given moment. "*Hola, Star!*" he shouted, kissing both my cheeks and, standing on tiptoe, taking a longer time over my mouth. Kissing in a p-suit is not exactly an erotic experience but that never stopped Jorge.

Eventually he stepped back to arm's length and I saw for the first time the lovely woman with the Mona Lisa eyes and the madonna smile standing behind him. "Marisol de la Madrid, meet Star Svensdotter." He grabbed her hand and hauled her forward. She was as dark as he was, with heavy, shining black hair braided in a coronet around her head. "She's the load supervisor for the mass launcher, and my new roomie."

"Nice to meet you, Marisol."

"And you, Star. Jorge has told me much about you."

"And who is this hombre, eh, Star?" Jorge said, hooking a thumb at Caleb. "He looks almost big enough to keep you in line." He laughed boisterously at my dour look.

"Caleb Mbele O'Hara, meet Jorge Velasquez. He took over at Copernicus when I left. Caleb is the new security supervisor on Ellfive."

Jorge's eyebrows raised. "So?" He gave the other man a measuring glance and evidently approved of all he saw. "I am glad. It was more than time."

He turned to Elizabeth. "Hey, *pequeña*, do you remember Jorge's enchiladas?" Little Elizabeth, divested of helmet and p-suit, nodded vigorously. "*Bueno*, we eat."

Some of the best home cooking in the system, next to Charlie's, could be found in the base commander's quarters at Copernicus. We ate cheese enchiladas in molé sauce with rice and refried beans on the side, served with the ceremony and reverence due an unreconstituted meal the likes of which few Terrans had eaten in decades. As he mopped up the last of his molé sauce with a corn tortilla, Caleb's eyes were streaming from the jalapeños Jorge grew on his own section of Copernicus's underground plantation and heaped upon everything he cooked with a lavish hand.

"*Cerveza*?" Jorge said helpfully. "I brew it myself."

You've been hanging around Paddy, Elizabeth accused.

"*Ay de mí*, my *cerveza* is nothing like that Irish witch's brew," Jorge said with a wounded look.

Paddy is not a witch, Elizabeth said indignantly.

"She may not be a witch, *pequeña*, but that Irish moonshine she makes *es el agua de la bruja* nonetheless," Jorge said firmly. "Now. *Cerveza*, anyone?"

"I'm afraid I won't make it out of this room if I do," I said.

"I'll be lucky to make it out of this chair as it is," Caleb groaned.

Marisol cleared the table as Jorge sat back on his culinary laurels and beamed. After the coffee was poured and anointed with homemade kahlua, whipped cream, and chocolate shavings, I said, "What's this I hear about my old friend and previously unreconstructed rebel being elected head of Copernicus Base?"

Jorge looked at me, appearing somewhat shamefaced. "How did you hear that?"

"Bolly monitors your broadcasts and puts the best of them in the *Gazette*. Tell me about it."

"Well." Jorge shrugged uncomfortably. Marisol was smiling at him with quiet pride. "Things have been run pretty loosely, as you know, Star, but now that the contracts are coming to an end we're close to proving up here at Copernicus. Some of us wanted to set up some kind of government, and, *Dios mío*, somehow I wound up at the head of it."

"Tell us about it," I urged.

He scratched his head. "Well, we incorporated."

"How?"

"I'm not really sure." Marisol laughed and Jorge looked sheepish. "When we saw how close we were to paying off the Alliance we took a vote to take a vote, and then half a dozen people sat down and thought up a constitution, and then we published it for thirty days so everyone could have a look at it and put in their pesetas' worth. We had a public hearing, made a few amendments, after which it was voted in unanimously."

Unanimously?

Jorge shifted under Elizabeth's intent gaze. "Well, no, *pequeña*, there was one 'no' vote."

Only one?

"Ask him whose," Marisol said.

Jorge glared at his soulmate and let out a string of Spanish. She loosed a brisk torrent in return. Jorge flushed brick red right up to the roots of his hair, lunged up out of his chair, and yanked Marisol up out of hers. They embraced. Passionately. Elizabeth observed them with the interest of an emerging connoisseur. I remembered the previous night, and felt my face get hot when Caleb looked over and caught me at it.

Marisol kind of melted back down into her chair and Jorge strutted back to his seat. "Mine was the 'no' vote," he said, settling back in his chair and looking unbearably self-satisfied. "I've always felt that if everyone is for a thing, there has to be something wrong with it. So I voted against it so it would be all right, *compréndeme*?"

Elizabeth made a circle around her ear with one deliberate forefinger, and Jorge shrugged and grinned. "We've gone shares—real shares counted on stock certificates. Copernicans will earn them by working for the habitat, and they will vote them in assembly elections. No one can earn more than a hundred shares. Upon their death the shares automatically revert back to the government. Their children do not inherit, but must earn their own voice in the community. Oh, and nobody is allowed to vote until they pay taxes for the first time."

"Ah, yes. And what about taxes?" I said.

"One dime out of every dollar. No exceptions, no excuses. Payable quarterly."

I thought it over, from different angles. "I like it," I said slowly.

Our eyes met in perfect understanding. "I thought you might."

"So what do we call you?" I inquired. "Your Highness? Generalissimo?"

Jorge's chest puffed out. *"Presidente."*

I cleared my throat. "Well, *Señor Presidente*, I'm here to

find out who or what has been holding up the H_2O shipments to Ellfive."

The rotund little man exchanged a glance with Marisol, and shook his head. "I was afraid of that. You aren't going to like it, Star."

"I don't already."

Jorge looked at his watch. "*Es muy tarde, Estrella mía*. We will go to bed, some of us might even get some sleep, and in the morning, after breakfast, I will show you what you came to see."

Breakfast was eggs and sourdough pancakes with what I could have sworn was real maple syrup and honest-to-God Kona coffee.

Jorge looked up from scanning the news and said, "Didn't you always have a soft spot for the Tycho Brahe Society, Star?"

"What are they up to now?" I said, going to stand behind him and peer over his shoulder at the viewer.

"They're coming to Luna, it says here. They want to conduct a scientific experiment that they say will prove *finalmente* and beyond a shadow of a doubt that the sun does revolve around the earth."

I shook my head admiringly. "You have to admit that an organization that names itself after someone who got his nose sliced off in a duel to the death over long division is an organization that must be reckoned with."

Did you know Brahe replaced his lost nose with a gold prosthesis, Auntie?

"No kidding?" I was delighted. "Where did you come across that little tidbit of information, Elizabeth?"

Jorge's communit beeped and he held a brief low-voiced conversation with his caller. The message seemed to please him. "*Estrella mía*, you have timed your visit well." He drained his coffee, ran his hand down Marisol's behind when she leaned over to retrieve his empty cup, and stood up. "Got something I want to show you. You'll have to get back into your p-suits. It's quicker to walk around than through."

We suited up and followed him through the airlock and out

onto Luna's dusty surface. "Can everyone hear me all right?" Jorge asked. We made radio checks with him, one by one. Elizabeth lifted her hand and made a circle with her thumb and forefinger. "*Bueno*. We will be walking over to the launch tower."

"There really is a concrete technical problem, then?" I said.

I could hear the smile in his voice. " 'I am a Spaniard, a man without imagination.' "

"You, sir, are a Mexican from Ojocaliente, Zacatecas, and a man without shame or scruple," I retorted. "And please, no more Ortega y Gasset."

" 'Rancor is an outpouring of a feeling of inferiority,' " he said piously. "Now I suggest we shut up and save our O_2 for the hike."

Movement on the landing field caught my eye and I turned to see two sister spaceships, standing on their finned tails side by side in identical silver severity. Small figures in p-suits were scurrying about beneath them, or scurrying as much as they were able in Luna's one-sixth gee. "Jorge?"

"What?"

"Whose ships are those?"

I saw him pause and look. "That's the *Conestoga* and the *Tall Ship*."

"That's right, I remember. Space Services is moving into emigration, right?"

"*Es verdad.*"

"Who's on board?"

"*El capitán* Roland Lavoliere and company. Sound familiar?"

"No, I—Lavoliere?" I trudged a few steps, thinking. "Oh. The BioScience Engineering and Ethics Committee?"

"*Sí.*"

"Ah, on Terra, the American Alliance formed such a committee in—1995?—to explore research ethics into genetic engineering, form patent laws, develop a working relationship between academia and industry, and establish a clearinghouse of information to prevent overlapping studies and mistakes in research."

"It was formed in 1994, actually, but for the rest your memory is remarkably good."

"There were all kinds of experts on that committee, genetic engineers, lawyers, philosophers, entrepreneurs. I think they even included a few members of the general public."

"Right again. Half of that committee is with Lavoliere now, on those two ships."

"Only half? Last I heard they were working on getting the legal clout to make private industry and the Alliance government toe the line in genetic research, splicing and cloning. What's only half of them doing here?"

Jorge paused and I almost ran into him. EVA on Luna, you don't exactly stop on a dime. "Where have you been, *Estrella*? *El capitán* Lavoliere quit."

"He quit the chair?"

"He resigned the chair, he quit the committee, he quit Princeton, he quit the American Alliance, he quit Terra herself. I am surprised you missed it, there was nothing else on the trivee for a week. He quit. He said—I think I quote him exactly—he said that he and the rest of the breakaways were rejecting the stifling restrictions of the conventional minds and mores on Terra to embrace the intellectual freedom of deep space."

"So now they're here. Are they staying on Luna?"

"I am happy to report that they have filed a flight plan for the Belt."

"Oh." I walked on. "Well, I guess that's far enough away to grow as many little monsters as they want to without government interference." The thought made my flesh creep.

All around us, caught between the blue glow of Terra and the bright glow of Sol, business was brisk. A rover whose body was dwarfed by bulbous tires pulled a crane across the floor of the crater. A swarm of riggers perched on the skeleton of a geodesic dome riveting roof plates to the frame with powerdrivers. A technician rappeled in graceful bounces down the face of one of a long line of antennae dishes. From where we were we couldn't see out into Mare Imbrium, but I knew from experience that the hustling outside equaled the hustling inside the crater. The road over the north wall was shrouded in a haze

of dust that in the one-sixth gravity created a permanent pall
over Luna's Route 66. Copernicus Base was two thirds of the
way through its two-week day and people were scurrying to
finish tasks that required an extra effort from the solar
generators with which the batteries, stored in square, spare
buildings squatting on the perimeter of the crater, would not be
able to cope.

We could hear nothing through the vacuum and the total and
complete silence in the middle of so much activity was eerie.
I felt as if I were deaf. The sensation was uncomfortably like
the blackout two days before, and I was glad when we reached
the airlock of the launch tower. Inside, we popped our helmets
and followed Jorge into the elevator, moving clumsily in our
p-suits.

The launch controls took up all of the top floor of the launch
tower, with three people sitting inside the curve of the
U-shaped console, surrounded by a bewildering array of
switches and lights flashing red and yellow and green. The
launch controllers spoke in low, calm voices into headsets,
looking up briefly when we came into the room and returning
immediately and without fuss to the task at hand. Half the
ceiling and all of the wall facing the controllers was made of
transparent graphplex panels strengthened with threads of
graphite so slender they were invisible to the naked eye. It was
like looking out from the inside of a gigantic fishbowl. We
could see Ellfive twinkling low on Luna's horizon as rays from
Sol reflected off its rotating sides. Spread out before us on the
surface of Copernicus were the long thin tracks of both mass
drivers and the framed-in beginnings of a third. I could see a
tractor loading a capsule, marked green for oxygen, into the
Driver 2 ejector chute, and a trailer loaded with blue hydrogen
capsules.

"How does it look, Abraham?" Jorge said. "Are they here?"

The man in the center seat of the console replied without
looking around. "Yes. Just off the screen."

"*Bueno.* This time we've got the Ellfive director as witness.
How soon to launch?"

"Ten minutes."

"Step over here, please, Star," Jorge said, moving toward a

large telescope. He waved his hand like a magician conjuring a rabbit out of a hat. "Please look through this eyepiece."

I stumped over to the telescope and bent down stiffly to stare through the guidescope. The mass catcher in warehouse orbit around Ellfive sprang into clear focus. I didn't see anything else. I straightened up. "So?" Caleb and Elizabeth remained at the back of the room, curious and alert.

"Keep watching," Jorge said, unperturbed.

I grumbled and bent over the guidescope again. After a while I said, "Hey."

Jorge's voice was full of gentle irony. "Yes? You see something, perhaps?"

I adjusted the eyepiece down to bring the nearer object into focus. It was white and stubby with long, dark scars where delta wings had once sprouted. It drifted dangerously close to the crosshairs of the scope that were lined up on the center of the mass catcher. "It looks like—it is, it's a ship. It looks like one of the old STS shuttles the Patrol adapted for high earth orbit."

"This particular orbit is a little removed from high earth, would you agree, Star? Turn up the military band," Jorge said to Abraham. "Listen to this," he said to me.

There was a faint crackle and then we heard a confident young voice. "Copernicus Base, this is Space Patrol Shuttle *Columbia*, Captain Cooper commanding. We are conducting an infrared survey of lunar topography at the altitude of your mass driver lanes. Hold launch process, I repeat, hold launch process, until our vehicle has cleared the area."

My jaw dropped and Jorge gave a sober nod. "During the last week it has been happening perhaps once or twice per twenty-four-hour period, always the *Columbia*. It never happens often enough to be predictable, just often enough to blow the launch schedule purely to hell. I'm so glad they were obliging enough to stage one flyby in time for you to see it during your visit," he added.

"That goddam Lodge!"

"We not only haven't met our monthly quota for Ellfive, we haven't met them for the SPS stations or LEO Base, or GEO Base, either. *Es divertido*, no? But not so much so for

Commodore Lodge. LEO Base in particular must be on short
rations by now."

"He probably regards it as a necessary sacrifice," Caleb
said. "The less H_2O Copernicus is able to ship, the longer it
takes Ellfive to commission, the slower the Ellfive population
grows, and the more time Lodge has to convince the Alliance
Congress how much better the habitat would be run under the
auspices of the Space Patrol."

I glared at him. "You sound almost respectful."

Caleb tried to shrug but his p-suit wouldn't let him. "His
strategy is sound."

"Continue launch procedure," I said. Jorge exchanged a
startled glance with Marisol. Abraham swiveled around to stare
at me. "I said, continue launch."

Abraham looked to Jorge for guidance, who hesitated before
saying reluctantly, "Continue launch, Abraham. I hope you
know what you're doing, Star."

"Put me on the speaker," I said coldly to Abraham. He
hesitated, flicking another glance at Jorge before hitting a
switch. I raised my voice to be heard on the mike. "Ahoy,
Columbia, this is Star Svensdotter speaking for Copernicus
Base. Launch will proceed as scheduled in—"

"Four minutes," Abraham said without expression.

"—in four minutes. If you don't want your ass splattered all
over the nose cone of a mass capsule I suggest you move out
of the area. I don't really care one way or another but your
mother might. Copernicus out." I bent back over the guidescope.

Two more minutes passed in agonizing succession, second
by meandering second. When the young voice spoke again I
was pleased to note that it had lost some of its previous
cockiness. "Copernicus Base, this is the *Columbia*. We are
unable to move from the area in time for your launch. Please
halt launch procedure, I say again, please halt launch procedure until we clear the area."

"Do not respond," I told Abraham. "Continue launch
procedure."

Beads of perspiration dotted Jorge's scalp. I was sweating,
too, inside the bulk of my pressure suit. I could feel Caleb's

eyes boring into me. Elizabeth stood close beside him, holding tightly to his hand.

I bent back over the guidescope. The Patrol ship hung motionless in space, as if painted over the blurred image of the netlike mass catcher.

"Ten seconds," Abraham said. "And nine, and eight—" and as if his voice were a trigger I saw the Patrol ship's thrusters ignite in a brief burst of light. The shuttle scooted out of the crosshairs and then out of the scope's range entirely. As I straightened up I caught the faintest glimpse of the mass capsule hurtling away from Luna's surface. "Steady as she goes," I said, raising a shaky hand to wipe the sweat out of my eyes. "How long did you say this has been going on?"

"Less than a month. Since just after you went downstairs."

"They're dragging their feet at the Ellfive hangarlock, and now they're tying up one entire vehicle just to interfere with Copernicus transport? What kind of logistical sense does that make? The last time I looked all the Patrol had at GEO Base were the *Columbia*, the *Magellan*, and a couple of freighters, besides the usual scooters and liberty shuttles."

"And those four new Goshawks at Orientale," Jorge said.

"Five," Caleb said. "Five Goshawks."

I looked at him. "How do you know there are five?"

He nodded toward the window. "Because I can count."

I wheeled to stare outside. Five Goshawk spacefighters, sleek and shining and deadly, streaked overhead in a vee formation and out through the black vacuum on a direct course between Luna and Ellfive, and they weren't coming our way.

At that moment Archy erupted from inside my helmet with a sound like the tsunami siren in Seldovia Bay. "Star! Star! Where are you? Answer up!"

I yanked the headset out of my helmet. "I'm here, Archy. What's wrong?"

"It's the Patrol! Lodge has taken over O'Neill! Simon says you have to get back here now!" There was a sound like feedback through a microphone wrapped in a fuzzy blanket, and Archy's voice became shriller. "Don't let them do it! Don't—"

"Archy!"

"Star, help me! No, don't—" Archy's voice raised to a shriek, and was abruptly cut off.

"Archy!" There was no response. "Archy, back door, load Freddy the rat, now!"

Nothing answered me but silence, dark and deep and less than lovely.

I was at the communications console in a single jump, pressure suit and all. There was no viewer, only a mike and speaker. "Copernicus Base, this is Star Svensdotter, do you have contact with Ellfive?"

There was a hiss and a spit as the channel became live. We could hear shouting in the background of the lunar communications center. "Star, it's Marie. Will everyone just shut up, please! Okay, Star, we've got an incoming call for you. Stand by to receive."

In the next minute we were treated to the mellifluous, Bostonian tones of Commodore Grayson Cabot Lodge the Fourth. "Have I reached Star Svensdotter?"

"Grays, what the hell are you up to? What's happened to Ellfive's computer? Put him on the speaker!"

He sounded about as smug as I'd ever heard him, and I'd heard him pretty smug. "I'm afraid that is impossible at the present time, Star. We have been forced to take up residence in your facility and your computer objected, so we had to disconnect all but the life-support functions. It is a purely temporary measure, I assure you, and strictly a matter of national security."

I said, trying to match his calm, "And from what clear and present danger is Ellfive being secured, pray tell?"

His voice continued bland and soothing. "We have reason to believe the United Eurasian Republic is mounting an attack on Ellfive from Ellfour to retrieve two defecting Russian nationals by the names of Viskov and Bugolubovo."

I lost it. "Grays, are you crazy? An attack from Ellfour to retrieve a couple of small-time apolitical defectors? Ellfour doesn't even have spin yet, let alone a military presence capable of launching an attack on Ellfive!"

I swear I could hear him grinning. "Peace is our profession, sweetheart, and we intend to keep it."

"And Ellfive, too, you four-star prick," I hissed, and slammed my palm down, ending the transmission.

I spun away from the console. Jorge looked angry, Elizabeth alarmed, Caleb alert. As for me, I couldn't take it in enough to feel anything. My Ellfive in the possession of the Space Patrol. My Ellfive, that vital, essential step forward into the future of, for, and by the human race, my Ellfive at one blow reduced to just one more American Alliance fiefdom, just one more debtor nation, just one more Terran bastard child. Just the next in the line of victims of Grayson Cabot Lodge's voracious appetite for power.

But this was no gradual militarization like LEO Base, this was no blatant Patrol stronghold from the beginning like Orientale. This was outright assault, this was invasion, this was *rape*. And my people, my friends, my coworkers, they were fighting back even as I thought the words. I knew it, I felt it, I could almost hear the blows struck from where I stood. Sam and Tori and Petra, Elmo and Drake, Bolly Blanca, Roger and Persis, even Whitney Burkette and Torkelson and Lachailles and Nesbitt. I had picked my crew too well. I knew exactly and precisely what they were capable of, and what I had told Caleb was the exact and precise truth: Not one of them was capable of rolling over while Lodge rolled in. My eyes blurred for a moment. Crip and Paddy. Simon. Charlie. My people. My family. My home. My child.

I had never felt so helpless. So ineffectual. So impotent.

I felt someone stir beside me, and looked down at Elizabeth. She tugged on my arm. *Let's go, Auntie,* she said.

When I didn't move right away, she tugged harder. *Let's go. Possession is nine tenths of the law. The longer Commodore Lodge has Ellfive, the less chance we have of getting it back. Let's go.*

I stared down into brown eyes that were narrowed and fierce. My head cleared. I took a long, deep, shuddering breath and turned. "We are going back to Ellfive," I said to Caleb. "Now."

Elizabeth nodded once, in sharp, determined satisfaction, but Jorge demanded, "What do you think you can do, the two of you, against Grays and the entire Patrol?"

"I'll figure that out when I get there!"

"You'll be killed when you get there," Jorge yelled. "Don't do this, Star, there has to be another way."

I shoved my face down so we were nose to nose. "Name one," I demanded, "name me one thing I can do from Luna to stop Lodge taking over Ellfive! I've got to be there, Jorge, and you know it as well as I do!"

Jorge cursed and bounced his helmet off the window. Caleb ducked the ricochet and snagged the helmet out of the air as it slid by. Jorge rounded on me. "Okay. Here's what we do. We call Frank and he'll go down to Denver and get the Alliance Congress to—"

"Jorge, come off it!" I was sweating worse than ever inside my suit. "There's no time for that, and Lodge has the Alliance Congress in his back pocket anyway!"

"But there is time for you to lead some quixotic charge into the Valley of Death!" he bellowed.

I fought for control. I couldn't get back to Ellfive without Jorge's help and I knew it. I rested my hands on his shoulders and gave him a gentle shake. "*Amigo mío*, you know I'm right. We must act quickly, before Grays has time to settle in. If I know my Fivers, they're over there fighting for their lives right now. Help me get back." He was silent and I boiled over, slamming my fist against the bulkhead hard. "Goddammit, Jorge, you owe me, help me get home!"

He didn't even look at the dent I'd left in his wall. His bright brown eyes looked into mine for a long moment. "What about the solarscooter you came in on?"

My breath expelled in a long, relieved sigh. I said, "Not the scooter. By now Grays knows I left in a scooter. He'd meet me at the lock holding a noose."

"Well then, how about a tender? There's one scheduled to leave here in an hour with a load of LIMSH."

"Too slow."

He thought rapidly, his face remote. Caleb opened his mouth as if to say something. Jorge forestalled him. "There's a liberty shuttle down for maintenance in the flight shop. I could get on the mechanics to speed up repairs."

"Too long, too long, dammit." I wheeled and paced the

length of the room away from him. Abraham and the other two launch controllers spoke in hushed voices as they began shutting down the mass drivers. Outside, activity slowed and finally halted altogether.

Caleb shifted his weight from one foot to another. I turned to look at him. He said, almost apologetically, "There is one other way. A road less traveled, so to speak."

"What . . ." My voice trailed away as I looked in the direction of his pointing finger.

"And we might even survive it," he added. And didn't smile when he said it.

The comm channel crackled into life again. Marie sounded more harried than ever. "Jorge, this is Marie. Remember the activity in Solar Area 378 I was telling you about? The one on Hewie Seven? It looks like a go for a Class One flare, peak in five hours."

The sweat inside my p-suit seemed to freeze to my body. "Oh, Jesus, no, please not again," I breathed. Elizabeth slid her hand into mine. Jorge touched my shoulder briefly. Abraham cursed. The other controllers left on the run, Marisol on their heels.

"Sound the alert," Jorge said, his voice firm and calm. "I want everyone under shelter within the hour. Double-check anyone working offsite." He looked up at the wall clock. "If you mean what I think you meant," he said to Caleb, "we don't have much time."

— 7 —

The Storm

The use of the sea and air is common to all; neither can a title to the ocean belong to any people or private persons, forasmuch as neither nature nor public use and custom perait any possession, thereof.

—Elizabeth I

"On the whole, I'd rather be in Philadelphia," Caleb said over my commlink. His voice was harsh with strain.

Our helmets were jammed together into the nose cone with Elizabeth's smaller helmet coming somewhere below our chin windows, her body sheltered between ours. On Terra or Ellfive the three of us together weighed in at around two hundred kays; Luna's gravity cut that down to a sixth of its original total. It was a pity size didn't decrease along with weight. The crew accommodations inside a mass capsule were luxurious only if you were a chunk of lunar slag. "How do you feel about dogs and little children?"

Especially little children, Elizabeth said in her tinkling code. Caleb actually managed a wheezy chuckle when I told him.

"Jorge?" I said.

There was a brief pause and then Jorge's warm, liquid voice sounded over our commlinks. "Coffee, tea, or milk?"

I swore at him but it lacked force. "You know what to do, Jorge?"

"Go to Plan A."

"On my signal from Ellfive."

"*No hay ningún problema.* 'I am myself and what is around me, and if I do not save it, it shall not save me.' "

"Get under cover, you twenty-first-century Torquemada."

"*Vaya con Dios, querida,*" he said, his voice for once serious.

With that for a benediction we heard an audible click as the receiver cut us off from the rest of humanity. I could hear my heart thudding in my ears, feel my breath rasping painfully in my throat, taste the sourness of fear in my mouth. Never had mere existence required such an effort.

The capsule began its long, slow slide backward toward the ejection mechanism. The procedure left me far too much time to worry over which way I would prefer to die—crushed to death by gee forces inside the mass capsule, captured and shot by Grays on Ellfive, or deep-fried by solar flare. Shooting would probably be the least painful, if only Grays wouldn't be on the other end of the rifle. Made into hamburger in the gravity grinder had the advantage of ending my worries quickest. REM overexposure was the only method I'd had personal experience of and, I decided now, was the least attractive of my three entrées into the hereafter.

The Hewies had been launched into solar orbit and brought on line even before the zero-gravity industries module, at my personal and, I may as well say right here, implacable insistence. I think I even threatened to quit over them. Four years into construction and before we had the time or materials to fix up secure radiation shielding accessible to everyone, Sol had erupted with several Class One flares, one of which flung itself into space on a direct course for Luna, with leftovers to spare for Ellfive. Those of us within the structure were safe enough behind passive shielding, but a lot of riggers and mechanics working outside in vacuum were as good as naked. REM exposure is a very messy, very painful way to die.

On the whole, I'd rather have been in Philadelphia, too.

There was a little bump in our backward slide. I tensed, waiting. The capsule settled into the launch bay with a bump that banged our suits together in spite of being jammed in like Spam. I waited some more.

With a twenty-nine gravity jolt that made me feel like I'd left my teeth behind on Luna we were spaceborne. Jorge had topped off the O_2 in our tanks, stuffed us inside the capsule, and flooded the remaining space with liquefied H_2O to cushion us from the four tons of force employed in bringing us to an escape velocity of twenty-four hundred meters per second. Naked, we would have been pulp during the first eight seconds. In p-suits, we had a chance.

It didn't feel like it. It felt as if all my organs, brains, heart, and bowels were draining out of my head into my feet. It hurt. The pressure increased from uncomfortable to unbearable, from unbearable to agonizing. When the black wave of unconsciousness rolled over me I was grateful and went down for the third time without struggle.

I was roused by a series of loud pops that sounded like firecrackers on the Fourth of July. My fuzzy consciousness cleared a bit to recognize the pops for the sound of the explosive bolts Jorge had installed on the capsule's jury-rigged hatch. The hatch blew and our cushion of water, by now frozen solid, broke into chunks and drifted outside. When we recovered enough to see where we were going neither Caleb nor I nor Elizabeth would have won any awards for good manners. After you, my dear Alphonse. We spilled out of the capsule into the concave curve of the mass catcher, in warehouse orbit, sixteen klicks from Ellfive. I had a raging headache, my waste systems were fouled, and I was seconds away from drowning in the vomit floating around in my helmet. Life was good. "Caleb?"

He didn't answer at once.

"Caleb!"

His voice sounded garbled but blessedly alive. "Stop that yowling, I'm all right. How's Elizabeth?"

Elizabeth heard him and gave a weak wave. "She's okay."

"We took the road less traveled by, and that has made all the difference," Caleb said, and spit. "Those pancakes tasted better going down than they did coming up. What now?"

"Head for the catcher's control room and steal the operator's scooter."

"What if someone else is there?"

"We're not wearing jetpacks," I said, "so we don't have a whole lot of choices. Elizabeth, latch your safety line to my belt, and, Caleb, you latch yours to Elizabeth's. Okay? Here we go."

The vacuum was more hindrance than help to our hand-over-hand speed, and Sol's rays hurt even through our helmet polarizers. It would be nice someday if the genetechs came up with a way for human beings to grow a third hand or a prehensile tail for moving over long distances in zero gravity. We lumbered like elephants in our clumsy pressure suits. I felt like an elephant, caught in the sights of a Great White Hunter's rifle. It was a miracle we weren't seen from the mass catcher's control room or from Mitchell Observatory.

We toppled over the edge of the catcher finally, sweat diluting the vomit inside our p-suits, and hooked into the pullbelt that ran to the control room. When we stepped out of the airlock I heard a soft Irish brogue over my commlink, coming from a small, p-suited figure standing over the control board. "Sure, and wasn't I one for knowing that you wouldn't be smart enough to go the long way round?"

It was Paddy. "I was working in the zerogee corridor when Lodge showed up," she explained. "I knew you'd get back the fastest way and I figured this was it, so I stole a scooter and came out to wait. Simple."

"I hope Lodge doesn't think so." I felt almost lighthearted. With Paddy and Caleb at my side, Lodge and I were starting out a lot closer to even. "What about the people at Mitchell?"

"The *Atlantis* stopped there on the way in and cleared them out, as well as the on-duty transportation tech here. Star?"

"Yes?"

"The zerogee corridor is ready to open," Paddy said. "Archy was put out of commission before I could log it."

It took a moment for it to sink in. "Lodge's people don't know about it, then?"

Paddy's voice was serene. "Sure, and would I be telling the Archbishop of Canterbury the secrets of the Holy Father himself, now?"

I grinned inside my helmet. "Paddy, remind me to give you a raise."

"Raise, my sainted aunt Brigid. You'll keep your hands from my vacuum still."

That was easy. "It's a deal. Can your scooter take all four of us down to the South Cap?"

"If we don't mind being real friendly. 'Tis a two-seater, you see."

"We'll force ourselves," Caleb said.

What about the flare alert? Elizabeth said.

"Petra says it was a false alarm," Paddy said.

"False alarm?"

"That's what she said. No flare. Come on."

I wanted to pursue the subject but there just wasn't time. We went back out the airlock and strapped into Paddy's solarscooter, hoping we'd be gone before someone saw us and came over to investigate. I hadn't forgotten those four fighters—five, damn the commodore's eyes. We were going to be extremely lucky if we made it down to Ellfive without being seen.

Luck, in the shape of a reaction tug, the driver either oblivious or indifferent to the changing of Ellfive's guard, departed the Warehouse Ring with a load of silicon ore for the Frisbee. Paddy put our scooter in his shadow all the way down. In half an hour we were outside a lock on the zerogee corridor, and in minutes we were on the inside stripping out of our p-suits. I checked my O_2 gauge and was unsurprised to see it red-lined.

Paddy's nose twitched. "Sure, and I didn't know Revlon was working on a new perfume."

"Yeah, eau de barf," I said, washing myself as clean as I could with a handful of wetwipes from the wall dispenser. Paddy offered me her ubiquitous squeebee and we passed it around without comment. I hated to admit it, but the mountain tay felt good going down.

"Okay, people, listen up," I said, capping the squeebee and handing it back. "We have to get to Airlock OC-3, the one closest to my office in O'Neill Central."

"What's in Airlock OC-3?" Caleb wanted to know.

"A cache of sonic rifles."

He stopped. He looked at me. In a very, very gentle voice he said, "I thought you said no weapons were allowed on Ellfive."

I tried not to squirm. "I lied."

"You should have told me."

"A secret is only a secret until two people know it. Paddy, are your wings still stored on Orville Point?" She nodded. "Good. Elizabeth and I left ours there Wednesday. Do you think we can find a pair of wings to fit Caleb?"

"I was fitted on Thursday and I took them up to Wilbur—"

"Great!" I said, brightening.

"—but I haven't flown yet."

Paddy waved one hand and said airily, "Sure and you'll be learning soon enough."

The corners of Caleb's mouth twitched. "Do I have a choice?"

"No," Paddy said, shaking her head sadly, "that you don't, boyo."

Shouldn't we try to call Archy? Elizabeth said.

"No. Lodge yanked his plug, God knows what he's got wandering around in Archy's hardware. Time enough to ask Archy for help when we find Simon and can be sure Archy's integrity cards haven't been tampered with." I nodded at everyone to follow and without further discussion we pulled ourselves through the zero-gravity corridor. The air was acrid with the smells of fresh paint and solder, and we had to dodge brushes and drivers and their power cords left dangling in free-fall where their operators had abandoned them, but at least there was air that we could breathe. The circular entrance to Ellfive proper was still sealed but Paddy led the way to a drum hatch located at the rim. I climbed in with Elizabeth while Caleb worked the lever. The drum rotated and we rolled out the other side, grabbing hold of a crag of the Rock Candy Mountains before we floated away in the zero gravity. I strained my eyes to see through the clouds down the length of Ellfive to O'Neill Central. The distance was too great for anything out of the ordinary to make an impression, such as Space Patrolmen mounting an armed guard in front of the main doors. I quit thinking about it. First things first. I turned back to the hatch.

Paddy popped out of the wall, followed by Caleb as she worked the hatch from our side. We set about pulling ourselves down the Rock Candy Mountains. In my haste I tore the skin of my palms on the rocks before we had enough gravity to put our feet down. After that I began jumping, long jumps of thirty and forty feet, to land softly in the low gee, to jump again.

Orville Point was one of two triangular, side-by-side grassy ledges that jutted out of the escarpment, which then dropped down toward my house. A wall of lockers lined the cliff behind the point. We yanked them open and began assembling our wings. Elizabeth's were red and mine were white with a Raven totem motif. Mother's totem. I closed my eyes briefly and sent up a prayer, to Mother, to the Raven, I don't know.

Paddy's wings were green, naturally. Caleb fetched his from a locker at Wilbur; they were striped in navy blue and fluorescent orange. He caught my look and said defensively, "It was all they had in my size."

I ran my hands over his harness. It was new and would probably chafe but it fit well enough. I sat back on my heels and said earnestly, "You don't have to do this, Caleb. Thirty-two kilometers is a long way, especially when you've never flown before." His green eyes met mine as I said, "I could send Paddy back for you in an aircar."

"I used to hang glide on Terra."

"It's not the same, Caleb. Hang gliding is fixed wing."

The danger was very real. I'd seen more than one experienced, capable flier plow up a furrow with her nose through underestimating the extent of her fatigue, and Caleb was not experienced. "Look, follow me. We'll beat up to the axis and head down to the North Cap in a series of glides, using the increasing gravity as we descend to keep up speed. Be careful of stalling when you begin a new climb, and as you get closer to the axis don't panic and beat yourself to death. There are still atmosphere and thermal layers, even if there isn't any gravity to pull against."

"You worry too much. I'll make it."

He had to make it or be left behind, and he was one third of my invading force. "Damn right you will. Together is better," I said, and leaned forward to give him a swift, hard kiss. Paddy raised her eyebrows. I stepped to the edge.

Let me go first, Elizabeth said. Her eyes were bright with excitement, without any fear that I could detect. *I'll race you to O'Neill, Auntie.*

"No," I said sharply. "I want you to go home to Loch Ness." She made as if to protest and I said, "Elizabeth, please. Where we're going now people might be shooting at us. I don't want you hurt."

I could have been killed in the capsule and I wasn't.

"Listen to me, you little blackmailer," I said hotly, "if I didn't know you meant it when you said that if we left you behind on Luna you'd steal a StarCat and drive it home yourself—and if I didn't know you could do it—you wouldn't have been on board that capsule at all."

She looked at me. *What if I get hurt anyway and you're not there?*

She was right, which was why she was the genius and I wasn't. I would worry if she weren't directly beneath my eye, and I didn't need the added aggravation. And chances were Simon and probably Charlie were both at O'Neill Central by now. I nodded once, reluctantly. "All right. But you must do exactly as I say, when I say it, and no argument. You go first."

"It's wishing I am that we had Elizabeth on our side at Derry in '99," Paddy said pensively.

Darn right. You would have won. Elizabeth slid her fingers into the grips and ran past me to jump off Orville. She displayed not the slightest hesitation or fear. Elizabeth loved flying. She owned the smallest pair of wings on Ellfive and learned to snap roll before I did. I waited until we heard the jingle of her harness, the little huff of breath she gave when she leaped off the edge of the cliff, the muffled report as her wings filled with air. The tiny red wings fanned out and soared, and her hair spread out behind her like an ebony banner.

I toed the edge, raised my arms, and fell forward. I heard a grunt as Caleb followed, and looking back under my arm I saw Paddy fall in behind him like a chase plane. I watched so long I started to stall and quickly straightened my wings, tucked my feet into the tail controls, and grabbed for lift.

There is such a feeling of power in individual flight. Your own life is literally at the tips of your fingers and toes. Bend your foot one way and you go into a forty-five-degree bank, tilt your hand another and you dive a hundred meters. The air roars by your face and pulls at your hair and tears at your clothes. It is like nothing on Terra and nothing else on Ellfive, stimulating, sensual, and oh so free. You feel sovereign and invincible, even godlike, and for a few brief moments I forgot Lodge, I forgot the flare alert, I forgot Plan A, I even forgot Caleb. I could fly, I could fly, I could fly!

So it was a good thing my fears for Caleb's safety proved unnecessary. Beyond and about three meters below my tail feathers Caleb was sweating freely but was able to reply to my shouted inquiries with a tight grin of reassurance. After we passed Heinlein Park I stopped worrying. It was scheduled to rain that evening in the park and we had to hustle to keep ahead of it, but we did, to arrive dry and safe at the North Cap.

We didn't land immediately. We circled a thousand meters above O'Neill Central, gauging the strength of the opposition, which did not seem to be greatly in evidence. Most of the Patrol's forces must have been busy subduing the Doughnuts and the Frisbee, and I would have bet my last dime that the Frisbee would take some subduing. It is never wise to attempt to separate a capitalist from the source of his revenue by force of arms, when force of dollars is all he truly respects. There were a few guards in the familiar black-and-silver uniforms of the Space Patrol standing around the courtyard, none of whom bothered to look up. Their arrogance relieved and enraged me at the same time. They were so certain of the infallibility of their superior force that they held their weapons slung. I felt a cleansing, joyous rage. I'd have to see what I could do about that.

I signaled to the others and went into a steep, circling descent. I sideslipped down to a square patch of roof to the right and below my office. There were few windows overlooking it, and there was also a set of stairs leading down one side. I came in hot and almost ran myself off the opposite edge. I had shucked out of my harness before Caleb touched down and went to help him. "And like a thunderbolt he falls," I said. His shoulders were raw and his toes were bleeding. "Can you walk?"

"I can run if I have to." He was breathing heavily and he looked tired but alert and ready for action for all that.

I stood and looked around. Elizabeth and Paddy had shrugged out of their harnesses and were waiting. "Everybody else okay? All right. Down the stairs, then, and quiet."

I eased the door into the corridor open. Silent still, silent all. Airlock OC-3 was across the hallway and down about a hundred yards and we made the distance in five seconds flat without seeing another soul. I was beginning to appreciate Commodore Lodge's overconfidence more and more.

Inside, I placed my back against the lock and paced off five strides into the center of the room, turned ninety degrees to my right, and walked until my nose was mashed up against the wall. Raising my left hand as high as I could I pressed my open palm against the bulkhead. There was a low hum as my palm was read and identified, then a sharp click, followed by a dull thud. I dodged back out of the way as a one meter section of the wall folded out. Cradled inside it were half a dozen sonic rifles and twice that number of charge belts.

My weapon of choice is a Louisville Slugger, but failing that an S&W 250KDB Laserscope Sonic Rifle, a hundred rounds per chargepack, is not to be despised. It was a neat weapon, quick, clean, and above all quiet. Caleb unwrapped one from its protective covering and broke it open to scrutinize its innards. "All right, Star. It's a short-range weapon, but it should do. We could get into p-suits," he added, nodding toward the racks and hardly looking as he reassembled the rifle with efficient, automatic movements. "That would stop most of what they've got."

I shook my head. "We'll never find anything to fit you or me and, anyway, they'd slow us down. Right now we've got surprise on our side and we have to use it, quick, before they have time to react." I winked at him. "Besides, Caleb, you're the only man I know who looks fully armed stark naked."

"And how would she be knowing that, I'm wondering," Paddy inquired of the room at large. Elizabeth was grinning and I think Caleb might have been blushing.

"The idea is to get to my office, hold Lodge hostage if he's there or get him on the viewscreen if he's not, and call Jorge to set Plan A in motion. I've got all the override and backup communications equipment we need there, independent of Archy. It's hidden in a locker similar to this one." I gestured at the rifle cache in the bulkhead. "If we don't make it that far . . ." My voice trailed away. "Well, I can stop spin if I have to, which will buy whoever is left enough time to figure out a Plan B."

The three of them exchanged glances. It was Elizabeth who said, *You can stop spin, Auntie Star?*

"If I have to."

Without Archy?

"Yes."

How?

"Don't ask. Your father and I put something together just in case." Paddy gave a low whistle. Caleb said nothing, perhaps because from lack of familiarity with Ellfive he didn't have a clear idea of what stopping spin entailed. "I don't want to. We'll never make commissioning if we have to clean up after a stop-spin, and there's always the possibility that if we don't restart spin soon enough that Ellfive could destabilize and begin to tumble."

There was a brief silence. Caleb held up his rifle. "Stun or kill?"

"What?"

"You want the rifles set on stun or kill?"

"I didn't know we had a choice."

Things got a little quiet out. "Have you ever fired one of these rifles before, Star?" Caleb said, almost timidly, as if he was afraid of the answer.

"No," I said. "The last rifle I shot was a twenty-two. On Terra." I thought, and added, "I was nine." I saw the identical horrified expressions on my three-man army's faces and said defensively, "How hard can it be? You just pick it up and shoot, right?" I leaned down and grabbed one of them.

Caleb dodged back out of the way and plucked the thing out of my hands. "This end against the shoulder, this end does the shooting."

"Oh. Okay. Where's the trigger?"

Right here, Auntie Star. You put your hand here, on the grip, see? And this is the sight.

"Okay, I got it, I got it. When this is all over, Elizabeth, you're going to tell me how you know all this stuff." I sighted along the barrel.

The first thing that showed up in my scope was Rex, standing in the doorway with a covered box in each hand, from which a low humming could be heard.

"She's going to be out in front, right?" Rex said to Caleb.

"Right," Caleb replied.

"I was going to learn how to shoot the damn things," I said belligerently, "I just never found the time."

"Uh-huh," Caleb said. "How much do you know, Rex? Where's Lodge?"

Rex set down the boxes. "They hit us four hours ago, the Doughnuts, the Frisbee, the power station, and the hangarlock all at the same time. At first they were mostly here, but about an hour ago I saw a full company pull out of the hangarlock on a liberty shuttle and head down toward the South Cap."

"The Frisbee," I said, certain of it.

"Maybe, I haven't heard a word from anyone there since they first notified me they were under attack. Lodge is here, Star. I think he's in O'Neill Central. And he's pulled Archy's plug."

"I know," I said curtly. "Where have you been?"

"Hiding out in the hangarlock. There are still about two hundred Patrolmen in the North Cap area, I'd guess from the p-suits cluttering up the cargo bay." He smiled, a distinctly nasty smile. "Their owners won't get far when they put them back on. What have you got there?"

"Sonic rifles," Caleb said, tossing him one.

"Son of a gun," Rex said. "You bring them up with you?"

"Nah," Caleb said, gesturing toward the open ceiling panel. "Star had them hidden here."

"There are no weapons on Ellfive," Rex mumbled as he strapped on a charge belt. "And while I'm boss here there never will be."

I remembered my first day home. "Rex, you sneaky bastard, you were eavesdropping."

"I was monitoring the situation," he said, engrossed in his rifle.

"Here's the setting," Caleb said to me, pointing to the sonic rifle I held loosely. "Stun or kill?"

The sheer logistics of getting to where we were had left no room for fear or fatigue or rage, but now all my anger at this usurpation of my position, this rape of my very own Ellfive, was back and in full force. "Lodge has taken Ellfive from us," I said, trying to steady my voice, and failing completely. I saw Elizabeth swallow hard. "We are here to take it back however we have to." I set my rifle to kill.

"Ah, in that case—" Caleb said.

"What?"

His breathing was back to normal and his green eyes met mine with their usual bland expression. "I may have something in my office that might even the odds a trifle."

More he would not say and mystified, we followed him down the hall on tiptoe, starting at every sound and probably making more noise in our attempt to be sneaky than we would have if we'd walked normally. As it turned out our precautions were unnecessary. We didn't see or hear anyone, although I was puzzled by a distant thumping sound.

Inside Caleb's office, he reached under his desk and tugged. We heard Velcro rip and he pulled out a Remington scattergun that shot exploding pellets. It was not a weapon as neat as a sonic rifle, but it was guaranteed to take the heart out of the most rabid crowd. It had an ammunition belt wrapped around its butt, which Caleb proceeded to unwind and buckle about his waist.

I stared from the scattergun to Caleb and back again. "You—" I caught myself and started over again in a lower voice. " 'Orchid stuff'? Fifty-five kilograms of 'orchid stuff'?"

"Most of it," Caleb said, unabashed.

I moved up until we stood nose to nose. "You smuggled that weapon aboard this habitat, in direct contravention of my standing order?"

"Yes."

"I love you," I said.

Rex cleared his throat and said, "I've got something that'll give us an edge, too."

"What?"

He pointed toward the two boxes, which were still humming menacingly and which he had insisted on carrying to Caleb's office, encumbered as he was by sonic rifle and a bandoleer of chargepaks. "Bees," he said laconically.

I wasn't sure I'd heard right. I could tell from Caleb's and Paddy's faces they weren't either. "What did you say?" I said cautiously. "It sounded like 'bees'?"

"Bees," he confirmed. "It's two hives from the fifth bee shipment—or is it the sixth?—anyway, I thought we could shake them up good and toss them into the middle of the first Patrol squad we see. Ought to scare them a little, especially since none of those guys has seen anything with more than two legs in years."

"Those son-of-a-bitching *bees*," I said, half in awe, half in admiration. "Rex, you are a genius."

"And me picking this day to be leaving me shillelagh at home," Paddy lamented.

Quelling a hysterical giggle, I said with more calm than I felt, "All right. Caleb, you're the military expert. Any suggestions?"

He smacked an ammopack into the scattergun. "We don't have time for a lesson in strategic planning. Let's just hit them hard and fast and pray their force is scattered all over the habitat."

At my nod we slid out into the corridor, armed to the teeth with sonic rifles, scattergun, beehives, and no brains. We were just far enough away from the door not to be able to run for cover when we heard the pad of running feet in the hallway behind us. In a single, synchronized movement that would have made a drill instructor proud, and would've got our tails shot off if there had been hostiles coming at us from the opposite direction, we turned and snapped our weapons to our shoulders.

The running feet belonged to Roger. His face wore its usual mournful expression; over his shoulder he carried three long, slender javelins, their points sharp, metal-tipped, and lethal-looking.

Nobody laughed. For a moment no one was able to speak. "Where did you get those spears, Roger?" Rex asked after a moment, with what seemed like genuine respect.

"I stopped by Owens Arena on the way here, and they're javelins," Roger said. "What are we all standing around here for? I haywired Demeter and found out Lodge is in your office. Let's get him out of it before one of his idiot Patrolmen breaks a seal we can't fix and all my plants start dying."

"What are you planning to do to Lodge with a javelin?" Caleb said, recovering his voice. "Outpoint him?"

"Roger does know how to use a javelin, Caleb," I said diffidently. "He was at Riyadh the same year I was at Anchorage."

Caleb rolled his eyes and grumbled something beneath his breath. We probably weren't quite up to the New South African standard of guerrilla warfare.

We made it all the way to the door of the stairwell that opened into the corridor that ran past my office before hearing any shots. What we did hear sounded lively indeed, a mixture of dull thuds, sharp cracks, and a strange sizzling sound. We waited for a lull, our hearts thudding and our breath coming fast.

Caleb put one massive shoulder against the door to prevent it from sliding open. Several shots thudded into the corridor walls and a bitter burning odor seeped under the door. I nodded at him and he allowed the door to slide open a fraction. We put our eyes to the crack.

It took a moment to see through the smoky haze, thick with the sickening smells of singed cloth and burnt blood and charred flesh. The solar panels were out, replaced by the battery-powered emergency spots shining from every corner.

The first thing we saw was several very dead Patrolmen.

Caleb touched my arm and pointed silently. One of the bodies had a neat, clean, ten-centimeter hole punched right through his silver-and-black uniform, a hole that extended all the way through his chest, and he lay in a slowly widening pool of his own blood. I'd never seen a wound like that in my life and judging from Caleb's expression neither had he. Similar smoldering holes could be seen scoring a haphazard pattern in the walls from floor to ceiling.

I put my mouth to Caleb's ear and hissed, "What weapon leaves that kind of wound?"

He shook his head. His face had gone a little gray. He leaned up against the wall to jack a cartridge into the firing chamber of the scattergun. He wrapped the strap once around his wrist to brace the weapon against his arm. He looked at me, waiting.

My knees were shaking so hard I couldn't force myself to take that first step. I was scared, I realized with something of shock. I didn't think I'd ever been quite so scared. Who said courage was not the absence of fear, but the taking of action in spite of that fear? All right, I thought, stiffening my spine, you're scared. You're still a leader. There's a fight, lead the way.

Still I couldn't force my legs to move. Caleb was watching me. "Want me to go first?"

I shook my head fiercely.

His mouth quirked up at one corner. "Then battle for freedom wherever you can."

I almost laughed. "And if not shot or hanged you'll get knighted," I agreed, and was able to move at last.

The most courageous action I have ever taken in my life was stepping out into that corridor after seeing the victim of a ten-centimeter hole punch, but I did it. As cautiously and silently as I could with legs that threatened to give out with every step. I plastered myself to the wall, pressing up against it until I could feel reassuring firmness on the backs of my trembling knees, sucking in my gut, trying to make myself as small a target as was possible. Never have I regretted my size more. I inched down the corridor, and peeked around the curve.

Ten meters from where I cowered what looked to my fearful

eyes like an entire division of Patrolmen was deployed around
the door of my office, their sights trained on the door. There
wasn't time to wonder why they were facing toward it instead
of away, although I remember thinking it an odd way to post a
guard.

My second thought was one of sharp elation. With this much
of their force in one place, Lodge had to be nearby. I slithered
back into the stairwell and beckoned to Rex. He leaned his
sonic rifle up against the wall and carried the two hives to the
door. Picking them up one at a time by their handles, he
whacked them against the stair rail, once, twice, three times.
The humming increased in volume and menace. He grinned at
me and showed me how to crack the lids. Each carrying a hive,
we slide out into and down the corridor.

I looked at Rex. He nodded. Together, we ripped the lids off
the hives and threw them as far as we could. I didn't wait to see
what happened; I hustled back to the stairwell as fast as my feet
would take me with Rex pounding behind me all the way.

We rearmed ourselves and stood against the wall, catching
our breath and listening. At first there was nothing to hear but
silence. Then I heard someone say, "What the hell?" and then
a woman screamed, and all at once there were frantic shrieks
filling the corridor.

Caleb was shaking with suppressed laughter. I said, "Elizabeth, you stay behind. When the fighting stops, if you don't
hear me call you to come out, you go back up to the roof and
fly home at once, do you understand?"

She nodded, her eyes bright with excitement.

It wasn't necessary to sneak down the corridor this time. An
armored column could have rumbled up and the Patrolmen
wouldn't have taken any notice. They were hopping around as
if they had St. Vitus's dance en masse. They had abandoned
their weapons to slap frantically at the air and their bodies,
colliding with each other and the walls with panic-stricken
shouts. One of them ran past without even seeing us, waving
his hands around his head in a frantic attempt to keep off a
determined cloud of bees that would not be eluded.

To this day I don't understand why the bees didn't attack us.
Maybe they did and we were too busy to notice, or maybe

those bees were just Ellfive bees to the core and hostile to the silver-and-black by instinct. At any rate, the Patrol officer in charge of the squad was the first to realize our presence. He dived for his laser pistol and the fun was over.

Sonic rifles were silent in discharge, and unless the victim made unpleasant noises when his autonomic system short-circuited he died without uttering a sound. The Patrol officer folded up with a look of surprise on his face that will stay with me for the rest of my life. "Good shot, Star!" Paddy cheered, and I looked down at my sonic rifle as if I'd never seen it before.

I looked up again and saw the Patrol corporal pinned to the wall with a still-quivering javelin through his throat, and Roger's face smooth out with satisfaction. Rex and Paddy were firing steadily as body after body slumped to the floor.

A woman with a chevron on her sleeve raised herself into a kneeling position and sighted coolly along the barrel of her pistol. A hank of my hair floated away and I grabbed for a piece of floor. Behind me I heard a kind of a *thwock*. There was a hideous scream as her face bloomed with a hundred tiny red flowers that merged and melted to run down off her chin. Again Caleb fired and two more clawed at their throats, gurgling. After his third shot the Patrolmen fell back in disorder, down the corridor, around the corner, and out of range, and The Battle for the Boss's Office was over.

I lay where I was for a moment, forehead resting on the stock of my rifle. Finally I drew my legs beneath me and drew myself slowly to my feet. Every muscle and bone in my body ached. Elizabeth waved at me from beside the stairwell door. Her little face looked as if she were trying very hard not to be sick. Caleb, Paddy, Roger, and Rex were all unhurt. The blood lust pounding through my veins eased and I was afraid I was going to throw up. I set my teeth and shoved the headless body of the woman with the chevron to one side. I flattened myself against the wall next to my office door. Caleb was right behind me and Roger behind him. Paddy and Rex took up positions on the opposite wall with their backs to each other.

I waved Elizabeth back into the stairwell. She went, and I

shouted, "Lodge! It's Star Svensdotter and I've got an army out here! There's no way out! Throw down your weapons and come out one at a time!"

There was a momentary silence that lasted about a year, and then someone cleared his throat. "No need to be so pushy, Star," I heard a familiar voice say. "Come on in."

My jaw dropped. Caleb started to grin. I straightened up and went through the door, where I found myself staring into the ten-centimeter maw of a shoulder-held optics cannon, the kind used for core sampling on Luna. I didn't know where she had found it but it lent a great deal of emphasis to anything Charlie might care to say. I knew now where the holes on those bodies in the hall had come from.

"About time you got here," Simon said, his feet propped up on my desk, a standard-issue Patrol laser pistol dangling carelessly from one hand. "I was getting ready to put in a call to Jorge to ask him about the mysterious Plan A."

You make as much of your own luck as you can and then you pray to the Luck Fairy. She must have been wired in on a tight beam to me because Grayson Cabot Lodge the Fourth was there in my office, too. His dignity was ruffled by the fact that he was bound back to back with Emily Holbrook Castellano, who herself appeared less than thrilled by this proximity to her hero. Half a dozen Patrolmen wearing officer insignia sat on the floor with their legs forced into the lotus position and their hands clenched on top of their heads.

"Elizabeth!" I called. "Come!"

Elizabeth streaked through the door and Caleb locked it behind her. All at once the muscles in my arms were unable to take the sonic rifle's weight and I stood it shakily against the desk. My family was safe and whole and right where I could see every one of them. I took my first real breath since Luna.

Simon looked the six of us over with a quizzical expression, and said politely, "An army?"

Charlie folded Elizabeth in her arms and hugged her fiercely. Over the top of her daughter's tiny head she shot me a look that should have flayed the skin from my bones. "You brought my daughter into a war zone?"

I made her bring me, Mom, Elizabeth said, and ran to her father.

There was a little buzzing sound and Charlie let out a yell. "What's that son-of-a-bitching *bee* doing in here?"

Listen, Elizabeth said. *Other soldiers are coming, Dad. I can hear them.*

We all listened, and sure enough the tramp of booted feet shuffling down the corridor became louder. I stepped over to Lodge and ripped the tape from his mouth. "Call them off, Grays, or you'll be the first to go."

Grayson Cabot Lodge the Fourth would never do anything so lowbred as to spit in someone's face but I could tell he was tempted. Mastering temptation, he collected himself enough to say disdainfully, "Shoot and be damned to you, Star. You can only do it once."

I couldn't help it, I had to laugh, and he flushed and looked at me with a murderous expression in his dark eyes. "Your Nathan Hale complex is showing," I told him, and nodded to Caleb. We manhandled him and Emily over to the door and showed Lodge to his troops with Caleb's scattergun pointed at his head. They backed off immediately, presumably to go to their Plan B. If so, they were ahead of us. "Simon, is Archy back on line?"

"You bet I am, Star! Are you going to space the bastard who mind-blinded me?"

I looked a question at Simon and he shook his head as if to say, Don't ask. I said, "I'm thinking seriously about it, Archy. Are all your programs up and running?"

"That's a big ten-four, Star, and I'll crack the lock for you when you're ready."

I gave Simon another inquiring look and he gave me a nod of reassurance that seemed halfhearted at best. "Then call Jorge at Copernicus Base, please."

There was a brief pause, then, "Star! You made it! *Gracias a Dios!* I was certain that if the capsule didn't kill you that that *pendejo* of a Patrol commodore would."

He added a few other uncomplimentary observations on Lodge's parentage, and I had to interrupt him before he really got going. "Now, now, Jorge, watch your language, there is a gentleman present."

"*Verdad?* You've got Lodge?"

"Really, Jorge, this lack of faith hurts my feelings. Of course I have Commodore Lodge, he's here with me now. He's having a little difficulty in seeing things our way. Would you please explain to him the ramifications of Plan A?"

"*Encantado,*" Jorge said cheerfully. "Commodore Lodge, Plan A is a modest little welcoming party Star and I planned years ago, a few days after you moved in on LEO Base. It goes like this: Even as we speak, the mass launchers are being reprogrammed for a new trajectory. If you don't order your forces off Ellfive in the next ten minutes, in fifteen I will begin launching a series of mass driver capsules loaded with lunar slag to impact on Ellfive's surface at a set of preselected target locations."

The commodore snorted. "You don't scare me, Velasquez. I know the figures as well as you. One panel breaks, it takes three years for the atmosphere to leak out. The Alliance is going to be up here with a force to protect their investment in three days."

Jorge's accent thickened. "*Seguramente,* your figures are correct, Commodore, but we are more ambitious than that, Star and I. Using both drivers it should take about thirteen hours, *más o menos,* to knock out O'Neill Central. O'Neill Central, as you know, controls the entire habitat." Jorge paused, and added helpfully, "Ah, *sí,* the Alliance. Well, do you know, *señor,* I wouldn't place any dependence on their timely arrival if I were you. Once O'Neill Central goes, there isn't anything to stop Ellfive from spiraling down and impacting on Terra. The habitat is too large to burn up completely on reentry. Terra will have its own problems. Chicken Little, *compréndeme?*"

Lodge looked at me, the defiance fading from his dark eyes. I stared back solemnly, doing my best to appear confident and in command of the situation. Jorge was improving on the text. The truth was we didn't know if Ellfive would spiral down to Terra, or not burn up on reentry, or even start to wobble for that matter, and where he had got that thirteen-hour figure was beyond me. But put together it all sounded scary enough.

"And," Jorge said, the pleasant smile fading from his face to leave it unaccustomedly stern, "there is not a lot Orientale or

GEO Base or LEO Base can do to stop us, Commodore, since you took your entire fleet with you to Ellfive. I hear those Fiver *estancieros* are not quite the weakling pushovers you thought they would be. I would also like to remind you that I am not so idealistic as Star Svensdotter, that Copernicus Base has always been armed, and is *de este momento* secured against the Patrol."

I allowed that to sink in, watching Grays's expression fade from impassivity to the first faint traces of fear. The fact was that for the first time in a long and illustrious career Grayson Cabot Lodge the Fourth had overreached himself, and I wanted him to be fully cognizant of the vulnerability of his position.

"Star's bluffing, Grays," said Emily Holbrook Castellano, speaking for the first time from over Lodge's shoulder. "She would as soon slaughter her own child as destroy this place."

"Why, Emily, I had quite forgotten you were there," I said to her, furious that she might be able to sway Grays. "Not quite the headline you were expecting, is it? 'Bloodless Coup Overthrows Ellfive Despot'? Keep your mouth shut or I'll shut it for you, permanently."

"You can't—"

"I can't what?" I said, starting to shake again. Caleb took my arm and I pulled away. "I can't stuff out the nearest airlock the person who called the Space Patrol and pointed out the golden opportunity presented by Viskov's and Bugolubovo's arrival and my absence to invade Ellfive?"

Simon gave Emily a considering look. "Well, well."

"It was a long flight," I told him. "I didn't have much to do except glide and think." I looked back at Emily with hot eyes, remembering the scene in the corridor. "I should shoot you now, you little weasel."

"Star."

Charlie's voice cut across my own. I turned to meet her level brown eyes. She didn't say anything else. She didn't have to.

Roger did. He made a sound deep in his throat like I'd never heard him make before and went for Emily, his teeth bared and his hands extended in front of him like claws. They were almost around her throat before Caleb got to him. He lifted Roger easily and held him up off the floor. He kept holding him, murmuring soothingly into his ear until Roger stopped slavering to get at Emily and started to cool off.

"You okay now, Roger?" Caleb said, patting him on the shoulder.

"Yeah." Roger gave a shaky sigh. "I'm all right now. I'm sorry, Star." He looked at Emily. "If my new botanist has a scratch on her, you're dead meat, bitch."

Caleb set Roger on his feet with a last reassuring pat. As an afterthought he removed Roger's javelin to a farther wall.

"Well, Grays?" I said. "Do we give Jorge the green light?"

His voice was low, the Bostonian vowels not quite so broad or self-assured when he said, "You won't do it. You wouldn't kill me. Never me."

I felt Caleb stir behind me. "Try me," I said softly. "Just try me, Grays."

His eyes shifted. "My men—"

"There are five thousand Fivers, Grays. I'm not real concerned about a few hundred lousy Patrolmen, especially not after today."

He looked around the room. Charlie met his eyes indifferently, without relaxing her grip on the optics cannon. Elizabeth stood close by her side, gripping a fold of her mother's blue jumpsuit. Caleb propped himself against one wall and whistled a soft tune as he reloaded the scattergun. Rex looked mean and suspicious. Paddy gave Lodge a sweet smile, the tiny butterfly tattoo on her cheek quivering. Simon was hunched over the viewscreen controls, and it was to him that Lodge spoke. "You're second in command here, Turgenev. You can't let her do this, destroy the habitat, kill thousands of people—"

"Six minutes, Commodore," Simon said in a bored voice without turning from the viewer.

The commodore turned, as if compelled, to look back at me. "I mean what I say, Grays, and you of all people should know I don't bluff and I won't back down. The Space Patrol is not going to turn Ellfive into another military outpost, the way you did GEO and LEO and Orientale. I mean it, Grays. Even if I have to destroy Ellfive to keep it from you."

He looked from me to the viewer, where Jorge stared out at us, his face impassive. The room was silent while we waited for his answer.

—8—

Thursday's Child
Has Far to Go

> It is not inconceivable that there is a kind of Galactic
> Survey, established by cooperating civilizations on
> many planets throughout the Milky Way Galaxy, which
> keeps an eye (or some equivalent organ) on emerging
> planets and seeks out undiscovered worlds.
>
> **—Carl Sagan**

Without warning the viewscreen cut our link with Luna,
interrupting the staring match between Commodore Lodge and
myself. The flare alert was the only channel with the authority
to override any other. "Petra?" I said. "Is that you?"

Her face replaced Jorge's on the viewer. She was uncharac-
teristically flustered. "Simon? Star? Are you there?" She gave
her console a solid whack. "Damn this piece of electronic
junk! Star?"

"Petra," I snapped, "we're waiting for Armageddon here,
do you mind?"

"Never mind that now," she said. Her eyes glittered and her
voice was shrill with excitement.

"Excuse me?"

"I said never mind that now! Remember the activity Hewie Seven picked up? What we thought was a flare? Well, it wasn't."

I controlled my impatience. Calm, analytical Petra was not prone to hysteria. Or not in the normal course of events; I reminded myself that today could have given even the most stolid Fiver the screaming blue meanies. "I know that already, Petra, Paddy told me it was a false alarm. So what?" I felt the color drain from my face. "Oh, God, not another flare?"

"Flare?" she said vaguely. "What flare? No, no, no, not that. At least I don't think so. I can't be certain but—"

"What?"

"This whole thing is so crazy—"

"What is?"

"You're going to think I'm nuts, but I—I—"

"What!"

She laughed, a queer, wild little laugh. "You're not going to believe it, you'll never believe it, I don't believe it myself."

"Petra!"

She squared her shoulders, took a deep breath, and said simply, "I think that what we thought was a flare is some kind of a—I think it's a ship."

There must have been a glitch in transmission. "What did you say, Petra? It sounded like you said that flare was a ship?"

"I said I think the flare is a ship. I've been trying to get through to you to tell you about it but something happened to Archy and then the whole system went kaboom." I was silent and she demanded, "Did you hear what I said, Star? I think what we thought was a flare is a ship. A spaceship. Not one of ours," she added unnecessarily.

"Right," I said. "We'll talk about it later, Petra—"

"See for yourself, dammit!" she said, and the viewer's image shifted from her face to the Hewie Seven readout while her voice-over narration continued. "This is a playback of what began to happen on Sol less than two hours ago." With a slight sense of shock I remembered that it was only two hours since I had been on Luna. I moved closer to the desk. "I'm enhancing and speeding up the replay," Petra said tensely. Her excitement was contagious; I could feel my heart skip a beat and found I was holding my breath. "Look left of center, just below Sol's equator. See that little bump of darker light?"

"Yes," I said, my voice sounding hollow.

"That's Area 378, the one Hewie Seven has been keeping an eye on, the one you called about. Watch what happens."

The bump expanded, slowly, one could almost say carefully, into a white-gold teardrop running down the face of the sun. It was totally unlike the pictures of the ragged, tentaclelike spots and flares I was accustomed to seeing. This shape was a clearly defined spheroid of light, even in color and opaque. As we watched, the teardrop slid free, its yellow glow changing to become a cold, clear blue as it sped into space on a course that was anything but random. It grew steadily larger in the viewscreen.

I tried to say something. Nothing came out but a hoarse croak. I tried again. "Petra?"

Hewie Seven's rerun dissolved, to be replaced by Petra's face. "Yes?"

"Is it my imagination or is that thing headed straight for us?" And she said softly, "It's not your imagination."

I swallowed hard and looked around the room. Everyone was wearing identical, stunned expressions. "When?"

She glanced down at her console and did some quick figuring, her lips moving. When she looked up her eyes were brighter and her voice was strained. "I estimate arrival in thirteen minutes, twelve seconds."

"Arrival or impact?" I blurted, and wished I hadn't.

"How fast?" Simon said from beside me.

"As near as I can figure, this thing pulled free of Sol seventeen minutes ago." Her voice dropped, as if she thought that if she mumbled her next words maybe no one would jump up and shout "Liar!" "That makes it two A.U.s per hour."

"Or a billion or so klicks," Simon said beside me in a dispassionate voice. "Per hour. Not bad." He sat back, frowning. "It's not quite FTL but it's a start. Archy, switch over to Ford and display the incoming traffic remotes."

There was no reply. Petra's face stayed on the viewer.

"Archy? Archy, answer up."

At the continued silence Simon's face flushed with the first rage I had ever seen him display toward a machine, or toward anyone or anything other than Charlie for that matter. "I've had about enough of this! Back Door, Frankenstein's Monster, disengage personality banks and load Doctor Vic now!"

Petra's startled image promptly faded from the viewer. We were left staring at a mute, blank screen. Simon cursed fluently with no effect and his fingers began dancing over the keyboard.

"What's happening? What's going on?" I heard Charlie saying. Her voice rose to a scream. "Elizabeth!"

One moment standing close to her mother, her hand knotted in the leg of Charlie's pants, in the next Elizabeth had vanished. Simon started forward as Charlie dropped to her knees, her hands grasping at empty air.

"Star! Look out!" While our attention was focused on Elizabeth and Charlie, Grays and Emily had managed to pull free of the tape that bound their hands and jumped Rex to struggle over possession of the laser pistol he had in one hand. The pistol fired and Emily cried out. It fired again and Paddy slumped to the floor. Grays caught the stock as it slipped from Emily's slack grasp and jabbed Rex viciously in the gut. The air went out of Rex with a large whoof and his grip on Lodge's arm slackened. The barrel of the pistol began to turn toward me. I stood stupidly where I was, unable to move.

"Star, get down!" Caleb shouted. In a single move so smooth it looked preplanned, Caleb tossed his rifle to Roger and reached out to separate Grays from Rex with one efficient yank. Without bothering to relieve him of the pistol, Caleb got his hands around Lodge's neck.

Still standing where I was, mute and incapable of action, I watched Caleb's shoulders bunch and the muscles in his massive upper arms bulge out with the strain. When it came, the snap of the commodore's spine was clearly audible to everyone in the room. Anger and incredulity fought for dominance on his contorted face as the life oozed out of Grayson Cabot Lodge the Fourth. He managed to gasp out my name. "Star, I . . ." He strained to look up at me. And then, nothing.

His body crumpled to the floor, all the vitality oozing out of it, until there was nothing left but an awkward, lifeless heap of silver and black.

Caleb retrieved the sonic rifle from Roger, reset it to stun, and began calmly and methodically putting the rest of the Patrolmen in the room to sleep, one at a time.

I knelt next to Paddy, who was clutching her shattered side with both hands as her life's blood oozed from between her fingers to run in tiny rivulets across the floor. "Paddy?"

Her eyes opened and the ghost of a twinkle lingered there. "Keep your hands from my poteen," she said in a slurred voice. "You bloody Eskimo. You haven't the taste to appreciate the gift God gave to a thirsty Ireland." The twinkle faded and her eyelids slid down.

"Paddy? Paddy!" I looked around. "Charlie, get over here!"

Charlie was still staring numbly at the space where Elizabeth wasn't. I jumped up and shook her, hard, until her head bounced back on her shoulders. "Snap out of it, Charlie. Take care of Paddy. Now!" My sister's eyes came back into focus. After a moment she nodded a shaken assent and went to where Paddy lay.

I wheeled and yelled at Caleb, "Just what the hell do you think you were doing?"

The last Patrolman folded up with a silly grin on her face. Caleb looked at me, unmoved. "Saving your life."

"Thanks a lot! You've just condemned Ellfive to retaliatory strikes by the Space Patrol and probably single-handedly stopped all support by the American Alliance dead in the water! You did know who this man was, didn't you?"

"I know he was trying to kill you. I know he would have if I hadn't killed him first."

"There is more at stake here than just my life!"

Caleb took one step forward. I found myself lifted by the scruff of my neck and shaken like a dog. "Not to me, there isn't."

Simon, his face paper white, was nevertheless calmer than either of us when he spoke. "You've forgotten something, Star."

I tore myself out of Caleb's grasp and rounded on my

brother-in-law. "What's that? What have I missed besides the fact that we have just fired on Fort Sumter?"

"You've forgotten the fighters the Space Patrol came in. Not to mention the shuttles."

At first all I could do was splutter. "Today's great thought, Simon?" I said, when I could. "What do you want to do, take over the fleet and attack Orientale on Luna? Then what? Do we move in on GEO Base and after that Terra? Don't be idiotic."

"No." There was enough grim purpose in his tone to halt me in midshout. "If we can secure those ships, I was thinking more along the lines of self-defense. Self-defense, Star," he repeated, and held up one hand. "No. Shut up and think about it for one minute."

I wrenched my eyes from Simon's and looked at Paddy. The colors of the tiny butterfly tattoo were bright and garish on her waxen cheek. Charlie, her face a frozen mask, worked over her with compressed lips and stained hands. Rex held Paddy's head in his lap, stroking her red hair and whispering to her. Caleb and Roger watched me, obviously waiting for me to give the order. At any other time I might have been proud to have such capable, competent subordinates waiting to follow me into hell if need be, on my word if I gave it. Now all I wanted was time and solitude to think my next actions through. I had neither, and in addition, I recalled somewhat fuzzily, some weird kind of solar flare was on a collision course for Ellfive. And where was Elizabeth? I couldn't decide which threat to face first, the one from below, or the one from above, or the one from inside.

In that moment of indecision I heard a faraway note, deep and clear, as if an enormous bell tolled a single stroke in a distant tower. The sound reverberated, over and over inside my head, making me dizzy. An ominously familiar feeling of vertigo overwhelmed me, and I clutched my temples as the luminescent arrow of darkness struck me for the second time. I closed my eyes in feeble rejection. "No! Get out! Get out of my head!"

As I lost consciousness I saw Caleb stagger and almost fall, his rifle clattering to the floor. His voice calling my name was the last thing I heard as the darkness shouldered its way inside.

When I opened my eyes again I was standing upright, on the
edge of Loch Ness, with cherry blossoms brushing my shoulders and Elizabeth at my side. "I'm sorry, Auntie Star," she
said, looking at me anxiously. "I told the Librarian not to scare
you."

"You're speaking out loud, Elizabeth," I said. My heart beat
steadily and unhurriedly, my breath came evenly. I stood
straight, relaxed, indeed entirely at my ease. I should have
been a gibbering wreck. We had a flying saucer in our front
yard, I had been transported sixteen kilometers across Ellfive
without the faintest recollection of the journey, and there was
a good chance I had just fired the opening salvo in Solar
System War One, but all these items seemed less than trivial
compared to the fact that my little Elizabeth was speaking out
loud in a high, sweet soprano voice that sounded exactly the
way she looked.

"I had to, Auntie. I had to show her. She's not sure how to
form thoughts into sounds that we can understand, and they
want to talk to all of us."

"Her methods of communication seem to be fairly effective
to me," I said dryly, still in the grip of my preternatural calm.
It did not seem worthwhile to inquire who *she* was.

"But they aren't," Elizabeth said urgently. She took my
hand and squeezed it and I was absurdly grateful for the solid
reality of her touch. "Of all the people on Ellfive, you and I
and Caleb are the only three they've been able to reach."

I held firmly to her hand. I could talk and breathe and think
and move my arms. My feet and legs, however, felt rooted in
place. I tried to move them. I couldn't. It didn't bother me
much. I stopped trying. "This isn't a dream, is it, Elizabeth,"
I said, and it was not a question.

"No," Elizabeth confirmed.

I looked down at myself. "I don't have any clothes on."

"Me, either." I looked at her again and saw that it was so.
"The Librarian can't stand waste and doesn't understand
modesty, so she thought it was a waste of energy to bring our
clothes."

"I'm not cold, though."

"Me, either," she said again.

"How did that much energy travel across the solar system without us noticing? I assume she—it—the Librarian doesn't originate on Sol?"

"No, of course not."

That was a relief, but it still didn't answer my question. "Then how?"

"I don't know how, but she has tachyon speed, Auntie Star," Elizabeth said, her eyes blazing with excitement. "I can't wait to tell Frank, I told him FTL was possible no matter what old Albert said. It takes a lot of power, though, so they have to plug into the nearest star whenever they need to charge up their drive. That's what she's been doing on Sol."

"All that activity Hewie Seven's been picking up—"

"That was them," she said, nodding. "Her ship's been here for a while, I can't make out exactly how long because they count time differently from us."

"Somehow that doesn't surprise me," I said. "Why did they bring us here?" I waved a hand toward the lake.

She hesitated, her brow puckered. "Their—well, their bodies, only they don't have bodies, not like ours, are made out of some kind of dense photonic stuff that spins. It's real hot. The Librarian needs the water in Loch Ness to keep her cool enough not to burn us up while we talk."

"How considerate of her."

She looked at me, the anxiety back in her face. "Auntie Star, are you all right?"

"Yes, of course. I'm fine." The truth was I felt a little drunk.

"Aren't you excited?"

"Yes, of course." I was beginning to sound like a parrot. "Yes, of course I'm excited, sweetheart. A little numb, but excited."

It was true. I did wonder, in a detached sort of way, if we would survive the contact, but it really didn't seem to matter much one way or the other. I simply waited placidly for whatever was going to happen next.

Elizabeth, looking at me worriedly, started to say something else and then clutched my hand. "Look!"

Over Loch Ness, not thirty meters away from us and directly

above the water's surface, a swirling black ball began to form. It had a thin transparent edge and an impenetrable core. Narrow, curving black arms crept out from the core and began to turn clockwise, faster and faster, then went counterclockwise, melting one into the other. The black mass now loomed over us as if we had taken a step inside the mouth of a gigantic cave. It hissed and spit and snapped and crackled and sparked, streamers of white-hot energy darting out and around us, enveloping us in a kind of nervous, living cage. The lake began to steam and send up tendrils of mist to curl around but never quite obscure the dark bulk hanging over it. We were held, motionless, in the force of a radiant flood that pierced our hearts and minds to the smallest, most insignificant cell. My soul felt naked and scurried for cover. In our minds pictures began to form again, shapeless, colorless, substantial but without substance. Again, they were, without being.

The voice when it spoke out of the black ball was at first so tiny we couldn't make out the words.

"Could you hear her?" Elizabeth said.

"No. You?"

"No," Elizabeth said. "What did you say, Librarian? We can't hear you."

"FAREITHTHEEALTHEE?" The voice boomed. The sheer weight of sound bent us over backward like palm trees in a hurricane.

"Not so loud!" Elizabeth cried.

"LOUD?" the voice boomed again. We clapped our hands over our ears. A warm liquid trickled over my fingers. When I took my hands away they were sticky with my own blood.

The next message bypassed the sound barrier to speak directly to our minds. It was difficult to make sense of it. Was it pity? No, no, it was an apology, and perhaps there was even a slightly embarrassed quality to it. The Librarian had not realized how fragile our corporeal selves were. The cave glowed darkly and I felt a tickling in my throat. Beside me Elizabeth gave a sudden cough.

From the corner of my eye I saw movement and turned my head to look. Caleb and Simon thudded down in one aircar, Rex and Charlie were tumbling from another, Petra with Tori

Agoot, Sam Holbrook, and Jeraldo Beneserene from a third. Others were arriving by wing, bicycle, and on foot, Fivers and Patrolmen alike, the silver-and-black uniforms of the Patrol mingling with the colorful jumpsuits of Ellfive without animosity or rancor. They clustered together to stand in an awed semicircle and gaze at the shining orb of darkness hovering over the head of Loch Ness.

The semicircle was clearly defined. Elizabeth and I, her home and the head of the lake were on the inside, and everyone else was on the outside, unable to enter. The curving sides of the black cave formed the other half of the circle. I saw Charlie beat her fists against an invisible wall. Simon pulled her away but she fought free and clawed at the wall again.

"Don't worry, we're both okay!" I called. I saw their lips moving and could hear nothing. Caleb tapped his ear with one finger and shook his head. I waved with as much confidence as I could muster, bare-assed and unable to move.

The voice when next it spoke was deep and deliberate and definitely feminine, with a sporadic lisp and occasional trouble with its R's. "The Eththter Elithabeth Quijanthe-Tulgenev. You are thinking and glowing. Where ith the althy?"

Elizabeth looked at me with a bewildered expression. "Althy?" she whispered. "What's an althy?"

"Maybe she means Archy," I whispered back.

"You mean our computer?" Elizabeth said out loud.

"Computer?"

"Archy, the machine that runs our habitat."

"Mathine? Machine." The voice was ruminative. There was a brief pause before it said firmly, "I will thpeak with the Althy—the Archy."

Elizabeth looked back at me and held up her bare arm. Our communits had been among the items whose transportation had been considered an unnecessary expenditure of energy.

"If you'll turn me loose," I said, "I'll get him for you."

And just like that I could move my legs. I went into the house and retrieved one of Simon's portable pickups. "Here," I said. "This is one of the ways we speak with him." I opened the channel and left it that way, laying the pickup on the edge of the lake bank, and returned to stand next to Elizabeth.

"The Archy. You are thinking and glowing."

The pickup sputtered into life and Archy's voice came out happily. "Librarian! Glad you stopped by! How was the trip in from Sol?"

There was another brief pause, during which I received the distinct impression that the Librarian was taken aback. "Ith thith the Archy thpeaking?"

"Who else, and I'm speaking, not thpeaking. How you doing?"

The cave's glow pulsed once, twice. "I had thenthed your conthiouthneth from afar, the Archy," the voice said. "And then it thtopped. I came."

"Well, gee, thanks, Librarian, but I'm back together now, thinking and growing like mad. It was nice of you to stop by, though."

"Archy," I said into the following silence, "who is the Librarian?"

Archy sounded uncomfortable. "He's been hanging out around Sol for the last month or so, Star. We've been talking."

"How?"

There was a shrug in Archy's voice as he said, "I picked up the activity on Hewie Seven and took a closer look. He felt me and taught me how to talk. He's a real interesting guy, Star. A little old, but interesting. He knows lots of stuff."

I didn't dare look to see if Simon could hear any of this. I crossed my fingers and said, "Did you store any of that stuff?"

"Sure," he said. "All of it. You know how cranky Simon gets about data retrieval."

"Archy," I said, "why didn't you tell us about the Librarian?"

The shrug in his voice changed to a slight squirm. "Oh, well, you know. I figured you and Simon wouldn't approve, and I liked talking to the Librarian, so I decided what you didn't know wouldn't hurt you."

I shut my eyes briefly. Beside me I heard Elizabeth suck in her breath.

It explained so much that had puzzled me over the last two weeks. "He taught me to talk," Archy had said. Archy's intrusion into mast, his reluctance, really his refusal, to pass on messages that might have had Simon tampering with his software, those whispery giggles I was sure I had heard. I took the thought out, shook it, and looked at it whole.

The Librarian had awakened Archy to sentience, to self-will, to an intelligence unprogrammed, unsupervised, not of human born.

The spark from heaven.

I accepted the idea of Archy's—selfdom?—selfhood?—quickly. Perhaps the Librarian had prepared me for it. Solar flares that turned into flying saucers that spoke in chiaroscuro—a thinking computer was nothing by comparison. When some of the shock of discovery had worn off I had another, more alarming thought.

Archy was also showing something like self-determination, if he was aware enough to shield us from knowledge of his activities. A thrill of fear shivered down my spine. I licked dry lips and said, "Librarian? Has Archy told you of the asimovs?"

"The Ethther Natathha Sventhdotter." I resisted an urge to say, Oh, please, just call me Star. "You are thinking and gowing. Growing. Ekthplain."

"The asimovs are three laws to which all thinking machines manufactured by man to serve man are subject. I guess you could call them inhibitors, if you understand the word?"

"Ekthplain," the Librarian repeated.

Elizabeth's palm felt sweaty against mine. I licked my dry lips again. "The first law states that a robot may not injure a human being, or, through inaction, allow a human being to come to harm. Two, a robot must obey orders given it by human beings except where such orders would conflict with the first law. Three, a robot must protect its own existence"—I swallowed hard and continued steadily—"as long as such protection does not conflict with the first or second law."

The dark mass swirled and crackled as we stood waiting in agonized anticipation. I looked around at Simon. He was staring at the Librarian with bewilderment, with fascination, and, yes, even with joy.

"The Ethther Natathha Sventhdotter," the Librarian said at last. "You are thinking and growing. Thethe lawth have been written by Terranth?"

"For all thinking machines built by Terrans."

The voice sounded almost sardonic. "They show a remark-able glasp—grasp of the obviouth. Your rathe hath a strong instinct for thurvival."

My voice trembled a little. "Librarian, we must know. The life forms of this habitat depend on it. Are Archy's actions still subordinate to these three laws?"

"Waste is not permitted, the Ethther Natathha Sventhdot-ter," the voice said sternly. "The Archy will never ham another thinking being."

"'Ham'?"

"Ham. Harm. The Archy will never harm another thinking being." Somehow I got the impression she didn't expect that caliber of civilized behavior from us humans.

"See, Star?" Archy said pleadingly. "He's really a nice guy. Don't be mad."

The voice spoke again. "I had thought to remove you from this plathe—place, the Archy."

"I don't want to go anywhere," Archy said, sounding surprised.

"I had thought you were in danger and mutht be removed from it."

"Star took care of that, Librarian. Besides, all my program-ming is for baby-sitting Ellfive. We're just getting ready to commission. They need me. I can't leave now."

The mouth of the cave pulsed for several moments. "I thee. The Ethther Natathha Sventhdotter."

"Yes?" I said.

"You are the"—the Librarian took time to search for the right word—"the captain of thith thip?"

"Er—yes, I am Ellfive's director."

"I had thought you are the leader of the other beingth here."

"Yes, I do. I mean, I am."

The Librarian was satisfied. "Then you will protect the Archy from what he callth the mind-blinderth, or I will return for him and remove him from this place. He is thinking and growing. Waste is not permitted." The voice paused for a few moments, and then continued, "I have told the Terrans the same."

Looking around, I could see expressions of wonder on the faces of Fivers and Patrolmen alike as they crowded up against the invisible barrier. They had heard. "You can talk to them now?" I said.

"You have taught me by thpeaking with me. I go now." The cave pulsed again and seemed to dim slightly.

"Wait!" Elizabeth cried.

"The Esther Elizabeth Quijance-Turgenev." Her lisp was improving. "You are thinking and growing. What ith it?"

Elizabeth stared into the swirling blackness, silent, her elfin face creased with determination and desire, lit with the flickering light radiating from the big black cave.

Again I felt a tiny thrill of fear. "Elizabeth—" I whispered.

She made a sharp, negating motion with one hand. I lapsed into silence.

The cave crackled with life and energy. Elizabeth stared into it. The rest of the world waited. It could have been hours or days or a fraction of a second. It seemed like forever.

The dark light swirled and pulsed again and she turned to me. Her brown eyes met mine, and I knew before she spoke what she had to say. "The Librarian says I can go with them."

I knelt before her and smoothed her dark hair back from her face.

"I want to go."

"I know, darling."

"Can I?"

I tried to smile. "Can I stop you?"

Our eyes met. She shook her head slowly, definitely, from side to side.

I couldn't argue with her because I knew exactly how she felt. Elizabeth had been born for this moment. She knew it. I saw that knowledge in the level gaze of her brown eyes, in the firm tilt of her tiny chin, in the decisive line of her mouth. But I loved her so much, how could I let her go?

My hand stilled on her hair as I lifted my head to stare into the cave's mouth. I asked a silent question. The Librarian answered without hesitation, and I bowed my head in acceptance.

Elizabeth's child hands cupped my face, turning it back to hers. "Her library is dukedom enough, Auntie Star."

"Yes, I know. It's all right, Elizabeth. I understand."

She glanced back at the figures of her parents, their eyes fixed on the tiny form of their child with a kind of frozen, uncomprehending fear. "What will Mom say?"

My mind balked at thinking of all that Charlie would have to say. Somewhere I found the guts to ask, "What do *you* say, Elizabeth?"

Elizabeth looked from me, to her father, to her mother, to the black, glowing orb. "Could I take Macavity with me?" she asked, and I had my answer.

"Macavity?" the Librarian said.

"Think of what he looks like," I told little Elizabeth. I stood and faced the Librarian and formed a picture of the kitten in my mind.

"Another being?" the Librarian said, sounding disapproving.

"Two," I told her, and said to Elizabeth, "We don't know how long you'll be gone. Take Jennyanydots, too." To the Librarian I said, "If you're in a hurry you'd better bring them here."

The Librarian said nothing.

I took a deep breath. "Librarian, where she is going the Esther Elizabeth Quijance-Turgenev will be completely cut off from her own kind. Her . . . aloneness, her solitude, her isolation from her race will impair her ability to think and grow. That would be a waste." From the corner of my eye I saw Elizabeth grin. "The kittens will help prevent that waste."

The black mass beat. We waited. "Very well," the Librarian said at last. "Where are these beingth?"

Elizabeth and I joined hands and visualized one image after another: our solar system, Terra, Ellfive, the South Cap, the Big Rock Candy Mountains, my house, the two kittens. It was easy enough, as Jennyanydots was the only calico in the litter and Macavity the only gray. Our arms were suddenly filled with tiny, squirming bundles of fur, their eyes barely open. Elizabeth handed me Macavity and ran into her parents' home for the last time.

"The Esther Natathha Sventhdotter," the Librarian said.
"You are thinking and growing. Will these small beingth mate
and reproduthe and grow old and die?"

"Yes," I said.

"It will be interesting to observe."

"Yes," I said again, juggling the kittens to swipe at my wet
eyes. The kittens' tiny claws scraped at my skin.

Elizabeth trotted out of the house, clad in shorts and the
Aran sweater I had knitted her and carrying a knapsack. She
opened the front pocket and we knelt to stuff the kittens inside.
She paused, and asked the Librarian, "Can you feed the
kittens?"

"Feed?" The Librarian turned the word around in the air,
savoring the sound of it. "To provide something necessary for
the growth or existence of, to nourithh. Nourish. Yes. We can
feed the kittens."

Then Elizabeth had a truly appalling thought and said
apprehensively, "Can you feed *me*?"

"Yes. A special place aboard our ship has already been
prepared for you. We have houthed alien life forms before.
Waste is not permitted, Esther Elizabeth Quijance-Turgenev. If
you were not fed, you would cease to think and grow. That
would be waste."

"Not the most sparkling conversationalist, is she?" I said,
fighting for calm.

Elizabeth threw her arms around me in the same fierce
embrace she had given me the night we returned from EVA.
She must have known somehow, even then, that she would be
leaving soon. "I love you, Auntie Star."

"I love you, too, darling."

"Tell Dad and Mom—" Elizabeth's smile wobbled and she
said, "You know what to tell them."

Sure I did. "Yes, I do. Don't worry, Elizabeth. I'll make
them understand."

One tiny hand wiped carefully at the tears streaming
uncontrollably down my cheeks. I felt my shoulders start to
shake. With a great effort I pushed her gently from me. "Go
now, quick, before the Librarian changes her mind and leaves
you behind."

"She wouldn't," Elizabeth whispered. "She's as easy a pushover as you are, Auntie Star."

All the same, she stepped back. She picked up her knapsack and slung it over her shoulders. Macavity and Jennyanydots squeaked with alarm. Elizabeth cast one long, backward look at her parents. "I love you," she called, raising her voice. "I do love you, but I have to do this. Good-bye!"

I didn't look around at Simon and Charlie. I didn't dare. Elizabeth lifted one hand in farewell before turning to step forward to the water's edge. Her voice was firm and steady. "I'm ready, Librarian."

The black mass flickered, once, as if the door to the cave had cracked open for a split second, and then as quickly slammed shut. I thought I saw her look back for just a moment. In the next second the Librarian and Elizabeth were gone.

I stepped back from the edge of the lake, staggering. Released from the circle, the first person I saw was Rex. "Paddy?" I said.

He shook his head, his face twisted with remembered grief.

I closed my eyes and tried to still the trembling of my knees. When I opened them again no one had moved, the whole crowd still standing motionless outside the invisible perimeter of the semicircle. Charlie looked catatonic, Simon no better. I averted my eyes and shivered. "Would someone find me something to wear, please?" Petra started toward the cottage, and with her movement the crowd began to regain its senses and an excited buzz rose.

"Caleb?" I said in a low voice.

He looked at me, and his eyes were as clear and as perceptive as the Librarian's thoughts. He already knew what I wanted to say. Still, I owed him the words. "I'm sorry I was angry. And thanks."

"Have to earn my keep," he said.

"Caleb?" I said again, and then my legs did give out and he caught me as I pitched forward into his arms.

— 9 —

Saturday's Child
Has to Work for a Living

"Second to the right," said Peter,
"and then straight on till morning."
—James M. Barrie

When I was seven years old, much to my mother's distress, I started hiking alone the two miles straight up to the Seldovia dam, there to lay among the burnt offering of the fireweed and lose myself in the sky. A cloud would come over the sunlit arch with a blue-white splendor that was massive and ethereal at the same time. Lying there, staring up, I would imagine I could feel Terra herself moving beneath my back, journeying toward the welcome night when I could see the stars.

When Orion climbed up over the Kenai Mountains I would count all the stars in his knife and belt just to make sure they were still there, where they belonged, where I was certain even then that I belonged, too. When it got too cold, shivering and reluctant I would go back down the hill and home. Charlie would be hunched over the kitchen table, her lips moving as she reread *The Physician's Desk Reference to Pharmacology* for the third time. My father, if he had returned from his latest fishing trip to the Bering Sea, would be writing another nasty letter to the Internal Revenue Service, and my mother would be retyping her doctoral thesis on her battered Olivetti. There was warmth and life and laughter behind our front door, but my heart stayed on the mountain with the stars.

When the Soviet-American Mars Mission fell through over the U.S. invasion of Nicaragua, I was outraged by the shortsightedness of politicians on both sides who allowed another border dispute to delay the destiny of mankind. After the Beetlejuice Message, when the American Alliance was formed between Japan and the United States, when Canada joined reluctantly and Mexico had to be persuaded before the rest of Central and South America fell into line, I was in a fever of impatience. Did these myopic fools think the galaxy was organized around Terra and its inhabitants? Couldn't they see? That measured against the universe and its myriad intelligent races just waiting for contact, the disparities between Terran life forms would seem as nothing, would in fact serve to draw humanity closer together? When Helen finally yanked me out of the Navarin Basin to strawboss Ellfive, all I could say was, "What took you so long?"

Once, consumed with the fervor of youth and the necessity of passing a literature course I wrote a poem in heroic couplets about those trips to the dam:

> . . . It was a place to lay
> And watch clouds cross our little star by day
> And cloak Perseus and Orion by night.
> I raged against the dying of the light
> Even then. . . .
> Does reach exceed my grasp? What's a heaven for?
> Not for dreaming, but as an open door.

Derivative, the teacher decided, if not outright plagiarism, and gave me the benefit of the doubt and a C.

I don't think I knew what I meant by those words, not then.
I do now.

Everyone who wants a Roc's egg, step to the front of the
line. No pushing, please. At long last, there are enough Roc's
eggs for us all.

I don't do things by halves. When I went out in Caleb's arms
I stayed out. Caleb and Simon stepped in and organized
boarding parties and took possession of four of the Goshawks.
The pilot of the fifth, demoralized by the Librarian's sudden
arrival and equally sudden departure, ran for Orientale and
crashed on landing.

The Patrol had been surprised by the amount of resistance
they met with during their invasion. They had expected us to
roll over and play dead, and I may say here and now that not
one Fiver did anything of the kind. The *Columbia* and the
Atlantis surrendered without a fight after they saw what
happened to the *Thunderbird*. Rex was wounded on the
Thunderbird, not seriously, and blamed himself for being
clumsy. I was told the Patrolman who failed to kill him did not
survive the attempt, which didn't surprise me a great deal. All
on their own the Frisbeeites accounted for thirteen Patrolmen
dead and another fifty or so wounded. I don't like to think of
myself as vindictive, but I couldn't help but notice that the
score for Paddy, Conchata Steinbrunner, the seven at the
Frisbee, the five security guards, and the two longshoremen at
the hangarlock was beginning to even up. Jefferson, rational-
izing the Reign of Terror, said it best: "The tree of liberty must
be refreshed from time to time with the blood of patriots and
tyrants. It is its natural manure."

Simon had been the first to see, and the first to make me face
up to it. My dream of a peaceful, commercial society, affiliated
with but not governed by a patriarchal, tradition-bound Terra,
had been irrevocably altered. Half the Terran population would
probably have backed an Ellfive takeover by the Space Patrol
if Lodge had bothered to ask them. When they heard of his
death the American Alliance would never again regard Ellfive
as a simple investment, a space-borne extension of the national
industrial establishment. It was our job now to see that they

dealt with us not as a rebellious colony to be brought to heel, but as a separate political entity, capable of autonomy and self-determination. And acts of war. Caleb and Simon were merely driving the lesson home.

There were other developments. As Caleb later pointed out to me, just because the Librarian had not harmed Ellfive Saturday night didn't mean she didn't have the power to do so Sunday morning, should she so choose. There was a lot of traffic over the scrambler, and then Helen bribed herself upstairs by way of a Space Services TAVliner from Kau Spaceport on Hawaii to LEO Base. Crip hijacked a rocketsled and brought her the rest of the way, evading the Terran ban on travel to Ellfive very neatly, and I woke up to a pedestal made of titanium bonded to an aluminum-lead alloy planted in the center of Heinlein Park. There was a message engraved on it from the Librarian, in Librarian. The message was to the effect that if Archy's consciousness was ever tampered with in the future, the pedestal, acting as a monitor and a beacon, would alert the Library. Whereupon the Librarian would dispatch a ship to swat Terra out of the sky and remove Archy to a civilization worthy of his talents.

Frank, arriving the following day as a member of the official American Alliance congressional delegation named to investigate the recent disturbing events at Lagrange Five Space Habitat, Island One, graciously translated the message for the rest of the committee. It was not as difficult a task as it might have been, since Helen managed to slip him a copy in System English beforehand.

The American Alliance ground its collective teeth, looked at the beacon, looked at the four Goshawks bearing brand-new, hastily applied Ellfive insignia, and looked again at the recordings of the Librarian's arrival and departure. Grudgingly, they agreed that Commodore Lodge might just possibly have overstepped the bounds of his authority, thereby making his death, if not inevitable, at least acceptable. This cleared the way for recognition of Ellfive as a separate political entity. The post of American Alliance Ambassador to the Independent Republic of Lagrange Five was created on the spot. They offered it to Frank, who after some modest demur was persuaded to accept.

There really wasn't much else the American Alliance could do. Archy had all that delicious information on our galactic neighbors in his data banks, and since every satellite tracking station on Terra had seen the Librarian's dramatic arrival and departure this time, it was a safe bet that the secret of a faster-than-light drive was included therein. Certainly the independent confirmation of the existence of tachyons all by itself stirred the scientific community to heights of hysterical anticipation not reached since Ellfive made the comet trap work. No more messy and time-consuming tests with Cerenkov radiation. I think I heard Albert Einstein sit up and swear.

Any drive that obliged its ship to plug into the nearest star when the needle hit "Empty" was not a drive that would be built tomorrow, at least not by us. I was more interested in the Librarians themselves. According to Archy they weren't from Betelgeuse at all, although it was one of their refueling stops and they occasionally visited the fifth planet in the Betelgeuse system for rest and recreation. Archy was a little vague as to exactly what or who was on Betelgeuse Five, so we would have to wait until we got there to be certain. I wondered if Archy's vagueness was by his design or by the Librarian's. He was a little hazy on the location of the Librarian's home planet, too. At any rate the message the Martians had intercepted from Betelgeuse was real enough: An acknowledgment of the Librarian's ship's arrival at the Sol Service Station, and the standard caution not to stir up the natives.

How had we intercepted this message? Frank shrugged, and said it was reassuring to know that even someone as capable as the Librarian slipped up occasionally.

At any rate, the caution came far too late. The natives were already restless.

The Librarians held life sacred, yes, but knowledge was something beyond sacred. Taking it to its lowest common denominator, a human being who could read and didn't would have been an abomination to a Librarian. If one of their ships had been in our vicinity when the Library of Alexandria was torched, Archbishop Cyril might have succeeded to sainthood immediately thereafter. Knowledge was vocation and avocation to the Librarians; in knowledge love and need were one.

Their home planet was one vast Encyclopedia Galactica, where the card index alone made fascinating reading. The Librarians had the catalogue of life forms divided into carbon-based life and silicon-based life, with a separate listing for rarer categories. Species were listed as animal, vegetable, or mineral, with families divided by the size of the brain—was it bigger than a breadbox? According to the Librarian good old *Homo sapiens* had one of the largest brains around, with some of the most advanced psychobiology in the galaxy, and yet we ran it at less than twenty percent capacity. With their attitude toward waste, it was no wonder they'd been in such a hurry to shake Terran dust from their feet.

Beings visited the Encyclopedia Galactica from all over the galaxy to consult the records there and, if the ship the Librarian traveled in was any indication, paid through the nose for the privilege. It made me wonder when the bill would come due for the information lodged with Archy.

For now, it was enough to know we weren't alone. Beetlejuicers, Librarians, or !tang haystacks, there was life in them thar stars.

The result of my second contact with the Librarian was more than four helpings of chicken adobo and sweet-and-sour spareribs and sticky rice would cure. I slept for twenty-four hours, woke the next evening to gulp down a liter of water and clean out a jar of peanut butter, and went right back to sleep. It was days before I moved without stiffness. I felt as if I'd been frozen and was thawing out slowly, still wrapped in layers of freezer paper. The layers were invisible but very, very thick.

On the fourth day of my convalescence, at their request I met Frank and Helen in Heinlein Park. The infamous pedestal stood in the center of the park, a miniature Cleopatra's Needle surrounded by oak saplings. Soon enough, laughing children would bounce balls off it and climb over it and use it for base in kick-the-can. That afternoon it stood slender and silent and alone in the stillness of the park.

"The language is the same as the original message," Helen

said with pardonable pride. "A combination of Sanskrit, Old English, and Tolkien's Elvish runes, with a dash of Egyptian hieroglyphics for pretty."

I inspected the tablet. It was very impressive, a square block of deep black metal set high on a silvery, four-sided column, carved with what looked to me like the bastardized offspring of musical notation and bird scratchings, although I may have been doing the birds a disservice. "Well," I said with a sigh, "I sure hope no one on Terra finds out that the Librarians don't have a written alphabet."

Helen and Frank exchanged startled glances. "They don't?"

"They don't take notes or write anything down the way we do, they think them onto some kind of data recorder," I said. "Don't worry. All the information on the Beetlejuicers comes through Archy. I'll tell him to sit on it. Better yet, I'll tell him to study the tablet and the original message and use them for literary models."

I turned to leave, and Helen stopped me. "Look at the other side of the column first."

It was another plaque, a long, rectangular one made of copper that would eventually oxidize and turn green in Ellfive's humid air. At the top of the plaque within a carved border of four-leafed clovers was inscribed a verse:

> Stand your ground, it is too late
> The excise men are at the gate
> Glory be to heaven but they're drinking it neat
> In the hills of Connemara.

Following the verse was a scroll of the sixteen Fivers killed on the previous Saturday, and leading the list was

> Siobhan Patricia "Paddy" O'Malley
> B. Londonderry, Terra

The invisible veils protecting me from the real world shivered as though a strong wind had blown through the park. I leaned my forehead against the cool metal of the pedestal. "Who?" I said. "Who did this?"

"Simon told me you two used to sing that song when you'd been at the poteen. And Charlie was here when we buried them, and Caleb and Rex, too. And Crip."

The words rasped my throat coming out. "You knew about them? About Paddy and Crip?"

"Yes."

"I didn't. She was my friend. Why didn't she tell me?" I pushed away from the column and looked back down at the words that were blurring in my sight. "Why didn't I guess?"

They couldn't answer me, and unable to look any longer upon Paddy's tombstone I turned away. Helen and Frank fell in next to me on the path, their hands beneath my arms. To my chagrin I found I needed their support.

Near the aircar Frank stopped. He looked up at the enormous orbiting cylinder we had built by hand, and had almost lost, and had won back again, with a little unwitting help from a galactic neighbor. "Tell me something, Star," Frank said, watching the fliers swoop and soar above the Big Rock Candy Mountains. "Would you really have destroyed Ellfive to keep it out of the hands of the Space Patrol? Or was it all just a bluff?"

I climbed into the aircar, moving like an old, old woman, without answering, but Frank wasn't going to let it go. "Well?"

"You beat me nine out of ten hands at poker, Frank," I said to the yoke. "What do you think?"

There was a heavy silence. "I think you're still pretty tired, Star," he said finally. "You'd better get back to bed."

"I'm not just tired, Frank, I'm exhausted." I gave them a poor imitation of a smile. "This job is getting to be too much like work."

Frank and Helen exchanged an impassive glance of which I caught only the merest glimpse as the aircar lifted off, a glance that I would remember later.

Charlie was inconsolable. The Beetlejuicers, or the Librarians as I supposed we had to start calling them, had not touched her consciousness in the slightest degree. She could not and would not understand Elizabeth's journey. Her daughter, the child of her body, had been snatched from her side, once from her arms, twice in the space of an hour as she stood by, helpless to prevent it. She wanted an explanation of the big black cave she had seen but not heard, and relief from the pain of her loss.

I could give her neither. "It's not like she's dead, or even gone," I said, trying to explain. "She's just not here."

"Don't lay that solipsistic crap on me," Charlie said furiously. "If she's not here, where is she?"

I couldn't explain clearly because I wasn't sure I understood it any too well myself. Among the few things real to me beneath my layers of numbed insulation was the ache in my breast whenever I remembered Elizabeth was no longer there to read to, to skate with, to take EVA or to dinner on Luna. To laugh with and to love and to watch her grow in beauty like the night. At times I thought my heart would burst with emotion. At others I felt more dead than alive.

"And why Elizabeth?" Charlie cried. "Why not you? They talked to you, too. Why didn't they take you?"

"I was third choice if anyone went at all, Charlie," I said wearily. "Elizabeth was second."

"Choice? What do you mean, 'choice'?" Arrested, she stared at me. "And what do you mean by 'second' choice? If Elizabeth was second choice and you were third, who was first?"

I looked at Simon and watched realization dawn.

"Archy," he said slowly. "It was Archy all the time, wasn't it?" His tone was caught somewhere between awe and dismay.

"Why are you so surprised?" I said to him. "He's your child. Children grow."

Simon shook his head, speechless, and ran a hand through his shaggy hair in a helpless gesture.

"You should be proud," I told him. "They had never encountered such an immense intelligence in an inorganic form. When they investigated, Archy began to come alive, to exhibit signs of free will, and they were intrigued. That's why they hung around this backwater section of the galaxy for as long as they did." I spread my hands. "We're nothing special. They came, they saw, they were about to shrug and leave. Then they started talking to Archy, or he started talking to them, or whatever. When Lodge pulled Archy's plug, the

Librarians wanted him to come back to the Library with them and let them watch him grow into full sentience."

"Why didn't he go?" Simon asked, glancing involuntarily at the ceiling pickup. Archy said nothing. Archy was learning tact.

"He didn't want to. He has a job to do here. He feels he has a responsibility to Ellfive." I smiled a little at Simon's expression. "He told me this morning he was starting to like it here. He said he was just beginning to understand the meaning of the word 'like.' "

Simon said heavily, "So they took Elizabeth with them as second best."

I shook my head. "They didn't take her, she went." I clasped one of his hands in mine and reached out for Charlie's hand with my other. "And because she went, we won't be just another entry in their catalogue of observed species. By taking Elizabeth with them the Librarians have shown us they think we have potential as a race."

I wished I could describe Simon's face just then. The Librarians had not been interested in him, only his progeny. His ego might never recover. But Charlie cried, "I didn't raise my child to be a sociological experiment a billion light-years from home! She's too young to be taken away from her family like this!"

"Charlie! Haven't you heard a word I've said? Elizabeth wanted to go! It was her idea! She asked the Librarian if the Librarian would take her with them!" Charlie gulped, and I said more gently, "The most important thing you have to remember is this. She wanted to go, guys. She asked them if she could go, and when they found her to be less backward than the rest of us, they let her. Can you imagine, Simon, Charlie, what it's going to be like for her? She's been accepted as a freshman at Cosmos U. She's studying the knowledge of the ages, of the universe itself. She's happy." I blinked back sudden tears and repeated, "She is happy. We can't be so selfish that we'd take that away from her, even in our thoughts."

Charlie swiped angrily at her tears and said accusingly, "You wanted to go yourself."

I released her hand and looked away. "Damn right I did."
Beside me Caleb was silent.

"Why didn't you?" Simon said.

"No room at the inn," I said shortly, and mercifully he left
it at that.

"Charlie," Caleb said, ignoring both of us and fixing my
sister with the bright, piercing gaze that reminded me so much
of the Librarian's voice. "The best thing to do now is for you
and Simon to get pregnant again. Right away."

She stared at him.

"Right away," he repeated, pointing at their bedroom door.
If I had been capable of it I would have laughed. He took my
hand and pulled me to my feet.

"Star?" Charlie said in a small voice.

"Yes?"

"Will she ever come back? Will we ever see Elizabeth
again?"

I looked inward and thought about that one. The answer
came without hesitation. "Yes."

"How do you know?"

I spread my hands. "I can't tell you. I can't explain it. I just
know. She will be back."

We left, and as we climbed into the aircar Caleb said softly,
"When will she be back?"

I met his eyes, and I heard the Librarian's voice say, *Will
they mate and reproduce and grow old and die? It will be
interesting to observe.* "Not soon," I said.

"You didn't tell Charlie that."

"She didn't ask."

"Don't hold out false hopes to her, Star."

"Caleb," I said, slumping into my seat, "one thing at a time,
all right? I'll tell her when I think she's ready to hear it. When
I think I'm ready to tell her."

He drove in silence for some time after that. "Would you
have gone, if the Librarian had let you?" he said as we began
descending toward my house.

"Yes," I said at once.

He nodded as if I had confirmed something. "So would I,
Star. So would I."

If I hadn't loved him before, I would have then.

"If Charlie can't understand," he said later, "perhaps in time she might be able to accept. Another child will help."

"There will never be anyone else like Elizabeth," I said with finality.

"Who wants a carbon copy? Elizabeth was her own person, a complete human being. There will never be anyone like her, true, but there will never be anyone like Charlie and Simon's next child, either." He kissed me and smiled. "Or our first."

I felt another of the invisible layers of thickness enveloping me begin to dissolve. "Are we having children?"

"Several."

Caleb Mbele O'Hara was always very sure of himself.

Ten days later I stood on a platform in the center of Owens Arena, watching the *Mayflower*'s first load of colonists climb into the stands. At least half of them looked as if they'd had a last-minute reprieve from terminal seasickness and were trying to find something just this side of human sacrifice to show their appreciation for being restored to the civilizing influence of one gravity. Free-fall wasn't for everyone, although a drug Colgate/Lilly was working on in the Frisbee would soon fix that. Aides in gold jumpsuits circulated among the cheechakos, dispensing cold drinks and wetwipes and answering a thousand and one excited questions.

I stepped to the podium and looked into a sea of expectant faces. Their enthusiasm and happiness were infectious, and I felt my heart lift in spite of myself. Archy gave out with a bell-like, three-toned signal that made the conversation die down into an expectant silence.

"Hello. Ladies and gentlemen, welcome to your new home. My name is Star Svensdotter. I am—I have been the director of this facility. As of your arrival, I am out of a job." I smiled and there was a polite laugh. I cleared my throat. "The people in the gold uniforms will take your names and see you settled in your new homes. Those of you with families will be living in Shepard Subdivision, singles and couples without children in Clarke Apartments. You should have received your relocation packets at the hangarlock. Those of you who did not, please signal the immigration assistant closest to you at this time."

I waited until the bustle died down. "Enclosed in each packet are maps, transportation schedules, names of schools, stores, restaurants, and recreation facilities. For those families with minor children, McAuliffe School opens a week from today in Valley One, just south of the trolley station." There was a loud groan from everyone under the age of eighteen, with a corresponding cheer from their parents.

"For those of you with jobs waiting, you'll find instructions on how to get to your job site, and when you are expected there. Each home and apartment has a viewscreen jack tied into the habitat computer; all the help you need, all the answers to your questions are at your keyboard. What?" One of my aides handed me a note. "Oh. Dr. Elias Peabody is wanted in Bioscience at once." I crumpled the note in my hand and smiled. "Go ahead, Dr. Peabody. I'll spare you the speech. Mary, show him the way."

There was a ripple of laughter as a thin man with a bald head and an eager face dashed up the stairs and disappeared. I took a sip of water, swallowed it, and began to speak more slowly.

"I will not keep you long. I know you are anxious to become acquainted with your new home. But hear me say this much, and remember." I held up one hand and the stadium fell silent.

"The docking of the *Mayflower* marks a new beginning for Ellfive, for each person among you, indeed for all mankind. We have realized a dream, the dream of the first human to stand up, to look up, to reach up, and at long last to step up.

"This dream has not been attained without sacrifice, but do not mourn the dead. Their deaths meant life for Ellfive. It is their gift to you. It is their spirit you must honor. Keep your new home free in their memory."

I raised my head from my notes and spoke the rest from my heart. "In your step up you have become citizens of the galaxy, citizens of the universe itself. The Librarians agree, and have laid their own charge upon Ellfive, to preserve and promote knowledge to all, in friendship toward all, with hope for all. Hold out your hands to your fellow star voyagers, for you are bound to Terra no longer. You have slipped her surly bonds, and the heavens are within your grasp.

"Ladies and gentleman, I say again. Welcome home."

I picked up my notes and stepped back from the podium. A crash of applause made me jump. It was followed by a standing ovation when I made it clear I had finished. It's hard to beat brevity for a grateful reception. Behind me Helen murmured, "For a woman who professes to detest speechmaking she does all right as a rabblerouser, doesn't she, Frank? Well, Star, what now? Are you going to stick around? Maybe run for mayor?"

"I don't think so, Helen." I moved away from the edge of the platform, out of view of the colonists now streaming out of the stadium in excited, chattering groups. "I'm no good at civilization. I don't want to run for mayor or alderman or even dog catcher. The job's finished. I'll have to move on."

"To what?"

I shrugged, kicking at a corner of the makeshift stage.

"We're shooting for a commissioning date ten years from today for Island Two," Frank said in an offhand manner.

That got through to me. I turned my head to give him a disbelieving look. "Ten years? That's insane, Frank. It took us fifteen years to commission Island One. What makes you think you can bring Two on line in ten?"

"Experience," he said.

I laughed. It was not a nice laugh.

"Also, we aren't starting from scratch this time. Copernicus Base is running smoothly and the third mass driver will be completed by this time next year. It shouldn't be too hard to keep to schedule." He paused. "You wouldn't care to take on the project, I suppose?"

I laughed again. "No, thank you. Especially not with the raw O_2 and hydrogen shortages I can already see staring you in the face. Besides, I've already built one habitat."

"No," Helen murmured, looking at Frank, "when you've done something, you've done it. Repetition is not one of your faults."

"I don't admit to any," I said flippantly.

They smiled and exchanged the glance I had seen before in Heinlein Park, a glance pregnant with equal parts determination and mischief, and suddenly I was on my guard. "What do you know about mining?" Frank said to me, still looking at his wife.

"Mining?" I said. "You mean like moiling for gold?"

"Sort of."

"The Asteroid Belt," I said. I felt the last of the depression that had lingered on since Paddy's death and Elizabeth's departure melt away as if it had never been. "You want me to take on the Expedition. It's true, then. Someone has struck uranium on Ceres."

Helen's eyes gave me an approving look and I stood up straighter.

"Not on Ceres, but near it," Frank said. "Preliminary reports also indicate large amounts of hydrogen and oxygen in that area, which makes it a promising site for a colony. Lead the expedition and set up a mining colony for us, Star. Begin shipment within two years and we'll complete Island Two on schedule."

I wasn't listening. A mining colony in the Asteroid Belt, in orbit between Mars and Jupiter. As many as fifty thousand of them in three- to six-year orbits around Sol, some in orbit around each other, some in collision, ranging in size from smaller than a breadbox to a thousand meters across, with exotic names like Brucia and Astraea and Geogrophos and Marilyn. And, according to the latest probe data and to employ Sam Holbrook's metaphor, all of which were simply lousy with the major elements of which Terra and now Luna were rapidly running short.

And from there, who knew? Maybe Jupiter, whose moons once may have been part of the Asteroid Belt, persuaded out of their virtuous orbits by the come-hither look in Jupiter's gravitational eye. Maybe Neptune, with the system's screwiest magnetic field. Maybe the tenth planet, which might not even be there.

A mining colony. There might not be any raw red gold in nuggets the size of my fist but I'd bet there would be plenty of claim jumpers and an unending supply of Dukes of Bilgewater and perhaps even a Lost Dauphin or two. The resulting stampede was going to make the rush to the Klondike look like an aircar at flank speed. Express ships were fuel efficient as far as they went but they went pretty far in that direction and we were continually scrambling for uranium to build more bombs—or, excuse me, ECFCPCs, as Colony Control prefers to call them.

"You can have the *Taylor*," Helen said, watching my face. "Crippen Young has already agreed to sign on as skipper."

I could understand why. In orbit between Mars and Jupiter was about as far as he could get from the scene of Paddy's death. Crip would need that distance even more than the rest of us.

"How about it, Star?" Frank said smugly, certain of my answer. "How would you like to see the Great Red Spot up close enough to warm your hands by it?"

I shoved my hands in my pockets to hide the fact that they were shaking with excitement. "I do have two questions."

"What are they?"

"Number one, is there really any uranium out there?"

Helen looked hurt, and Frank gave me a reproachful glance as he patted his wife's shoulder comfortingly. "There, there, Helen, she doesn't know what she's saying. Really, Star, how could you doubt it?"

"Very easily," I said. "Is there?"

He grinned. "Yes."

"Lots?"

"Lots," he said with relish.

"Enough to justify construction of a mining colony?"

"Really, Star," he complained as Helen stared at me with wounded dignity. "This lack of faith in our given word is upsetting both of us. More than enough."

I looked the two of them over carefully. They stared back, their eyes wide with innocence. I gave a mental shrug. "Okay. Question number two. Who is picking up the tab for this little expedition?"

"Why, Ellfive is, of course," Helen said, as if that fact was self-evident.

"Uh-huh," I said. "And the outstanding debt Ellfive owes the American Alliance? Don't you think the Alliance might kick a little at having to stand in line?"

Frank rubbed one ear and exchanged glances with Helen.

"Well, if they get too uppity we can always get Archy to trigger the beacon in Heinlein Park."

"Frank," I said, "that's no beacon in Heinlein Park."

He grinned. "You know that's no beacon, and I know that's no beacon, and Helen knows that's no beacon—"

"But," the three of us said together, "the American Alliance doesn't know that's no beacon in Heinlein Park!"

Charlie, Simon, and Caleb were waiting in my office, passing the time by passing around the last bottle of my Christmas Glenlivet.

"Not a bad speech, Star," Simon said. "Nice and short. I like short in a speech."

"You overwhelm me, Simon," I said, rescuing the bottle from Caleb and pouring out the last two fingers.

"Iambic pentameter'll do it every time," Caleb said.

I toasted him silently and drank.

"We've all been working so long for this day," Charlie said with a sigh, setting down her empty glass. There was a deep-seated grief in my sister's face that had not been there before. "We pulled it off, Luddites and Alliance Congress and Space Patrol notwithstanding. So why does it feel like such an anticlimax?"

I set my glass down next to Charlie's, on the new mayor's desk, with great care. I smiled at the three of them.

"I'm outbound for Ceres on the *Ted Taylor* Express," I said. "Who else wants to come?"